POTTER'S FIELD

POTTER'S
FIELD

ROB HART

Copyright © 2018 by Rob Hart
Cover and jacket design by 2Faced Design
Interior design and formatting by

ISBN 978-1-943818-93-8
eISBN: 978-1-947993-03-7
Library of Congress Control Number: 2018944550

First hardcover edition July 2018 by Polis Books, LLC
1201 Hudson Street, #211S
Hoboken, NJ
www.PolisBooks.com

POLIS BOOKS

ALSO BY ROB HART

remember the ones who descended here
into the mire of bedrock
to bore a hole through this granite

to clear a passage for you
where there was only darkness and stone.
Remember as you come up into the light.

—**"Subway" by Billy Collins**

To Jason
For letting me finish

ONE

A S WE PULLED to the curb, I vaguely wondered who I was going to beat the shit out of that day.

Samson parked the car but didn't turn off the engine. He let the air conditioner run because it was a hundred-and-fuck-you degrees out. So hot that for the first time in our brief history together, he wasn't wearing his leather duster. That day, he wore black jeans and black boots and a black tank top, his huge arms glistening with sweat. Some might call Samson overweight, but that would be a mistake. Bite him and you'd likely chip a tooth.

He was wearing wrap-around polarized sunglasses that would shift between blue and purple and pink depending on the angle. I'd never seen him without his sunglasses. Not even at night. And he spoke to me in a tone that made me wonder if I'd murdered a member of his immediate family.

"Glove box," he said.

"What's in the glove box?"

1

Like I didn't know.

"Open it and find out," he said.

I touched the black plastic latch, clicked it toward me. The glove box fell open, a silver handgun cradled in its mouth. I closed the compartment with care, not wanting to jostle the gun.

"Nope," I told him.

"The fuck you mean, nope?" he asked. "You're here to back me up. That means you go in with a full hand."

"I don't mess with guns."

"What are you going to do when these motherfuckers start shooting at you? Is your moral superiority bulletproof?"

There was a lot I could say in that moment. About how I thought a gun was a weapon for cowards. That they tore apart lives and destroyed families. That they made me queasy. That in a town like New York, if someone pulled a gun, it wasn't about hunting or tradition, it was about instilling fear or hurting someone.

Case in point.

That would have taken too long to explain, so I just placed my hand on the umbrella attached my belt. Kevlar canopy, steel baton, able to be carried in plain sight without anyone asking questions. Sure, a deadly weapon, but it required some degree of skill and a bit of proximity to use, which made me feel like I wasn't full of shit for using it.

"This is all I need," I told him.

"You and that fucking thing."

"Are going to tell me a little more about what we're doing?" I asked.

"You back me up. All you need to know," he said, killing the engine and cracking the door, cold air rushing out, replaced by blistering mid-afternoon heat.

We stepped to the curb, stood on the sidewalk. Surveyed the

block. A quiet stretch in Flatbush, brownstones on either side, street stuffed with cars. So hot you could smell the blacktop. Some dude was standing outside a bodega at the end of the block smoking a joint. That skunk smell of weed so thick I could taste it. He was giving us a vigorous eye-fuck, which wasn't lost on Samson. Then the dude pulled out his cell, dialed a number, and raised it to his face.

"Lookout?" I asked.

"Figures," Samson said. "No sense in waiting."

He crossed the street and I followed, bounding up the steps to our target. He slammed the flat of his palm against the blood-red door of the brownstone. The shades were drawn and an air conditioner was humming in a window. The guy across the street crossed toward us. I went back-to-back with Samson, put my hand on the umbrella.

"Open up," Samson yelled at the door.

The guy crossing the street, he was a big dude. Shaved head, heavy beard, built like a fighter jet. But all that upper-body muscle was stacked on a lean, skinny frame. Someone was skipping leg day. You can have the biggest arms in the world, doesn't matter one damn bit. Power comes from the core and the legs. I probably wouldn't even need the umbrella.

Still, I flicked open the button on the leather strap, just to have it handy, when a couple of things happened at once.

The lookout stepped into the street, but he was looking at me, not paying attention, so a car tearing down the block nearly creamed him. The driver slammed on his horn and brakes at the same time. The guy jumped back just as the door behind me creaked and someone said something, but then there was a crashing sound and a yell as Samson pushed his way inside.

I gave a quick glance over my shoulder, saw the door was open, and went in just as the lookout got his bearings. I slammed the door closed. There was a chair in the hallway next to the door so I wedged it underneath the knob. One less person to worry about. Within seconds the doorknob was jiggling and the lookout was yelling something.

The inside of the brownstone was dim. Blank hallway, staircase to the left, archway to the right that should have led into the living room but had been bricked up. Down and to the right I heard the sound of a scuffle. The place reeked of cleaning supplies. I passed a door under the staircase that looked like a bathroom. It was cracked open. Someone peeked out. A green eye and a flash of blonde hair. The door slammed, lock flipped.

At the end of the hallway and to the right was a dining room-living room combo. Leather couches, coffee table, beige walls, stacks of magazines, a flat screen television playing a baseball game. The sound on the television was off and the captions were on. Vibe like a waiting room. There was a nice fish tank, too, right across from the entryway. Big, clean, glowing blue, filled with shiny fish darting through clear water above rainbow-colored rocks.

Samson was standing over a couch, his girth blocking the view of what he was doing. He was yelling something at someone but it was hard to make out, because whoever he was holding down was thrashing and yelling, plus there was the sound of the guy at the front door, who now seemed to be trying to break it down.

I got closer and found Samson holding a man by the throat. The man was wearing white linen pants and a black pinstripe vest over a tiny bird chest. Expensive leather sandals, silver chain around his neck, lots of gold on his fingers. All that gold wasn't enough to save him from Samson, and he appeared frustrated by that.

"You know what the rules are," Samson said. "You think you can pull one over on us?"

The man struggled to respond. Samson let off a little pressure. With some room to speak, the man said, "Fuck you, and fuck that faggot."

Which was not the right answer.

Samson balled up his fist, reared back, and smashed it into the guy's face. It sounded like raw meat hitting pavement.

I figured it best to let Samson do his job, so I checked the hallway, heard the lookout smashing the door. Over the racket I thought I heard footsteps upstairs, but if no one had come down yet, I probably had nothing to worry about.

At the rear of the brownstone was a kitchen. Just as tidy. Like it was barely used, except for the microwave, which was sitting open and splattered with baked-on streaks of yellow and red sludge. There was a pile of plastic microwave dinner platters, rinsed and stacked neatly next to the garbage can in the corner. I popped open the fridge, found it was full of more TV dinners. The smell of cleaning supplies was even stronger in here. Everything in the house meticulously scrubbed.

When Samson wouldn't tell me the nature of the gig, I just figured we were going into a drug den or a gambling parlor. Those tended to be in Ginny's wheelhouse. This was different. The guy Samson was bracing had a certain flair that, coupled with the sound of footsteps upstairs, was opening a pit at the base of my stomach.

That pit opened wide when I returned to the hallway, looked up the staircase, and found a skinny Asian woman in a barely-there black dress leaning down the stairs, trying to get a good look, but then darting back into the darkness like a frightened cat when she saw me.

Before I could return to the waiting room, the front door splintered and broke and the lookout came tumbling in with two more guys behind him. I ducked around the corner and yelled, "Company."

Samson turned to me, nodded, threw another punch at the guy on the couch.

I took advantage of the fact that our attackers were probably hopped up on adrenaline and not really thinking. Pressed myself against the wall and stuck my foot into the doorway. The first guy hit it hard and flew head-first into the fish tank. The glass exploded and water rushed over the hardwood floor. I felt bad for the fish.

The next guy stopped in the doorway, surveying the damage, but by then I'd had enough time to pull the umbrella off my belt and flick it out to full length. I swung it into his gut. He exhaled hard, folded over it. I wrapped my arm around his neck and bucked my hips, yanking him into the room. He crashed onto the coffee table, the glass shattering but the frame holding, so that his body was draped like a rag doll over its remains.

That left the third guy, the lookout, who was smart enough to not come in. I was wondering about his plans when the sheetrock a few feet in front of my face exploded, dust rocketing into the air. I threw myself onto the ground to get out of the line of fire, landing in a pool of aquarium water. Something squished under my palm.

Poor fish.

I looked across at Samson, who was also on the floor, straddling his prey, eyebrow raised.

"Wish you had a gun now, huh?" he asked.

"Still no," I told him.

After a couple of more shots through the wall there was a stretch of silence. Samson pulled himself to his feet, said, "Six-shooter." Though I didn't know if he was saying it to me or himself. He disappeared into the hallway and I heard some heavy thuds. I didn't need to look to know who was winning.

I climbed to my feet, checked the two guys I brought down, found neither of them were interested in taking things further. Patted them down to make sure they weren't strapped. They just put their hands up in a peaceful gesture.

By the time I got to the man in charge, cowering on the corner of the couch, Samson was back. He grabbed the guy by the back of the neck and dragged him into the kitchen. I glanced back toward the front door. The lookout was twisted up like a pile of old laundry.

"The money," Samson said, tossing the man onto the tile floor.

"Nothing on hand. Deposited my weekly this morning."

Samson picked the man up and pushed his head into the wall, leaving behind a bloodstained dent.

"The money," Samson said, same register as before.

The guy put his hands over his head, crawled to the fridge. Climbed up against it and shimmied it out from the wall. Underneath, offset against the white tile, was a bare patch of wood, which the guy pulled up to reveal large stacks of wrapped bills piled in an alcove. Samson looked around the kitchen, found a discarded delivery box, and tossed it at the guy.

"Fill it up."

From behind us: "'Scuse me?"

Standing in the doorway was a slender blonde in red lingerie. Barefoot, hair falling over her face, hiding what looked like a constellation of bruising around a green eye. I recognized that eye. It was the eye from the bathroom door.

"Are you okay, Dixon?" she asked, looking at the man on the floor.

"Get the fuck upstairs."

The woman looked from me to Samson. "I just wanted to make sure…"

"Get the fuck upstairs, you dumb bitch," the man said, spitting, showing her the back of his hand.

She twitched. It wasn't the first time she'd seen it.

I kicked him in the face.

He went down hard, grabbing at his head. It felt good to hurt him. Pimps have carved themselves a pretty comfortable niche in pop culture. Halloween costumes and fast-talking movie characters. They're supposed to be suave and cool. Except, in real life, they're pieces of shit who coerce and abuse women into making money for them. So it felt good to kick him, even though Samson was pretty annoyed that I did. No making this guy happy.

"You don't talk to women like that, fuckhead," I told the pimp.

He moved quickly after that, filling the box to the brim. When he was done, Samson put the box on the counter and pulled out his own gun, a heavy-duty silver behemoth tucked into his jeans. I don't know much about gun calibers but it was clearly designed by someone with a deep fear of Bigfoot. He leveled the gun at the guy's head, but before he could fire, I grabbed his arm and jerked it up, the gunshot exploding in the small space, blasting into the top of the kitchen wall. The sound of it filled my brain with a shrill hum.

Samson threw an elbow and caught me on the side of the head. He knew all about getting weight behind a blow. I hit the ground hard. That bomb I carried in my chest went off and I had a very immediate and visceral fantasy of getting into a knock-down, drag-out fight with him over this, but I also knew enough gunshots had been fired that the cops couldn't be far behind.

"We have to go," I told him, climbing to my feet, arms up to protect my head in case he couldn't let it go.

He took one last look at the guy on the floor, then at me, like he was thinking it over, then nodded. We booked for the door. Leapt over the lookout, ran across the street, got in the car, and drove a few miles before he stopped in the shade outside a park. Not twenty feet from us were kids playing in a water fountain, like everything in the world was normal. We sat there for a little while, letting the adrenaline wear off. The angry insect buzz of the gunshot still drilling into my brain.

When Samson could hold the steering wheel without making the leather creak, he asked, "The fuck is wrong with you?"

"Not gonna stand there while you shoot someone."

"You all high and mighty. You think it's okay to beat on him but not kill him?"

"Everyone's got a line," I told him. "That's mine. Ginny has a problem with it, she'll have to be a little more judicious on when and where she sends me out."

Samson pulled the box of money off the back seat, pulled off a thick stack of bills, and smacked it hard against my chest.

"Services rendered," he said. "Get the fuck out."

"What happens to the girls?"

"What girls?"

"The ones who work there?"

Samson turned and stared at me long and hard. "Ginny's going to give them all an envelope of money and a pat on the head and tell them to go live their best lives on some motherfucking farm somewhere, far away from the harsh city life they've come to know."

"Asshole."

"The fuck you care?"

"I care."

"Do you? Because you're sitting in the car holding a pile of money. I don't see you running back."

"Are they going to be okay?"

He paused. That pause stung.

"Sure," he said. "Now get the fuck out of the car."

I did. He swung the car into the street and slammed the gas, tires spinning dust in his wake. I went looking for a subway station.

It was the first and last job Ginny sent me on with Samson.

A few times, usually late at night, with a head full of booze or drugs, I would go to that neighborhood, wander around, try to find the brownstone with the red door, but I never could. Samson was the one who drove and I didn't know the address. The door had probably been repaired and repainted.

I would try to remember the bodega on the corner, the look of the street, but the details of that day got lost in a haze of fear and adrenaline.

I think part of me didn't want to find it, because I was afraid of what I would see when I got there.

What would happen, or more specifically, what would be true.

TWO

THE PLANE BANKS. New York City's skyline appears outside the window, blue and steel and concrete, gleaming in the sunlight. The way the buildings peak at downtown and midtown makes the island of Manhattan look like a great beast that's opening its maw to devour us upon landing.

That's a little what it feels like, too.

My face stretches into a smile before I realize I'm doing it.

Fourteen months. A lot has happened, so it feels even longer.

According to the screen on the seat in front of me it's 3 p.m., and I try to figure out what time my body thinks it is. I left Prague sometime yesterday, which is six hours ahead of New York, but then spent nearly seven hours on a layover in the Frankfurt airport. Like being in purgatory. I didn't want to sleep because I was afraid I'd miss my flight. I didn't want to go through security again, so I wandered the airport, a cavernous structure devoid of soul and decent places to eat.

I know I'm tired. I know the first thing I want to do is get off the plane and climb into bed, except I don't have a bed, or a place to live. I've got money so I could get a hotel, but I hate the idea of getting a hotel room in the place where I was born. I'm tired of them, anyway—everything borrowed, disposable, temporary.

I'm tired of temporary.

After more than a year, I want some permanence.

The woman in the aisle seat leans over to look out the window. She's been asleep for the majority of the flight. Her eyes are soft and hazy, which confirms the theory I formulated when I climbed over her to hit the bathroom a few hours ago and she didn't stir: popped some sleepytime pills before we took off. I don't blame her. Nine hours is a long time on a plane. At least we were granted the mercy of an empty seat between us.

I tried to sleep myself, but found I couldn't—part discomfort, part anticipation—so I worked through four seasons of *SpongeBob SquarePants* on the seatback television. My brain feels like pudding that's sat on the counter too long.

"About to land?" she asks, stretching her hands above her head.

I nod at her. "Just about."

When we got onto the plane, we did the dance of strangers seated in close proximity—smiled and nodded without looking directly at each other, before she turned into a lump of frizzy blonde hair and purple eye mask and gray airline-issued blanket. Now she's all warm and smiles, like we're pals.

She does a doubletake when she gets a good look at my face. Patch-worked with bruises, fading from eggplant purple to snot yellow. She can't even see the full tapestry: there's plenty more covering my torso, visible through the plastic wrap cinched around my waist holding together what is either a broken or a badly-bruised rib.

At least, that's what the stabbing pain when I cough or laugh or breathe too hard makes me figure.

Souvenirs from my time in Prague.

She notices I've noticed her looking at my face so she goes looking for a more comfortable topic of conversation. "How was the flight?" she asks.

"Uneventful. Dinner options were chicken or vegetarian. I got the chicken."

"How was it?"

"Not terrible."

She nods. Glances out the window again, watches as the plane descends, details coming into focus. The thickness of traffic on the Belt Parkway. We pass over Coney Island, the Wonder Wheel like a child's erector set from this height. My heart flips in my chest.

"Coming or going?" she asks.

"Sorry?"

"Are you coming home or going someplace else?"

"Coming home," I tell her. "You?"

"Visiting family. What do you do?"

The real answer unspools in my head: amateur private investigator, though for a long time I preferred to think of myself as a blunt instrument. Point me at a job—carry something, find someone, scare someone—I got it done, and usually accepted cash upon completion. Though I would gladly take drugs or alcohol because I was fine operating on a barter system.

That answer used to tickle me. It felt cool and dangerous. Now it seems silly.

I settle on telling her, "Still trying to figure that out. How about yourself?"

"Paralegal," she says. Extends her hand. "Ashley."

I laugh. Pain shoots through my midsection, like someone

digging a pen into my side, and I wince. Take her hand and shake it. "Me, too," I tell her. "But everyone calls me Ash."

She chuckles. "I've never met a male Ashley before."

"It used to be a boy's name. Good Irish name. That changed around the 1980s."

She nods. "So you're from here, then? From New York?"

"Born and raised."

"Been traveling?" she asks.

I nod, not really wanting to expand on that.

"I was born here," she says. "Had to leave though. It just got to be…too much."

"It can be that," I tell her, watching as we hurtle toward a runway at JFK. "And sometimes it doesn't feel like enough."

She smiles like I said something clever, though, truthfully, I'm not entirely sure what I meant. It just slipped out. The important thing is, the only thing that matters as the wheels touch down and the plane jolts and shudders is: I am home.

THE LINE THROUGH customs feels nearly as long as the flight. Once I clear that, I hunt for a place to exchange my Czech crown, pulling thick wads of bills out of my toiletries bag, feeling a little sad to part with it because I really came to enjoy the Monopoly-money aesthetic of European cash.

I end up with a little over four grand. Which is not great. In this town, that's one month's rent and a sandwich. Not even a good sandwich. I've got a little money in the bank, but all together I'm not sure it could cover first, last, and security on a new place. I plan on being careful with my money, but then see an electronic kiosk offering no-contract cell phones, so I stop and navigate the touchscreen until it spits one out. On the way to baggage claim,

I toss my useless European-band phone into an electronics-recycling bin. No great loss. It was a burner anyway.

After retrieving my duffel bag from the carousel, I head to the cab line, step into the kind of cold that makes it seem like the air is angry with you. Climb into a yellow cab, suck in the smell of body odor and spilled food and old leather.

May as well be perfume.

"MacDougal and West Third, please," I tell the driver.

He says nothing and drifts from the curb. The television screen screeches at me with some cutesy news program aimed at tourists. A perky woman sits on a stoop, interviewing a celebrity I don't recognize. I jab at the corner until the touchscreen registers my frustration.

The cab speeds through the arteries of the airport until we hit Linden Boulevard and things slow down. I pull out my new phone, get it set up, check my e-mail—finding nothing—then key in the only two phone numbers I know off the top of my head: Bombay and my mom.

I open up the text message screen and type '*Mom*.'

Hover over the message field.

Think about my face. The bruises. Having to explain them.

Delete '*Mom*' and type '*Bombay*.'

Write: *Home.*

Almost immediately he writes back: *What's the plan?*

Need a place to crash.

Last time you stayed here someone trashed my apartment.

You're right. I'll get a hotel, like a fucking tourist.

Living in St. George now. I'll send you the address.

Love you.

Bombay responds with a smiley-face emoticon, followed with an address on St. Mark's Place.

Last I heard, he'd moved to Brooklyn. Moving back to Staten Island might be a money thing—the rents are cheaper—or a nostalgia thing. I wonder which.

The driver picks up speed and I doze until we hit the Manhattan Bridge, and even though its freezing outside I tap the button for the window to bring it down a little, let the air wash over me and wake me up as the city roars in our path. It is old and grand and dirty and beautiful and I have missed it. I didn't leave on the best of terms. All problems of my own making, and it's probably been long enough that nobody really wants to do me harm anymore. Still, it raises the question of what kind of welcome I'm going to get.

I think back on my conversation with Ashley. About what I do. About not knowing. That wasn't entirely true. I know what I want to do with my life. Now, after all these years, running around like I owned this town, playing games and acting like a tough guy, I get it. Where I fit. What I want to be.

A private investigator.

No more "amateur". No more moonlighting as a hired thug. No more barter system.

This is what I want to do with my life.

Now I just have to figure out how to make that happen.

THE CAB STOPS. I hand the driver a wad of cash and climb onto the street, the sidewalk so crowded I immediately have to duck and dance to avoid getting trampled.

The sun is setting. MacDougal doesn't look much different. A tangle of restaurants and shops, kids from NYU who haven't yet gone for the holidays wandering around like insects afraid of the lights, on the hunt for a sloppy drunk. Yellow cabs speeding down the block to catch the green at Bleecker. Filthy snow on the ground, collected in thin strips along the edges of the sidewalk.

The night before I got on a plane and left New York, I sat in the middle of this street during a freak snowfall. Early for the year, and a hell of a thing to see. No cars, no people, nothing, just the vast emptiness of MacDougal covered with a layer of white. Seeing it now makes it feel like I went to sleep and woke up and found everything like I left it, the snow cleared and trampled and the city going on with its business. Just another day. Like the past year didn't happen.

How sometimes when you're having a dream where you're late for something, and you wake up angry at yourself for being late, but then you realize: no, I'm not late. I'm here.

Then I look across the street and find the coffee shop where I spent years of my life sitting on the worn armchair in the back is now a Korean barbecue joint. My heart shatters on the asphalt.

Before I left, that would have sent me into a spiral of drinking and yelling at people. Now it's just a heartbreak. It's sad, for sure, and I wish I could have been here to say goodbye, but that's the nature of New York. We are constantly losing the things we love in favor of whatever can afford to take their place. It's not the reality I want, but it's one I have to accept.

Mamoun's, at least, is still here.

I've been thinking about this place the entire flight home. I'm glad to have access to decent pizza and bagels again, but right now all I want to eat in this world is a shawarma. Roasted lamb and lettuce and onion and tomato in a pita with tahini sauce. The most perfect thing in the world. Doesn't matter how hungry you are, just one and you're content. Not hungry, not stuffed, just satisfied. And even though it's fast food, there are vegetables on it, so you can feel good about yourself.

There are more falafel and shawarma joints in this city than there are rats, roaches, and tourists, but none of them come within screaming distance of Mamoun's. The line is long and the price has gone up by a dollar but I don't care. I get my shawarma, wrapped in foil and shoved in a brown paper bag with a pile of napkins, then step outside, stand at the curb, drop my duffel bag to my feet, and dig in.

It tastes like I remember. Like a million nights standing in this spot, being happy, but not happy like the way I am right now, which is the kind of happy you only get when you know the things you love were almost lost to you, but you found them again.

As I'm finishing off the last of it—still proud of myself for being able to eat one of these things without getting my hands covered in tahini sauce—a black Escalade with tinted windows pulls to the curb. It stops in front of me and the flashers go on.

Out steps Samson.

Still big like a childhood nightmare is big. Still wearing his leather duster and sunglasses.

Still doesn't seem to like me either.

"Ginny would like a word," he says.

I take the remains of the aluminum foil, stick it in the paper bag, ball the whole thing up, and toss it into the trashcan next to me. "My plane isn't even refueled. How does Ginny know I'm back?"

"Ginny knows all." He opens the back door. "Get in."

"And if I don't?"

He doesn't answer, because he knows I already know what he would do.

I grab my bag, toss it into the car. It has that new car smell. Vinyl and plastic. That smell is actually volatile organic compounds. Toxins seeping into the air. Most people find that smell comforting, but it's not good for you. So, pretty much the perfect analogy for getting into this fucking car.

The door slams and Samson lumbers into the driver's seat, the car dipping down under his shifting weight.

This ought to be interesting.

Because the last time I saw Ginny, she tried to kill me.

I was wondering what kind of welcome I'd get. It matches the air temperature, which numbed my fingertips and burnt my earlobes while I ate my shawarma.

Cold as fuck.

THREE

I HAD FORGOTTEN A notebook in my locker. My teacher let me duck out to grab it. Gym classes were over so the locker room was silent, that lull before the end of day, when various teams would file in to get ready for practice.

I was just closing my locker when I heard the sound of a thud. Something heavy hitting something flesh.

The locker room was laid out like a barbell. A room filled with lockers and benches on one end, connected by a narrow corridor of showers and toilets, with another set of lockers and benches on the other end. Beyond that, a special locker room reserved for the football players.

I stuck the notebook in my pocket and wandered to the other side of the locker room. Curious more than anything. As I got closer, I heard more sounds. The kind of sounds you hear and they set you on edge.

Heavy breathing.

A low, raspy growl.

The register that accompanies violence.

I peeked into the football locker room, saw one of the linebackers. I didn't know his name, didn't care to know his name, all I knew was he looked unfrozen from a block of ice. The kind of person you can figure sometimes misspells his own name.

His beefy arm was wrapped around a scrawny kid's neck. The kid was clawing at the linebacker's arm, trying to get free, but it may as well have been a cat swiping at a brick wall. The kid's face was purple and his eyes were rolling back in his head.

The bomb I carried in my chest went off. This was when I was angry in ways I didn't know how to handle, except to be constantly looking for an outlet.

"Hey, dummy," I said.

The scrawny kid looked at me, on the verge of passing out. The linebacker didn't acknowledge me. So I picked a helmet off the floor and flung it at him. It smacked him on the forehead.

That got his attention.

He threw the kid into a bank of lockers hard enough I winced, and then came at me like a locomotive.

I'd heard rumors about kids on the football team taking steroids and the coaches looking the other way. I'd heard another rumor about a linebacker having a roid-rage freakout on a teacher and the whole thing getting brushed under the rug because he was a D-1 recruit.

Given the steam coming out of the guy's ears, I figured the rumors were true.

In a fair fight he would have eaten me as a snack. But the thing about roid-rage is, it doesn't make you smart. So it was a simple matter of sidestepping and using his momentum to ram his face

21

into the exposed brick wall.

There was a wet smack and his head snapped back, his nose gushing red. He stumbled to get his footing so I kicked the back of his knee and he went down. I threw a hard right into his chin, which spun him around so that his face cracked off the bench. As he tried to get up, something small rattled on the stone floor.

I thought it might have been a chip of stone off the wall but it turned out to be a tooth.

Before he could stand up to full height, I proceeded to stomp him. Aiming for body shots. I didn't want to kick him in the back of the head and sever his brain stem or anything, but I wanted to make sure he would remember how it felt.

The pain. The helplessness.

I wanted him to remember.

After a little while, the scrawny kid grabbed me. Pulled me away. Said, "You'll kill him."

I snapped out of it. Turned to look at him.

"Yeah, I guess so," I said. Not really sorry. The linebacker wasn't moving, so I knelt down and checked to make sure he was still breathing. Which, yes.

The scrawny kid was Italian, with aquiline features and more five-o'clock shadow than you'd expect on a high school student. He was angry, too. Like he wanted to get some stomps in himself but knew the guy wouldn't notice at this point.

"Thank you," he said.

"What happened?" I asked.

The kid's eyes darted around the room, like he was trying to come up with an excuse for being in the locker room with a football player at a time that probably no one would stumble across them. It took me a second, but then I put it together myself.

"You know what?" I told him. "We don't need to talk about

that."

He smiled. I figured at that point we should leave, but reality was setting in: the football players were going to want revenge. I had probably benched this kid for the season. I could have argued self-defense, but that was before I beat him into putty. And if history was any indication, the administration would take his side.

"We have to protect ourselves," I said.

The kid nodded. "Don't worry about that. We'll be fine."

"How can you know that?"

"Oh, I have contingencies."

I raised an eyebrow.

The kid smiled again. This time it was sharp.

"Pictures," he said.

He leaned down. The linebacker stirred and groaned as the kid poked him in the shoulder.

"You hear that?" he asked. "I've got pictures."

The linebacker seemed to nod.

"Well, that's good," I told him. "Now we need to go."

As we made our way toward the exit, the kid put his hand on my chest to stop me. Looked me square in the face. I knew what he was going to say before he said it.

"You're that guy. Your dad…" His eyes went soft and his hand went to his mouth. Involuntary.

I expected him to say what most people said—some pabulum about my dad being a hero, about how sorry he was—but he didn't. He studied my face, which was revealing way too much about how I was feeling in that moment, about how much I hated being an object of pity and curiosity. That bomb in my chest ticking again.

Finally, he said, "You know what? We don't need to talk about that."

My shoulders dropped. "Thank you."

"Why did you do it?" he asked.

"Do what?"

"Intervene."

I glanced back toward the locker room. "I don't like bullies."

"You could have gotten hurt."

"I didn't."

The kid nodded. Offered his hand. "I'm Paul."

"Ash."

"Ash? Like short for Ashley?" He laughed, and all the fear fell away. He stood up a little straighter, taking on the quality of something I didn't know then, but looking back now I can say was the poise of a confident women holding a martini glass. He said, "That's a girl's name, darling."

"Thanks," I told him. "No one's ever pointed that out."

Paul continued walking toward the door. "A tough guy with a heart of gold and a fast mouth. Could you be any more of a cliché…"

I laughed.

Then he laughed.

And like that, we were friends.

SAMSON PULLS THE car to the curb on Broome Street and sits silently, the engine running, the only sound the aggressive whoosh of the heater from the front of the car. I think this is my sign to exit, but maybe this is the first step toward building a gentler, more thoughtful life for myself.

See if the two of us can bury that hatchet.

"So, how've you been?" I ask.

Silence from the front.

Maybe this was not a good place to start. The only hatchet

Samson wants to bury is a real one, in my face. Which bothers me more than it should, probably.

"Can you at least tell me why you dislike me so much? Was it something I said?"

"The fuck do you care?"

"I've been gone for a bit. Figured we could take it as a chance to start over."

He twists in the car to look at me. All I can see is his face in profile. "I do not like you because you're a dumb motherfucker thinks he's a smart motherfucker. That's the worst kind of motherfucker there is."

"People change."

He shows me the back of his head. "No, they don't."

"Fine. I tried. But one day, Samson. I'm gonna crack you." I stop as I'm climbing out of the car. "I don't mean crack you like hit you. I mean crack you like one day we're going to be pals. Just wait and see."

I think it's pretty funny, but he doesn't say anything. I step into the gripping cold, and as I'm closing the door, Samson says something. I open the door wider. "Come again?"

"Penthouse."

"Great." I slam the door shut, a little harder than I need to. Since the windows are tinted, I can't see his reaction but, I doubt it's favorable. Turn to face the building. It's big and ornate. Beige stone with green accents. I don't know the name for this style of building, except that it's the kind of building that doesn't get built anymore.

There's a set of double metal doors. A buzzer sounds as I get close. Must be cameras. I step into a small lobby that's all marble and mirrors. There's an elevator across the way and, standing to the side, an old Latino couple, leaning into each other, sobbing.

I can't see much about them, the way they're pressed into each other. They're wearing coats and the man has the woman's face nestled in the crook of his shoulder. He glances at me with sad, tired eyes. The naked display of emotion makes me want to turn around and leave, but the door clicks behind me, which presses me forward. I feel like I'm intruding so I hurry into the elevator and the doors slide shut, cutting off the muffled sounds of their crying. That much is a relief, though the feeling of sadness lingers like a smell.

There are four floors and a P. Before I can press anything, the P lights up and the elevator ascends. It stops and opens into a vast, darkened room. Everything is white—the walls and the floor and the domed ceiling, featuring three large skylights. The apex of the dome has to be thirty feet high, maybe more. The room is broken up by pieces of art and stylish but comfortable-looking furniture— couches and easy chairs and wingbacks grouped in patterns that feel both haphazard and deliberate.

Toward the back of the room there's a staircase leading to a loft, and underneath is a passageway. I step into the room and the sound of my footsteps echoes off the walls. The floor is a stone tile, and the whole place feels like the owner wants to recreate the feel of being in a museum.

"Darling."

It comes from everywhere and nowhere.

The word she hangs on like a portrait.

Ginny Tonic materializes out of the darkness under the stairs. Her hair is held in a tight bun, and she's wearing a surprisingly drab outfit—charcoal slacks and jacket, light purple blouse, light purple pumps. Like she just left a business meeting attended by people she didn't feel the need to impress. As she steps into the light, I can see a whisper of her five-o'clock shadow showing through her foundation.

"Please, have a seat," she says, sweeping a sharp-nailed hand toward a couch facing two wingbacks.

She doesn't attempt to shake my hand or lean in for a kiss on the cheek, and I don't move in to make the attempt either. There's something about the intimacy of it that would be inappropriate given how we left things.

She sits on the couch and I sit on a chair. Between us there's an oval coffee table holding a sea-glass green ashtray and a black leather cigarette case. She picks up the case, clicks a button on the side. The white butt of a smoke pops out and she places it between dark red lips, then presses another button. A flame leaps from the corner and she inhales, the cigarette crackling to life.

She holds the contraption toward me.

"No, thank you," I tell her.

"If you prefer your own…"

"Not smoking these days."

Her eyebrows go up. "Can I have my girl get you a drink? Jameson rocks still your poison of choice?"

I thought we were alone. Guess not. "Not drinking much either."

The cigarette nearly falls out of her mouth. "You. Ashley McKenna. Not drinking or smoking. Were you in rehab? Or is this an *Invasion of the Body Snatchers*-type scenario?"

"Like I tried to explain to Samson, people change."

Ginny nods, takes a deep drag, exhales, places the cigarette in the ashtray. Leans back and puts her hands on her knee. We sit there for a moment, occupying our space. I honestly don't know what to make of this. I don't think she does either. The anticipation is toxic. Like fumes you're afraid to breathe in.

There's a clicking sound from the other side of the room. Heels.

27

A woman appears from the darkness. Redhead, severe makeup, blue-sequined dress. Her Adam's apple casts a shadow across her pale throat. She reaches the table and places down a rocks glass in front of Ginny, containing fizzing liquid, ice, and a lime.

Ginny clears her throat, not taking her eyes off me.

The queen presses her hands to her mouth and reaches toward a cedar box, pulls out a coaster, and places it under the drink.

"I am so sorry…" she starts in a husky, put-upon voice.

"It's okay," Ginny says in a tone that makes it clear this is very much not okay.

The queen throws a frightened glance at me, like somehow I might be able to fix this, but I don't know where to start.

"That's all, darling," Ginny says, still not looking at her.

The queen nods like she's accepted her fate and disappears into the gloom. Ginny takes a sip and places the glass on the table, not on the coaster.

Finally, she says, "It's good to see you."

"Is it really?"

She puts her hand on her chest and her mouth forms an O. Like I've insulted her. "Why would you ever think otherwise?"

I laugh. Ribs ache. "You tried to kill me last time I saw you."

Ginny rolls her eyes. "Still on that, are you? I wasn't trying to kill you. I was trying to teach you a lesson. One you obviously learned. You are much more at peace than the last time I saw you." She squints. "Though I can see you're still up to your old tricks. What happened to your face?"

"Stopped an assassin. Foiled a terrorist plot."

"Tell me the real story."

"Just did."

Ginny taps ash off her cigarette. "At least your sense of humor is intact."

"What do you want, Ginny? How did you even know I was in town?"

She extends her hand, palm out, and fans her fingers so she can inspect her nails. "I know everything."

"Stop that."

She takes out her phone, cradled in a glittery purple-pink case. She regards something on the screen, taps a reply, the subtle movement of the phone catching the light and making it sparkle.

"Even if you knew I was coming home, how did you know I was at Mamoun's?" I ask.

"One of the employees there is on my payroll. He texted me soon as you walked in. As it happens, I've been looking for you."

"That's not creepy," I tell her. "So, I'm here."

Ginny leans forward, stamps out the cigarette. Picks up the case like she's going to extract another, thinks better of it, and places it back down. "I regret how we left things."

"You want something."

"We've been friends a very long time," Ginny says. "Truth is, I probably owe you my life. I know things got a little out of hand the last time we saw each other. I was in a tough spot. Everything that makes me *me* was under threat. This machine I had spent years building was on the verge of being smashed. It made me…cruel."

"Not the word I would use," I tell her, unable to offer another suggestion.

Truthfully, I wasn't blameless. The memory of Chell gets caught in my throat. I loved her so much it hurt. She loved me, too, just not the same way. After she got killed, after I tore through New York City like a wrecking ball trying to find the person who did it, I ran afoul of Ginny and she handed me my ass.

Ginny is a district leader. There are at least a dozen scattered around the city. The job description is as vague as the title, but it generally means anything that's fun and illegal, she gets a cut. At least, anything fun happening in her district, which used to be: 14th Street to the north, Delancey to the south, the Bowery to the west, and the FDR to the east. I expect, given the location and opulence of her new digs, her territory has expanded.

Point is, I was making a lot of trouble at a time when she was fighting for her business. I made the mistake of taking a swing at her in a blind rage, and that's when things went south. The next morning, when I came to, I apologized. Figured I owed her that much.

Because I sort of used to work for Ginny, too.

When I was playing the amateur PI thing, people would hear about me and hire me, but that's no way to make a living. I supplemented my income by working for Ginny. Mostly carrying things. Sometimes I found stuff and occasionally I hit people— though I always made sure they had it coming.

That was a life I was happy to leave behind.

It's why I left.

I was running from the giant clusterfuck of a mess I had made.

And it was time to grow up and I needed a little time away to do that.

But mostly, the clusterfuck, at the center of which, dictating the choreography, was Ginny.

I wave my hand around the apartment. "It seems things worked out."

"Do you like it?" she asks. "It's a little more befitting of my status. This building used to be an NYPD training facility before it got broken up into apartments. This here was the gymnasium."

"I'm happy you're happy."

"And I you," she says. "Your travels in the Orient have been fruitful."

"I wouldn't call it that. You didn't invite me over to reminisce."

She smiles. Gets up. Walks across the room to a table in the corner. Picks something up and carries it back, her heels clicking against the floor, the sound echoing in the cold void of the room. She puts down a folder.

"I need your help," she says.

I pick up the folder. Inside are some pictures. A young, skinny boy with mocha skin and a mop of dark hair. His eyes are red, a flare from the flash of the camera. Taken at a party by a cheap disposable. He's sweaty, smiling, wearing a tank top. There's another photo, too, this one a glamour shot. It's the same boy, wearing a brown wig, dress, heavy makeup.

"Jacqueline Coke," Ginny says. "Her straight name is Spencer Chavez."

"One of your girls."

Ginny nods gravely. "She's missing."

"And?"

"I want you to find her."

I close the folder, toss it on the table. "You have people for stuff like this."

"You're good at finding people."

"I don't work for you."

Her face falls a little bit, but rather than respond, she leaves me space to explain.

"I'm trying to walk a straighter path," I tell her. "I can't do that if I'm working for you."

Ginny sighs. "Did you happen to see them in the lobby? The Chavez family?"

The sobbing couple. "Yes."

"Spencer's parents. He's been missing for weeks. They're bereft. I've had one of my people looking for him and he hasn't been able to shake anything out. Last anyone saw him was on Staten Island. Wrapped up somehow in the heroin scene. To be honest, I was going to tell them it was a lost cause, but you being home, it strikes me as fortuitous. You know I don't hand out compliments like lollipops. You *are* very good at this. And it's your home turf. If anyone's going to find her, Ash, it's you."

"Staten Island has a heroin scene?"

"Clearly you haven't kept up with the news," Ginny says, standing, pacing around the room, raising her voice so it'll carry. "Heroin is experiencing a renaissance across the city, but on Staten Island it's reaching epidemic proportions. More than eighty overdoses this year. The police can barely keep up."

That, I did not know. And frankly, it's surprising to hear. Staten Island is the Smalltown, U.S.A. of New York. Lots of picket fences and modest suburban homes. Little leagues and church functions. But there are bad neighborhoods, too, and it's not like crime and addiction discriminate. Those things tend to latch on any place they can get a fingerhold.

I feel for the family. Really, I do. But it's Ginny. There's got to be a catch.

"I don't think I'm the right person for this," I tell her.

I think she's about to turn to face me, but she keeps walking, back to the table. Returns to the coffee table and places down a small leather toiletries case and a thick stack of bills. The bill on top is a hundred. It's held together by a yellow paper band that reads $10,000. My eyes go so wide they ache.

"Twenty thousand. There's ten to start, you get the rest at the end. Even if at the end you don't find her. I trust you to be thorough. If you can't find her, she can't be found. You get paid either way."

"She must be important to you."

"She's my friend."

32

"What's in the bag?"

"Naloxone. It's a nasal spray. Stops an overdose dead in its tracks. Figure where you're going, you might need it."

Ginny smiles. She sees it. Stubbornness giving way to curiosity.

That's a lot of money.

First, last, and security for sure.

But the money isn't the thing that's got the gears in my head turning.

I can't shake that image of the Chavezes, standing in the foyer, like they were the only thing in the world holding each other up. Crippled by grief over their missing kid. It makes me think of my dad. I know how and where he died, but we never got his body. Lost when the towers fell. No final resting place. Which means I'll never have a full sense of closure.

It's different, but it's not.

That little piece never feels like it's not missing.

My conscience is telling me this is a compromise—that for all my bluster about walking a straighter path, I'm full of shit because I'm back to old habits.

But it's for a good cause.

It makes me wonder if Ginny timed the Chavezes' exit with my entrance.

Probably.

Not that it matters.

"Okay," I tell her. "I'll do it."

She claps her hands and smiles. "Marvelous."

FOUR

THE DIM SHORELINE of Staten Island squats in the bay before us. The rest of the city radiates light and energy the way the island doesn't, like an empty patch in a star-filled sky. I can barely make out the curve of the eastern shore, the lights on the boardwalk at South Beach lit up despite the weather.

To the right, the waterfront neighborhoods of Rosebank, Stapleton, Tompkinsville, St. George. Closer to Brooklyn in feel and density. As you travel south on the island, it fades to a New Jersey aesthetic—strip malls and cookie-cutter houses—until you get to the southern tip, which feels like 1950s Middle America.

It's too cold for the air to hold any humidity so the view is crisp. A ferry pulls out of the terminal in the distance, bringing people into Manhattan for the evening.

New York City is home but Staten Island is *home* home. Where I was born.

I once read that if you took a pie graph that broke up the country by ethnicity, and laid it over the same graph for Staten Island, the numbers would be nearly identical. America in microcosm. With all the bullshit that brings.

A place I'm not always excited to visit.

The car drifts through the toll plaza to a cash lane, where the driver—not Samson, mercifully—forks over the $15 tab. It almost makes me feel bad, but not bad enough to dig into the stack Ginny gave me. I figure the toll is included in the trip.

When I got in the car I told the driver the address and he didn't ask questions, or plug it into his phone, or acknowledge me. I figure he knows where he's going.

We pull onto Bay Street. The island doesn't look much different than I remember it, though I haven't been here in long enough that I'd be able to point out things that have changed. Nothing looks new. Not the way it does in Brooklyn, in the gentrified neighborhoods, Williamsburg and Bushwick, where a block might be blown to shit but then suddenly there's a fancy bistro with modern design sensibility, stuck in between a run-down bodega and an abandoned building.

The infection of gentrification hasn't reached this far.

But then the driver cuts down Front Street. A good shortcut, saving you five minutes or so because there are no traffic lights.

Except, now there are lights. Three of them, plus a mammoth apartment complex on the water where the old Navy base used to be. The building is modern and boring with wood accents and a big courtyard in the middle. Bright orange loungers. I guess the infection has metastasized. Staten Island may be the least-cool borough, but as the rest of the city fills up to bursting, it was only a matter of time.

As we approach Bombay's building, I realize I don't know his apartment number, so I text him and he writes back immediately: *4B.* When the car pulls up, I thank the driver and climb out and he peels off, leaving me on a quiet street, the apartment building in front of me, a high school behind me, everything lit yellow by the sodium streetlights.

I feel lightheaded from anticipation. Step into the foyer, hit the bell for 4B, and the door buzzes. Press the button for the elevator but it's frozen on the third floor, so, fuck it, I take the stairs, moving faster up the landings until I'm nearly running, and I step into the hall and the door is opening and Bombay steps out and I throw my arms around him, almost knocking the two of us off our feet.

He slaps his hand against my back. Once, then twice. We stay there like that.

Bombay is my best friend in the world. Another person I met through an act of violence—in his case, a bunch of dumb kids in a post-9/11 frenzy smashing him into a locker because he committed the crime of being dark-skinned. I made them stop. It got bloody. We've been inseparable since.

He's the only person I maintained regular contact with while I was gone, and being here right now is the best I've felt since I got home, because he looks the same—shaved head, day-glo polo shirt. That smell. I don't know what the smell is. It smells like Bombay.

He pulls back, gets a good look at my face, frowns.

"What the fuck happened to you, bro?" he asks.

"Long story."

"Well," he says, stepping into the apartment. "I ordered pizza and I don't have to work tomorrow."

Something else to fill me with light and happiness: pizza. Real pizza.

The apartment has a tidy kitchen right off the front door. Tidy in a way like it barely gets used. A living room crammed with bookshelves, laptops everywhere. Stuff Bombay is repairing or tinkering with. Discarded bags of chips and bottles of diet soda.

I toss my bag on the floor and he turns on the television, switches it to a hip-hop radio station. Mos Def's *Black on Both Sides* plays as I settle into a chair. Bombay sits on the couch across from me.

We stare at each other for a second, until his face cracks into a smile and he says, "What the fuck, man! You're home."

"I know."

"Do you want something to drink? I don't have any whiskey, but I have some beer, and I think there's a bottle of merlot…"

I shake my head. "I'm good."

Bombay freezes. "You don't want a drink?"

"Jesus, is it that shocking? No, I don't want a drink."

He puts his hands up. "I'm not judging, man. It's a good thing. What took you so long to get out here?"

"Detour to Mamoun's," I tell him.

I leave it at that. I don't want to get into the meeting with Ginny. I don't want to explain it to him. Because I was barely in town for a half hour before I'm back in her employ. It's for a good cause, but Bombay is a worrier.

There's a knock on the door. Bombay runs over, exchanges cash for pizza, and comes back with two boxes. Sets them down on the coffee table.

"You want something non-alcoholic to drink?" he asks.

"Water is good."

He disappears to the kitchen and I flip open the top box. Steam curls off molten cheese. I know this is going to hurt but I don't care. I know it's rude but I don't care about that either. I pick up a piece and cram it in my mouth and it singes the top of my mouth and burns on the way down, but it is so delicious and I love it.

Bombay comes back, sets down two blue plastic cups full of ice and water. I tell him, "I hope you ordered some pizza for yourself."

"Fuck you, man," he says. He reaches for a slice. I bat his hand away and he raises his fist. We laugh and he takes a slice, holds it aloft, allowing it to cool.

"Now, fill me in on what happened," he says. "Starting with Portland."

I tell it between bites. Figuring I owe it to him, because a couple of times I tapped him for favors—Bombay works with computers, which are not really my forte, so if ever I need some light hacking or some research, he's my man.

It's a Holmes/Watson-type scenario, but with less sexual tension.

I tell him about Portland, where I was working in a vegan strip club. About Crystal, one of the dancers. Her shitty ex took their daughter from day care. It turned out to be at the behest of her estranged father, a politician running for higher office. He wanted to bury the skeletons in his closet by putting Crystal's daughter, Rose, up for an off-the-books adoption, and running Crystal out of town. I found Rose and put an end to all the rest. I don't tell Bombay the part about how I accidently killed the politician's right-hand man and buried him off a hiking trail in the woods.

I tell him about my stop in Georgia, where I was waiting for my passport to come through so I could flee the country for a bit. Hiding out at South Village, a hippie commune owned by Tibo, a mutual friend. How a militant environmental group wanted to kill some folks to make a name for themselves and me and some other people at the commune stopped them. I tell him how I was self-medicating with alcohol, then stopped drinking, then got hit with a case of delirium tremens in the middle of the woods. It's why I ramped way down on my alcohol intake. He's proud of me for this.

I tell him about Prague, where a spy—or at least I think he was a spy—blackmailed me into working for him, and the whole thing went sideways, and I ended up on the radar of an assassin, and that's why my face is battered. The U.S. bank that's currently under investigation for colluding with a terrorist group to push into oil fields in Iraq to drive up barrel prices—I'm the reason they got found out.

He takes all this in, nodding silently, smiling or laughing at a few points as he puts together the points where he came into play.

At the end of it all, the two of us having worked through a pizza and a half, he sits back.

"That all sounds completely ridiculous," he says. "Especially the last one."

"Yeah, it kinda does when you lay it all out like that," I tell him.

"So what's next? What are you going to do now that you're home?"

And here's the test.

Bombay has always been good at calling me on my bullshit. When you're standing on the edge of a four-story roof and looking down at a dumpster and you're drunk enough to believe you'll survive the fall—he's the friend who pulls you aside and explains why you shouldn't jump off roofs.

Which is a thing that actually happened to us once.

So part of me is a little afraid to say it because if he laughs at me, I have a problem.

"I've been thinking about becoming a private investigator, officially," I tell him. "Like, as a career."

He nods, like he's contemplating a dinner order. I tense up.

"Makes sense," he says.

Huh. "Really?"

"Helping people has always been your thing," Bombay says.

"You've got too many issues with authority to be a cop or a firefighter. You don't have the discipline to make it in the armed services. And you could be a social worker or something but that doesn't seem your speed."

"Well shit," I tell him. "I was expecting some pushback."

"No. In fact, I'll help you with what I can. It makes me happy to see you thinking about tomorrow. You didn't used to do that." He leans forward. "I really missed you this past year, but I'm glad to see it was good for you. Aside from you getting your ass kicked and then making up stories about assassins."

"There's a lot to do," I tell him. "First on the list is I've got to find a place to stay. I'm sure my old apartment is long gone. It'd be nice to find something in Manhattan, but I feel like Brooklyn might be more affordable."

"Plenty of units in this building," he says, swinging his arm.

"I don't feel like coming back."

"You're going to stay with your mom for a little bit?"

"I want to give it a few days."

Bombay grimaces. "Dude, if your mom finds out you're home and you haven't gone to see her, that'll kill her. Actually, she might kill *you*. And then she'll kill me for letting you hide out."

I gesture at my face. "What do I tell her about all this? That I fell down some stairs? I'm no good at lying to my mom. Another few days to heal and I'll go."

He shakes his head. This, he disapproves of. Which is fair.

"I have a spare room, and you can crash until you get on your feet," he says.

"Thanks."

"I'm going to get a beer. You want some more water?"

I consider packing it in. I've been up for too long. But I'm home, and I'm safe, and it feels good. My second wind is long spent but I feel a third one coming on, so I tell him, "Grab me a beer, too."

"I thought you weren't drinking."

"I said I wasn't drinking much. I'm not a fucking monk."

He disappears, returns with a brown bottle. The label says Flagship and features an outline of Staten Island. The colors match the Staten Island Ferry—orange and blue.

"Brewery just opened down the block," Bombay says, cracking the top for me.

I take a swig. It's good. "Speaking of, fill me in. What have I missed?"

TURN THE FAUCET for the shower. It starts cold so I give it some time to warm up. Strip down and look at my phone. Four hours since that beer—my one and only for the evening. I wanted another but I didn't take one and that's progress. Glad being home doesn't make me slide. Not yet.

Bombay turned in and I am desperate for sleep, but after being in planes and airports for the better part of a day, I need to clean up. I expect to sleep for at least twelve hours after this. More if I can manage it. I unwind the plastic wrap around my midsection, poke at the rib I think might be broken. Getting better for sure, but still not pleasant. My torso is covered in bruises. I lean into the mirror, which is slowly fogging up, but there's enough of me visible that I know I don't want my mother to see my face in this state.

Bombay is right. I can't put off seeing her, and anyway, if I'm going to be roaming around Staten Island, it won't be long until someone spots me and lets her know. It's sort of incredible how a borough with a population of a half million people can be so small like that.

After the shower, I head into the spare bedroom. It's more a storage room—computer guts on metal industrial shelving, some blinking equipment on a rack, a small twin-size bed in the corner. Which looks like heaven to me right now. The apartment is hot—one of those old brick buildings with a steam-engine boiler, so the heat builds up and stays in like a pizza oven. You end up sweating your way through the winter. I pull on a pair of shorts. Take the wad of cash out and flip through it. That's nice. I'm going to start apartment hunting, tomorrow or the day after, and this will help.

I take out the bag of naloxone. Inside are a dozen syringes. At the tip, instead of a needle, there's an inverted plastic cone, so you can press it into someone's nostril without stabbing them in the brain.

I grab the laptop Bombay lent me, swing my legs onto the bed, and open it up. Take the folder, look at the pictures again, poke around a little for Spencer. Find his Facebook profile and spend a little time reading through it. There's not much to see—most of the posts are marked off as friends-only, not for public view. There's a stray photo here and there where somebody tagged him.

I do find one video of him. He's sitting in a dressing room, laying foundation on his face, his hair pulled back and covered with a hairnet, like he's getting ready to put a wig on. He's talking to someone off camera, giving them a tutorial on how to apply makeup for a drag performance. High, sing-song voice, full of warmth. It tugs at me a little. I remind myself: this is what I'm doing. Helping him. Not Ginny. Him.

The video is five minutes long, parts of it sped up. I watch him transform from a funny, shy kid with delicate features into a striking Amazon done up in war paint. Side by side, you wouldn't know they're the same person.

Spencer Chavez as Jacqueline Coke turns to the camera and

gives a giant wink, twisting her lips into a razor smile.

The video ends.

Doesn't seem like there's much for me to do otherwise. And I know I should sleep but a fourth wind is whistling through the window. I think it's my body, knowing it's home. I want to leave here, get on the boat, go to Manhattan, wander around, see what's still there, who's still out, what's happening.

What I missed.

There'll be time for that. I know that.

I poke around on Google. Look for Crystal.

The other thing I didn't tell Bombay is that we had a thing.

Chell getting killed really messed me up. She loved me, but not the way I loved her. She carried my love like a burden. And even after I found the guy who killed her, even after I chose to dime him out to the cops rather than rip his throat out with my teeth—my attempt to end the cycle of violence—I was reeling. Crystal put my pain in perspective. Both with Chell and in a larger sense.

After I buried Wilson and got her daughter back, I figured the safest thing was for her to leave town and for me to disappear. Maybe that wasn't the right call, but it's what we did.

I thought about her a lot in the weeks afterward.

I thought about her in the months, too.

Her number was saved in my old phone, which got trashed in Prague. I could call Tommi, at the club where we worked. They've probably been in touch, and Tommi would at least let me leave a message for her. But I wonder if I should. That was a tough period in her life and I'm sure she's trying to put it behind her. I don't know what me getting in touch with her would help. Anyway, I tend to make people's lives harder.

Still, it'd be nice to hear her voice.

To know she's okay.

Nothing on Google. Can't find her on Facebook either, but given how things ended in Portland, I have to figure she's using a fake name. I find the number for Naturals, the strip club where we worked together, and sit there staring at it. It's only 11 p.m. in Portland. They must still be open. Must be.

I shut the laptop. Put it on the floor. Stare at the ceiling.

Close my eyes.

FIVE

THE FRONT DOOR creaked, barely audible over the music playing on the speakers. An orchestral piece meant to make a person want to sink into a plush chair, which is exactly what I was doing. I looked up and there was Bombay, brushing snow off his shoulders, eyes darting around Esperanto until they settled on me.

It was around four in the morning. The bars were letting out and MacDougal was growing thick with drunken idiots. I sipped my green tea and put my hand in the air so Bombay could find me, not that he wasn't already headed to the alcove in the back corner, to the two chairs we probably should have been paying rent on.

As he sat, the waitress who knew our faces but not our names asked if he wanted anything. He asked for a cappuccino and she turned to the coffee station to put it together and Bombay offered me his hand.

"So what's the good news?" he asked.

"Found an apartment."

"No shit. Where?"

"Little bit east of here," I told him. "One bedroom. It's a walk-up and the shower is a closet in the kitchen, but hey, you do what you have to. It's rent-controlled. Under a grand a month."

The waitress put down his cappuccino. He picked it up, held it to his lips, and blew, which did less to cool the drink and more to push a little furrow in the foam. "How the hell did you swing a sweet deal like that?"

"Luck, for the most part."

I didn't want to tell him the truth: that an old lady with a rent-controlled apartment had died. That a friend of mine had an arrangement with another friend at the city morgue. When a person died with no next of kin, he got a tip that maybe a rent-controlled apartment would be opening up.

Once a tenant is dead and an apartment is cleared, a landlord can jack up the rent to meet the market. But the clever and morally flexible can take over the lease and, along with it, the bargain-basement payments.

"Well, good on you," he said. "I know how much you've wanted to live in Manhattan."

"Not just me. You want to live here, too, right?"

"Well, yeah, but I'm not as viscerally unhappy as you are on Staten Island."

"Fuck Staten Island." I took a sip of tea, watched as a trio of drunken goons spilled into the café, stumbling toward the only available table left, close to us. I lowered my voice because I didn't want to invite their attention. "Living on Staten Island is like living behind a velvet rope for the best party in the world."

"It's not so bad."

"It's pretty bad."

Bombay shook his head. "You're being dramatic."

"Keep it up, I'm not going to make you my offer."

"What's that?"

"Come live with me."

Bombay put down the mug, suddenly interested. "I thought you said it was a one bedroom."

"It is. So we throw up a wall or something. It won't be comfy, but we'll be living in the East Village."

Bombay smiled. "You'd let me cramp your style like that?"

"C'mon, it'll be fun."

"Nah, man, I love you and all, but I like having my own space," he said. "Anyway, I'm making good money now. I won't be far behind you…"

"Hey, Habib."

Our conversation slammed into a brick wall. We both turned to look at the three goons sitting across from us.

The one who spoke had soft, boyish features. A mop of brown hair. A look like he came from money he didn't earn.

"They let you out of the Kwik-E-Mart for the night, huh?" he asked.

I looked at Bombay and raised an eyebrow. "May I?"

He shook his head. "Ignore it."

"Oh, c'mon."

"Dude, ignore it. It's not worth it."

I wasn't happy to defer to him, but I did.

For as enlightened as New York is supposed to be, it's often not. Bombay developed a thick skin over the years and didn't much care about the harassment. I tried to pick up the pieces of our discussions. "So, do you at least want to come look at the place…"

"Seriously though," the guy said. He shuffled in his seat, turning toward us.

They were older than us. Their eyes bloodshot. The guy's words were slurred. His friends were smirking, not doing anything to dissuade his shitty behavior. Which made them complicit.

The guy said, "How come all you Habibs works at gas stations and 7-Elevens and driving cabs and shit, huh? Like, it's kinda weird, right? Do you have like a special website that's only in Swahili, or whatever language you speak?" He pointed a finger. "That's gotta be it, right? Kind of like how all you fucking towelheads knew how to get out of the towers on 9/11, right?"

My temperature was rising in direct contrast to the temperature of the room, which was dropping fast. People were pretending not to look. Doing that thing where they were hoping someone else would intervene.

Bombay dropped his head. More frustrated with me than them.

"Please?" I asked.

He raised his hand. "Fine. Go ahead."

I stood up. The three guys shuffled in their chairs a little but remained seated. Tried to keep it cool. Figured there were three of them and only one of me, and we were in the middle of a crowded café at four in the morning.

They thought they had the advantage.

The guy opened his mouth to speak again. Before he could get a word out, I drove my fist so hard into his face it sent a jolt up my arm. His nose crunched and he fell back, crashing against the floor.

Everything in the café stopped, everyone turned to look at us, the orchestral music still playing. A lovely soundtrack to match the pain blooming in my knuckles.

His two friends looked at him instead of me. I picked up the ceramic container holding packs of sugar and smashed it onto the face of the guy to the left, then grabbed the guy on the right behind the neck and got close to him.

"You and your friends ought to leave right now, or things are going to get a lot worse," I told him. "This is me being polite."

The guy I hit with the ceramic was dazed. The guy I punched in the face, despite the blood trickling from his nose, looked ready for a fight, but the third guy, the guy I didn't hit, knew how to read the room: no one stopped me, the waitress was standing with her arms crossed, so maybe this wasn't a friendly environment for them.

The third guy pulled the first guy to his feet and led him to the front. The second guy followed. I looked at the waitress and shrugged. She rolled her eyes and went into the back room. She returned with a broom and a dustpan. I took them from her and got to work cleaning up the shattered ceramic and sugar packets.

"You gonna pay for that?" she asked.

"How much?"

"Couple of bucks."

"I'll leave a nice tip."

I sat back down, my fist aching. I rubbed my knuckles with my good hand. Bombay was looking at me with that mix of frustration and concern, with a very slight dash of bemusement.

Usually, that was the end of it, but I guess one of those dummies decided to be a baby about it, because ten minutes later a pair of cops came in and pulled me outside. Brought me down to the precinct, fingerprinted me, stuck me in holding. Only night I ever spent in the Tombs, the detention complex in Lower Manhattan where you wait until it's time to appear before a judge. It's a big, brutal monolith of a building, which is probably meant to give you a sense of what's waiting inside. I say this now like it makes me a tough guy, but truth is, I was scared shitless in there. Literally. I had to use the can so bad but wasn't prepared to do it in front of a crowd.

The next morning, I appeared before a judge next to a Latina woman in a rumpled suit—my public defender—and learned the charges were being dropped. As they led me out of court, she told me the guy I popped had gotten himself turfed from two bars before our paths crossed. At one of them he groped a waitress. He had enough to deal with, so he declined on pressing charges against me, and it made me feel even better about my choice to hit him in the face.

Lucky me. I made my way to the closest bathroom, my stomach twisted in a knot.

My first, last, and only night in a cell, surprisingly enough.

I hadn't slept well. And not because I was on a cold, hard bench, surrounded by the kind of guys who would carve out your eye to see what would happen. The thing that was keeping me up was what Bombay said after I sat back down at our table.

"Did you really need to do that?" he asked.

I nodded. "You know my philosophy on this. Some people need to get hit in the face. Next time he decides to be a bigot, he'll remember that. Now, do you want to come live with me, or what?"

"No," he said. "Because you like that stuff too much."

THE SUNLIGHT COMING through the blinds wakes me up. I climb to standing, feel my ribs shift. Stretch, but not too hard. Pull on a shirt and head into the living room. The apartment is empty. There's a note on the kitchen counter from Bombay, letting me know he had an errand to run and he'd be home later. Sitting on top of the note is a key.

The cupboards are bare so I figure on heading down the block.

There's a small diner by Borough Hall. Eggs and bacon and coffee sounds about right.

The sun is blinding. I pull down my newsboy cap to make a little shade. My hand drifts to my pocket, like there might be a pack of cigarettes and a lighter there. I laugh. Quitting wasn't so bad. I only occasionally want to trade a kidney for a smoke, but being home is already sparking old habits.

It's after lunch rush and the diner is empty, save a few people in suits sipping coffee and taking refuge from the jumble of government buildings and offices surrounding us. There's a lunch counter along the left side and tables to the right. I take a table at the back, figuring it'll give me some room to spread out.

A teenaged girl comes over and takes my order, which ends up being half the breakfast menu. By the time she brings over the coffee and a glass of ice water, I've got the loaner laptop set up. There's a chalkboard behind the lunch counter with the wifi password. I log in and try to figure what I should do first. Which is plunk some of the ice cubes into the coffee and take a sip, the contact to my lips alone making the neurons in my brain spin faster.

First, I should figure out all the things I need to do.

I take the laptop bag I swiped from Bombay's, dig around until I find a fresh yellow legal pad and a pen. Make a list:

Find a place to live
Get a job
Find Spencer Chavez
See my mom
Check on Crystal

There's some other stuff I could probably add to this, along with various subcategories, but it's nice to have something written down. The last one surprised me a little because I wrote it without really thinking about it. There are a lot of people I'd like to check on, but it would be nice to know she and Rose are okay and settled.

But that's also a little less pressing than the other stuff on the list.

It makes me guilty that seeing my mom is fourth. She should be first. But I need a little more time.

First up, find a place to live.

The waitress brings over the first of my plates and I alternate forkfuls of eggs and hash browns and sausage with clicks on Craigslist. I figured it wouldn't be pretty. It's worse than I thought. I search for the East Village, because it'd be nice to get back to the old neighborhood, but the first result is a studio going for $3,000 a month. And it doesn't even look like a nice studio. The one-bedrooms are north of that, which is sending my heart due south.

That puts Brooklyn on the table. I check Park Slope, because I've heard that's the cool neighborhood where everyone wants to live these days. Studios starting at $2,000. I don't want to live in a fucking studio. Not that I wasn't expecting this, but Portland and Prague spoiled me. Apartments with actual rooms.

Forget it. I'll come back to that.

Next up: how to become a private investigator.

This one, I know where to start, because I did look into it a few years ago.

According to New York State law, I have to be at least tenty-five, which is the only requirement I meet. Without a law enforcement background, you need three years' experience doing work relevant to the job, or apprenticing with an actual private investigator. You also need to take a test.

The waitress brings over a thick stack of steaming pancakes, which cheers me up.

A little clicking around and I reaffirm my understanding that I need real, on-the-books experience in the field. Then I learn that acting as a private investigator without a license is a class B misdemeanor, which is good for up to a year in jail.

The most sensible thing to do would be to apprentice. I do a search for private investigators and find a few offices in the immediate area. Click on one and it takes me to a slick website with a picture of a stone-faced guy sitting at a desk, the bay behind him. His name is Jay Gunner and he's a former NYPD detective. Seems like the perfect job for him. Jay Gunner is a cop name. Retired after thirty years on the job. He looks like a no-nonsense guy. I like no-nonsense. I bookmark the website.

Next up, Spencer Chavez.

I have the list of places he frequents, but figure it would be best to learn a little more about the local heroin scene. See if it matches up with Ginny's apocalyptic warning.

Typing "Staten Island heroin" into Google returns pages upon pages of links. Most of them from the local paper. Little things, like task forces and community meetings and arrests. But also some bigger pieces—obituaries and interviews with families whose kids had overdosed. Then: deep dives by glossy magazines. There's a big piece in *The New Yorker*. If *The New Yorker* cares about shit happening on Staten Island, it must be a big deal.

I forward that and a few other articles to my e-mail so I can read them later. Then I click through the local paper's stories. Look for common names and threads. If there's anything familiar.

Because I need to talk to someone, and after reading through two dozen articles, I know exactly who: Kathryn Petersen-Wichnovitz. Director of an organization in Port Richmond called Project Sanctuary, a treatment and recovery center. She's quoted in most of the articles I read and has a strong grip on the scene.

Plus, she's not a cop, which means she might actually talk to me.

My phone buzzes. A text from a number I haven't plugged in yet: *Are you fucking kidding me with this bullshit? Bombay tells me you're home and you haven't called me? The fuck is wrong with you?*

I write back: *Sorry. Where are you now?*

On the ferry to see your stupid ass.

I'll head down to the terminal and meet you.

I flag down the waitress and ask for the check as I pack up my things.

This is good. Lunette can probably help with at least one of the items of my list.

THE FERRY TERMINAL has a Dairy Queen. After all these years, New York has arrived—at least, for people who measure economic success by the influx of shitty chains. I stand outside the storefront, across from the set of doors where passengers will disembark from the next boat.

The wave that comes through is mostly tourists, wandering in a daze, looking for their path back to the Manhattan. Most tourists don't come to the island and stay—they take the ferry because it's free and there's a nice view of the Statue of Liberty. They turn right back around, much to the chagrin of basically every business and arts organization on this island.

I see Lunette before she sees me. She's got new glasses—big clear plastic frames on her small face, her blonde hair stuffed up under a gray cap. Long wool jacket a color somewhere between maroon and purple. I move toward her and she sees me and breaks into a run, slams into me. I wince as pain echoes through my torso, but I shrug it off and pull her close. Cigarettes and perfume. That

Lunette smell.

"You're home," she says. That little hint of a Russian accent slipping between her words.

"I'm home."

"And you didn't call me."

"It was on my list for today."

She smiles, smacks me in the arm. "How is Stanislav?"

Her cousin, Stanislav, who gave me a job at his apartment-rental company in Prague while I was living there. Great guy. Voice like a cartoon bear. One of the few things I'll miss about that town.

"He says he misses you," I tell her. "He said you should come visit."

"Maybe one day," she says. "So can we go outside? Have a cigarette?"

"Sure."

We walk through the terminal toward the promenade, exit through the doors and walk to the railing, the skyline crystal across the calm water. A lot of construction next to the terminal. Something's going up in the space between the ferry and Staten Island Yankee stadium. Lunette offers me a cigarette and I wave her off. She puts it between her lips and lights it. I'm thankful at least someone doesn't have an outsized reaction to me not smoking.

"What's the story here?" I ask, nodding toward the construction.

"Outlet malls," she says. "And a wheel. Like the London Eye, but bigger."

"Good god."

"Only a matter of time, right?" she says. "The tide was due to crash here."

We lean against the railing, look out over the water. The next boat is pulling out. The horn sounds, thrumming across the bay. It's cold, but that pleasant kind of cold where you feel good to be outside. Maybe a little invigorated.

"Where will you live?" Lunette asks.

"Don't know yet."

"I can help."

"Can you?"

She nods. "My new lady friend does real estate. She can find some places. What's your budget?"

"I'd like to keep it to under two grand a month. Fifteen hundred would be ideal. No roommates."

Lunette huffs out a little cloud of smoke and laughs. "You think you'll be able to live in this city at that rate?"

"Hope springs eternal. Where you living these days?" I ask her.

"Brooklyn," she says. "Bushwick. I don't like the apartment. I don't like my roommate. I'll probably leave soon."

"Where to?"

"Bombay's building, probably."

I look at her, smirk. Bombay is from Staten Island so it's not entirely out of bounds he'd end up here. "That's a little surprising."

"Why?" she asks. "I can get a two bedroom for what I pay for a studio in some shitty neighborhood. And in Brooklyn, anything worth doing, you have to wait in line for an hour. It's quiet out here." She takes a long, thoughtful drag of the cigarette. "I could do with some quiet." She flicks the cigarette to the ground and crushes it under the toe of her leather boot. "I could also do with a drink. Let's take a walk."

IT TAKES TEN minutes to walk to Cargo, a bar I used to frequent when I lived in this neighborhood. We grab a booth in the back. A waitress comes over and takes our order: coffee for me, Pinot Grigio for Lunette. We glance at the menus but I don't think either of us is hungry. Me because I just ate and Lunette because she's never hungry.

On the walk over we made it through most of the catching-up stuff. When I left, she was dating my cousin Margo. Things fell off and Margo is currently home for the holidays. I'll see her when she comes back. By the time our drinks arrive, I'm ready to get down to business.

"So," I tell her. "I'm working for Ginny again."

"That's stupid."

"It's not like before," I say. "One of her girls is missing. This is on the up-and-up."

"Is it ever that way with Ginny?"

"Kid is missing, parents are upset. I'm sure there's more to it than that, but that's enough for me to at least poke around a little. And she's willing to pay me a ridiculous amount of money to do it. Thing is, you might be able to help."

"How so…"

"He's into heroin."

Her back goes rigid. Eyes cold. "I'm clean."

I reach across and put my hand on hers, losing my train of thought for a second. "How long?"

"Four months."

"That's great."

"It is," she says, pulling back her hand to take a sip of her wine. "It's also real fucking hard. Do you know how many people I had to cut out of my life? I can't even think about them. So this is the first and last I'm going to say on the subject: find someone else to help you. I love you, but not even for you."

I put my hands up. "Say no more. Topic off limits."

She nods. "I'm sorry."

"Don't apologize. I'm happy for you. It's a good thing."

We sip our drinks, using them to fill the silence. I go looking for a lighter subject, figure on telling her my new career aspirations, when someone yells out, "Hey!"

We both look up. Standing over the table is a skinny kid with shaggy brown hair and thick black-framed glasses. Behind him is a heavyset Hispanic cook, arms folded in a don't-fuck-with-me manner. The skinny kid looks at me and nods, confirming a suspicion. "I remember you. You have to leave."

"Why?"

"You came in here last year," he says, his fists clenching and unclenching. "That stupid fucking game. You came in and attacked me."

It takes me a second, flipping through memories in my head like cards, until I find what I'm looking for. When Chell got killed, she had been working in a hardboiled live-action role-playing game—this goofy thing where you went around the city "shaking people down" for information. I figured someone involved in the game had killed her, so I played along for a bit. Problem is, I'm not very patient and no good at rules.

I remember this kid. I wouldn't say I "attacked" him, but I didn't leave him untouched. Didn't hurt him, but made it clear I was ready and willing. I cringe. Put up my hands in a "calm down" gesture and tell him, "Look, it's a really long story, but first off, I want to apologize…"

"Fuck off," he says. Points at the door. "Get out."

I look at Lunette. She shrugs and downs the rest of her glass of wine. I take out my wallet, peel off more than we owe, like a fat tip might make up for me being an asshole, and slide out of the booth. He steps aside as we make our way for the door.

Halfway there, I stop and turn. "I'm sorry. I know that might not mean anything."

He doesn't respond. Just stares at me like he thinks it might make me catch fire.

Back in the cold, Lunette puts another cigarette between her lips, lights it.

"Well," she says, smoke spilling out of her mouth. "That was fun."

"I guess I deserve that."

Lunette leans against the side of the building. Says, "You didn't think leaving was going to let you outrun karma, did you?"

"I don't know. Maybe."

"Doesn't work like that."

"Apparently not."

"What?"

"It's weird," I tell her. "So much has changed since I left. And yet it's like nothing did."

"The way it goes," she says, flicking her half-smoked cigarette into the street. "Now walk me back to the ferry. I've got some stuff I need to do."

We turn and make our way down Bay Street. I've got work to do, too. The ferry terminal is where I need to be. It's where I'll get the bus to Port Richmond so I can find Kathryn Petersen-Wichnovitz.

I'm happy for Lunette—I really am—and maybe this is selfish, but I was hoping she'd be able to help me.

Something. Anything.

I think she senses my disappointment, because halfway back to the ferry she says, "Brick."

"What?"

"Guy named Brick," she says. "I never copped from him, but I know some people who did. He's supposed to have the best shit. Might be a place to start."

"Thank you," I tell her. "You didn't have to do that."

"I know. That's the last of it. I'm serious."

"Sure thing."

I put my arm around her shoulder, pull her close, kiss her on the side of the head.

SIX

THE S46 BUS never gets above first gear. It inches down Castleton Avenue, coming to hard stops that make the people standing nearly topple onto one another. I manage to score a seat in the back but don't have it for long, because an older lady gets on the bus and I wave her over. As she makes her way through the crowd, some high school kid thinks I'm vacating for him, so I get between him and the seat until the old lady is set. He's annoyed but backs off when it dawns that I am literally twice his weight.

I catch glimpses of the street outside the windows, obscured because I'm stuck in the middle of the scrum, trying desperately to hold onto the overhead bar by my fingertips. Things look the same. That much is nice.

We pass the stop where I could get off and walk up to my mom's house and that makes me feel guilty. I wonder if I should go now. If she's not home, wait. I don't have my keys on me but

I know where she keeps a spare hidden: in the garage out back, underneath an old planter half filled with stale dirt.

It would be so easy.

But then I'd have to tell her some hard truths about my life, and that feels impossible.

I tell myself that if someone else selects this stop, I'll take it as a sign. The universe telling me to stop being such a fucking baby. But there's no ding. The sign over the driver doesn't light up. The bus shelter flashes by.

I pull out my phone and use the remaining time to brush up on the articles I sent myself.

By the time we approach Project Sanctuary, I've learned a couple of things:

When pharmaceutical companies introduced opioid painkillers, they downplayed the addictive nature. Doctors prescribed opioids like candy, so people got addicted. Eventually, those addicts couldn't get refills, and pills are expensive on the black market, so they turned to heroin, which was cheaper, widely-available, and close enough in terms of the high.

Capitalism in action.

That explains, in a general sense, why heroin is making a comeback.

Why it's hitting Staten Island so hard is a little less clear.

I have some theories. There are a lot of civil service workers in the borough, given the lower cost of living. Cops, firefighters, sanitation workers. People who break their asses in half just to make a living. They have high rates of injury and good health insurance. With good health insurance come good painkillers. But part of the problem, it seems, isn't the workers—it's their kids. The average commute time for Staten Island residents is among the highest in the nation, given the shit options for public transit and the poor road infrastructure. So kids have a lot of time unsupervised.

I feel like, too, there's an element of hiding in plain sight. Staten Island has a lot of wide open space. A lot of suburbs. The police out here, I'm sure they all do their best, I'm sure they're nice guys and gals, but the island has a reputation for being the kind of place you go when you're put out to pasture, or seeking a lighter workload. I remember hearing a story a long time ago about how the police precinct on the South Shore had a screen door.

"Quaint" is not the kind of descriptor you'd think to assign to any part of the NYPD, which is bigger than the armed forces of some entire nations.

Point is, if I were still doing illicit shit, this would be a good place to do it.

Ultimately, I think the problem comes down to isolation. The island is so cut off from the rest of the city. It feels lonely. You're a mile or two away from everything and you feel like it may as well be another galaxy. The times I felt alone were always when I fell the hardest. Propped myself up with booze and coke and cigarettes. Things that offered me temporary relief.

I get it.

Thinking you're helping yourself by hurting yourself because at least you feel *something*.

The bus approaches the corner of Port Richmond Avenue. Someone already pulled the cord, so I wait for the bus to pull over, climb out with a handful of people, stand there in the cold and try to orient myself.

Port Richmond is one of the neighborhoods that could most easily be mistaken for Brooklyn. Latin music blares from the cars that whiz by. Dilapidated storefronts with cheap apartments above them. Lots of dollar stores and Spanish restaurants. My favorite: 5-Eleven convenience stores. It's like Staten Island doesn't even rate for the full brand.

The Project Sanctuary building is across the street. Low, brick, mirrored windows. I wait for the light, cross over, push through the front door.

Inside is a small lobby with a scuffed tile floor. I can see the sidewalk clearly from in here. The mirrored coating on the windows outside is one-way, so the people inside have privacy. The space feels so much smaller because of how packed it is. The chairs in the waiting area are cheap wood and cushioning, like in a college dorm. They're filled up with a cross-section of the island. Every race, every gender, every class—from the gangbanger with teardrops tattooed under his eyes, to the guy in rumpled suit and wingtips, to the suburban mom with her daughter in tow. The daughter is too young to be in a place like this and I whisper a silent prayer that she's just tagging along.

A few people glance up, but quickly return to what they're doing: zoning out, dozing off, playing games on their phones, flipping through magazines. No one talks. The feeling of standing here is like being at a wake.

The walls are covered with pamphlets and posters. Multiple languages, from Spanish to Russian to Korean, advertising health services and housing programs. The light is gray, some of the bulbs blown and not replaced. Behind the reception desk, which looks pulled from a dumpster, is a short Spanish girl with red, red lips and a big smile. I approach the desk and she shifts in her seat. "Hi. How can I help you?"

"Kathryn Petersen-Wichnovitz, please." Had to practice that a couple of times in my head on the bus ride over so I could say it right.

"Do you have an appointment?"

"I do not."

She nods, picks up the phone, murmurs into it, listens, and looks up. "Can you wait a few minutes?"

"Sure." Since there are no open seats I stand and lean against the wall, next to a poster in a cheap plastic frame—a cloudy sky with "Let It Begin With Me" written in ornate black script.

I use the time to explore my new phone. Find some games. I'm halfway through a solid round of Solitaire when an e-mail notification pops up from my mom. I open it up to find a blank e-mail, before remembering that she sometimes puts the whole message in the subject line, like it's a text. It's adorable.

So when are you coming home?

My heart jerks a little.

I'm, what, three miles away? I could walk there. But she doesn't even know I'm in the country yet.

Soon, I write back.

"Hello?"

I look up, see a woman with frizzy black hair streaked with gray. Her shoes are worn. Her clothes—slacks and a blouse and a sweater—are more durable than stylish. There are deep lines at the corner of her eyes but her face shines like a star. She is ready, weight shifted forward on her toes. The way she looks at me is: *Can I help you?* And she means it. My bruised-up face doesn't throw her, but I guess that's not entirely uncommon here.

I walk over, offer my hand. She shakes it hard. "Ms. Petersen-Wichnovitz? Ash McKenna. I was hoping I could have a few minutes of your time."

She's suddenly unsure. "Please, call me Kathy. What is this in regard to?"

"I'm looking for somebody."

"Do you have identification?"

"Like, a driver's license?"

65

Her tone is sharp. "No, like a badge."

"I do not, I'm sorry."

She raises her eyebrow at me. That shining star dims. I can see the wheels turning—she's trying to figure a polite way out of this conversation.

"It's a friend," I tell her. "He's missing. His parents asked me to look for him."

She nods. "Okay."

"Thank you."

She leads me down a hallway. There are doors, some of them closed, some of them not. Most of the doors lead to offices and classrooms, but there's also a cafeteria. A dozen people silently eating or reading at long tables. Heads down, avoiding contact with each other. Spinning on their own orbits. People drift past us like ghosts.

Kathy leads me to a small room at the end of the hall. The lights are off. I think there's a desk sticking out from underneath the mounds of paperwork. Kathy points to a chair on the other side of the mound and I sit, take out the photo of Spencer, and place it on the pile. She picks up a pair of reading glasses, puts them on, and holds the photograph at arm's length.

"His name is Spencer Chavez," I tell her. "If it's helpful, he's in the drag community and performs under the name Jacqueline Coke. I know he's an addict, and the last anyone heard from him, he was on Staten Island. Sadly, I don't have much more to go on than that."

She takes off the glasses and raises a sharp eyebrow. "I thought you said you were friends?"

"It's been a long time."

She nods. "He looks familiar. We get so many people through those doors and I try the best I can. But he looks familiar. I think he came in a couple of weeks ago." She thinks, nods. "A few weeks ago, he was in the waiting room."

"Do you know why?"

"That, I can't remember. And I'm sure you understand but there are confidentiality issues here—I don't know if he has a file here, but even if he does, I can't pull it for someone who claims to be a friend. If you were law enforcement, I might be able to help some more. But even then…"

"No, I get it," I tell her. "It might be helpful to know his state of mind. Maybe if he was seeking treatment…"

"If he was, I would definitely remember him," she says. "He might have been meeting someone. He might have been getting clean needles or a health screening. We offer a lot of services here."

This isn't going as well as I'd hoped. There's a sound out in the hallway. Doors opening and closing, shoes squeaking on the linoleum. Kathy looks up and over my shoulder. This meeting is just about over. I make one more stab at it. "Does the name Brick mean anything to you?"

She nods. "He's a dealer. A very dangerous one."

"Do you know where he operates?"

She frowns. "If I knew that, he wouldn't be in business anymore.

"I do not doubt that." I stand up, push in the chair. "I'm sorry to have wasted your time."

She pauses, thinks. Says, "It wasn't a waste. A lot of people go missing. Not a lot of people come looking for them. It's a good thing. It's just…there are so many. If you find him, bring him here. We'll do what we can. Prepare yourself for what you might find."

"What do you mean?"

"The hardest kind of person to help is someone who doesn't want help," she says. "If there's one thing I know without any doubt or question, it's that. Unless someone wants to make a change, they won't do it. They'll dig in deeper. He has to want to be helped. So make sure when you find him, you give him what he needs. It might not be to drag him here kicking and screaming."

I laugh a little. "You sound worried about what I might do."

She raises that eyebrow again. Doesn't say anything. I get what she means.

"I understand," I tell her.

"Good," she says. "I have to make a call. Can you find your way out?"

"Sure." I shake her hand and take my stuff. She turns to the phone. As I step out of the office, I nearly knock down a scrawny black guy in a red do-rag. He's pushing a broom and gives me some serious stink-eye, like I should have known better than to fuck up the part of the floor he'd just cleaned.

"Sorry," I tell him before making my way to the front.

I T WAS PARTLY cloudy when I got off the bus, but the rest of the sky got filled up with gray while I was inside Project Sanctuary. There's a stiffness to the air, like it might snow. I look at the bus stop but don't really feel like standing still right now, so I walk down Castleton Avenue, in the direction of my mom's house. Just to have a direction to walk.

That wasn't terribly helpful. I guess I made a few mistakes. One, being some asshole off the street who has no authority of any kind to be asking questions. Two, assuming that any random person is going to have a lead on a needle in a stack of needles. Once again, I am not as clever or resourceful as I think I am.

I call up the website for Jay Gunner's office, click the link to his phone number. Goes straight to voicemail. Hang up instead of leaving a message, because I don't know what to say. *Hi, I'm a lunatic kid with dreams of being a PI, can I come work for you so I can get the requisite experience and that way I can stop working for a drag queen kingpin? Queenpin? Whatever.*

There's a shuffle behind me. I turn, find the sidewalk empty. We're away from the main drag now, in a more residential area. The occasional car cruises past but otherwise it's quiet, people locked inside, away from the cold.

I keep walking. Hear another shuffle.

Still no one behind me.

Because he's to my left.

There's a burnt-up house looming over me, red brick charred and windows boarded up. There's shrubbery around the property, about ten feet tall, blocking the view of the lawn from the street. It's so overgrown there's barely space left to step between the hedges.

Slightly past those hedges, a few feet away, is the guy in the red do-rag. He pulls up the bottom of his shirt and shows me the butt of the gun tucked into his waistband, resting against well-defined abdominal muscles. He raises his hand and waves me toward him.

As I step through the hedges, branches smacking at my face, he says, "Tell me what the fuck you know about Brick."

SEVEN

I PUT MY HANDS up as I step onto the unkempt lawn, frozen grass crackling under my boots. The man doesn't reach for the gun, but maintains the grip on his shirt so I know it's there.

"I asked you a question," he said.

It hangs in the air. I shrug a little. Try to get him angry.

Which may seem counterproductive. But angry is distracted, and he still hasn't reached for the gun, which is a big mistake on his part. Guns are only a problem when they're pointed at you. Up close, they don't matter for much. I'd rather go against a gun than a knife in close quarters.

The anger is bubbling up now, and he's about to say something, but before he can get the words out, I launch forward and put my hand on the gun, keeping it pressed into his midsection.

"Motherfucker," he yells, using both hands to try to pull it out. But I'm pressing down with all my weight, which means I have all

70

the leverage. I pop him in the face with a quick jab.

He stumbles backward and I wrap my fingers around the pistol grip. I step back and yank it free from his pants, put a little distance between us. Eject the magazine and toss it into the bushes alongside the house, pop the loaded bullet out of the chamber and let it fall to my feet, throw the gun over his shoulder.

The guy's nose is bleeding but it doesn't look broken. He's even angrier than before but I can't blame him for that.

"You want to make this into a thing, we can make it into a thing," I tell him. "Or we can be gentlemen about it."

He touches his fingers to his nose, looks at the blood on his fingertips.

"Yeah, real fucking gentle, asshole," he says.
"Don't get all indignant. You pulled a gun on me," I say. "I could have made that a lot worse."

"Fine," he says, shaking his head. "What the fuck you want with Brick?"

"Nothing in particular, just a name I heard." I reach into my pocket, pull out the photograph of Spencer. Hold it up. "I'm looking for this kid. He's missing. I heard Brick was a player. I'm guessing he's pretty important if you braced me for dropping his name."

"Well, you ain't a cop," he says. "Figure guy who ain't a cop show up asking questions about Brick, got to find out why."

"Sure. With a gun. How come you know I'm not a cop?"
"I didn't take the motherfucking gun out, did I? We could have had a perfectly pleasant conversation if you didn't need to go Jackie Fucking Chan on me. And I know you ain't a cop because you told Kathy you weren't. You were a cop, you would have used

I gesture with the picture. "You seen the kid?"
He shakes his head.

"Where can I find Brick?" I ask.

At this, he laughs. Long and hard. "You think you're gonna roll up on the hill and he's going to invite you in for tea? Maybe some scones? You a dumb motherfucker, or else you got a death wish. That ain't how it works."

"I guess we're done here," I tell him. "Sorry I hit you in the face."

He nods slowly, holding my eye with his. As I step through the hedges, I hear him say, "You'd better hope we don't see each other again."

Something tells me we might.

Because now I know where to find Brick.

IT TAKES AN hour of playing bus hopscotch to make it to Park Hill. Could have driven here in ten minutes probably. I'm hoping this'll be my last job on Staten Island for a while.

When I get off the bus, I walk through the parking lot of a Home Depot, toward Park Hill Avenue. It's a long street, with apartment complexes on either side. Privately owned but federally subsidized. Birthplace of the Wu-Tang Clan, which even stuffy white people who hate rap music will brag about, because it's about the only positive claim to fame Staten Island has. That, and David Johansen from the New York Dolls lives here. I saw him in the supermarket once. He was wearing sweatpants. Punk has been dead for a while but that was another fistful of dirt on the grave.

When the guy in the red do-rag referred to "hill" I have to imagine this is what he meant. That's what people call it. And no, I don't plan to go looking for Brick. My plan was never to track him down. At least, not yet. I'm not a complete idiot.

I only wanted to know where he operated.

Because if this is where Brick works, he'll have customers.

And customers, I can work with.

Given my history, I feel slightly more comfortable around drug users than I do trying to work with people like Kathy. May as well lean into that.

There's no good place for me to camp out to keep an eye on things, so I walk down Park Hill Avenue. Keep going until I get to the end, then circle back. Probably bringing too much attention to myself. A white face in Park Hill usually means one of two things: I'm a cop, or where do I score?

Luckily, it's winter. The street is abandoned, except for an older lady pushing a grandma-cart of groceries and a young guy hustling out of a building like he has someplace to be. I do see a flash of movement on one of the rooftops. A lookout, maybe, reporting back to someone that there's a goofy white kid outside.

I make it halfway down when a doorway at one of the buildings opens. A big man in a heavy denim jacket steps out. He looks at me like I'm food. Wants me to know that's how he's looking at me.

I keep walking.

This isn't going to work.

I go back to Home Depot. There's a food truck parked outside, so I get myself a dirty water dog and a bottle of water, stand there and eat in the cold. Look out over the parking lot.

The cars are arranged funny.

There's a bunch close to the entrance of the store, then a big stretch of empty spots, then more cars crowded together, all the way on the other side of the lot. As far from the front door as you can get, closer to the apartments.

Maybe people who visit the apartments use it for parking. It would be a good spot if you were stopping by for a short while. That's promising. I go back to the truck, get another hot dog and a pack of chips, climb onto the bench of a picnic table and sit on the top, someplace that I've got a good view of the landscape. Eat the food slowly, so even though it seems a little crazy that I'm sitting out in the cold, at least I'm doing something other than nothing.

My phone buzzes. Message from Bombay: *What's the word?*

I reply with my free hand. *Doing a thing.*

Coming back soon?

Later.

New Thai place down the block. You game?

Duck yeah.

Stupid autocorrect. Not worth fixing. He'll know what I mean.

Once I'm done with my food, I sit there, cinch my jacket around my throat, pull down my hat, think warm thoughts.

Pizza. Coffee. Aruba. Smelting.

An employee in an orange vest helps an old lady carry heavy bags to her car. He gives me a funny look on his walk back.

I don't know how much longer I can realistically do this. Either they're going to give me shit for loitering or I am going to freeze to death. I look at my phone, pledge to give it five more minutes. After two, there's a flash of movement, and then a stream of people moving toward their cars. Young, mostly. They come all at once, like a bar just let out.

A few of them don't get into cars, they veer toward the bus stop, so I figure on heading that way, but then one person breaks off from the crowd and makes his way toward the food truck.

And he looks familiar.

Small kid. Sandy hair. Freckles. Gaunt. Wearing a black bubble jacket and brown, beaten construction boots. He stops at the truck and mumbles something to the old man inside.

When I knew him, his face wasn't gaunt.

I hop off the bench, get a little closer.

"Timmy?" I ask.

He turns, surveys me. It's him. I know it's him. I don't know if he knows it's me.

But after a moment, his face splits into a grin.

"Ash McKenna," he says. "Where the hell have you been?"

I walk over, take his hand, smack him on the shoulder. I'm surprised it doesn't knock him to the ground. He's so much smaller than the way I remember him; the kid I sat near in high school a lot because his last name is Murphy. If we were in a class together, the alphabetical draw would put him behind me.

He was a nice kid. Smart, quick with a joke, friends with everyone. The kind of person you have a perfectly pleasant relationship with in high school and never see again. And then you run into each other in the supermarket or something and reminisce briefly before making plans to get together and catch up, and you both know you're lying but it still feels nice to pretend like you're not.

"Long time," I tell him.

The guy in the food truck hands him a bottle of water. He takes it and pats at his pockets. It might be a ploy to get me to pay but I do it anyway. He smiles as I hand over a bill. "Thanks, man. Yeah, it's been a long time, you know? What you been up to?"

"Traveling a bit. You?"

"Eh, out of work. It's a long story. If you're back on the island, why don't we catch up sometime, huh?"

"How about now?"

He pauses. I've broken protocol. He looks nervous.

"Look," I tell him, lowering my voice. "I'm not here to judge. I'm not here to give you shit. But it's not hard to guess why you're here. I'm trying to find someone who's missing. He travels in circles I don't have access to. So...I know you don't owe me anything, I know you might have shit to do. But it would be a big help if I could pick your brain for a couple of minutes. We can grab something to eat."

He hesitates.

"My treat," I tell him.

He nods, smiles. It's a painful smile, like he doesn't really want to be doing this, but at least there's something in it for him. I don't know if it's the chance to help someone or the food.

"Okay," he says. "You got a car?"

"Nope."

"I'll drive," he says, turning toward the jumble of cars on the other end of the lot.

H E DRIVES US to Bay Street in a white Dodge Neon that's beat to shit on the outside but pristine on the inside. We catch up a little. Where-you-been, how-you-doing stuff. He's happy to hear that Bombay is well, and that I just got back from Prague. I leave out the sordid and violent details and tell him I had a good time. It's not entirely a lie.

We find parking on a side street and head onto Bay, the corridor that runs along the northeastern shore of the island. Head into a small diner that looks like it hasn't been updated since the 1950s. Take a booth in the back. Pick up our menus. When the waitress comes over, I settle on coffee and a cheeseburger deluxe. Timmy asks for the same and ducks off to the bathroom. While I'm waiting, I shoot a quick text to Bombay, let him know to eat without me.

Timmy returns tens minutes later looking quite content. The tension in his shoulders is gone. His eyelids look heavy. He's smiling. He half-sits, half-falls into the booth. I think about making a smart comment about his drug use, but realize that would be hypocritical, and anyway, it'll be more helpful for me if he's not sitting here jonesing.

He sighs with his entire body and says, "So."

I take out the photo of Spencer, put it on the table. He takes it, gives it a good look, shakes his head. "Never seen him."

"Been missing for a bit. Trying to find him. He's tied up in the scene."

The waitress comes over, pours opaque coffee into ceramic mugs. I plunk some ice cubes into mine. Timmy slides the cup close, inhales the steam. Part of me regrets doing this. He looks like a shell of himself. Like the inside parts of him, the parts that make him a person—hopes and dreams and wants and needs—have been carved out. I'm about to tell him this was a mistake and that I'm sorry, but he starts talking.

"My folks died," he says, his voice even with acceptance. "Car accident. About five years now."

"I'm sorry to hear that."

He waves me off like he's shooing away a fly. "You know how it feels. A little, right? Your mom okay?"

More guilt. "Yes."

"That's good. Hold her tight, man. It's weird how losing your parents upends your life. I mean, you get it, I don't have to tell you."

"I only lost my dad."

He laughs a little, takes a sip of coffee. "It's not a competition. I'm just saying, you know how your parents are your parents? They're like this anchor. Regular as the sun. There since the day you're born, and then they're not. It's like this big hole in the world you don't know how to fill in."

"That how it started?" I ask.

He shakes his head. "No, first thing I did was throw myself into

77

work. I was doing construction stuff. Managing sites and stuff, but after they died, I needed something to do with my hands. Noise to fill up my head, y'know? So I started pitching in on every little thing I could. Worked too much. Eventually fell and hurt my back. Then came the pills." His voice drops. "Then came the rest."

Timmy looks up at me, eyes misting.

"I didn't mean for it to get like this," he says.

My heart twists. When my dad died, I threw myself into some very bad things—violence, drugs, alcohol. Timmy did something so much more constructive—threw himself into his work. And yet here I am, sober-ish, and he's the addict. Started out and ended up on opposite ends.

"You don't need to justify anything to me," I tell him. "I know the feeling. And I know how hard it is it cover up that thing that's missing. It's like…you know how they say time heals all wounds? Even when a wound heals, it leaves a scar, right? And that scar never goes away. You can always feel it. Sometimes it tugs when you move. Sometimes it aches. It's always with you, no matter what you do."

He nods. "That makes sense. That's a good way to put it."

The waitress interrupts with our plates. Timmy tears into his burger like he hasn't eaten in days. We eat in silence for a couple of minutes, but then I figure it's time to get down to business. I put down the last quarter of my burger so I can dump some ketchup onto the plate for the fries. "So what was with the procession?"

Timmy looks up and raises an eyebrow, his mouth full.

"All these people coming out at the same time," I say. "Looked like a wave of zombies."

Timmy finishes the food in his mouth. "Guy makes us wait. We line up in the stairwell. Sometimes an hour or two. That way he only has to come out once."

"Brick?"

"How do you know about Brick?"

"I'm resourceful."

"One of his minions," Timmy says, laughing at the term. "I don't even know what Brick looks like. He has a guy. But everyone wants his stuff. Quality is always good and he keeps us safe."

"How so?"

He pops some fries into his mouth. "Never gotten jacked in that neighborhood. Once you're a customer, you're protected. No one will touch you. I used to cop at the Berry houses. Got rolled four times 'cause the dealers there did not give a fuck."

"So I want to find this kid," I tell him. "You tell me. What do I do?"

"Best bet? Check out the shooting galleries. Highest concentration is down in South Beach, because of Sandy."

"The hurricane?"

"Yeah, fucked up the island good. Ruined a lot of homes down there. Made them unlivable. The government is supposed to be renovating and fixing them, but they're dragging their feet, so there's a lot of empty space. Plus, if it gets found out, it's easy to pick up and move to another one nearby. You got a pen?"

I hand him one from my bag. He pulls the paper mat out from under his plate and writes down some street names and addresses. When he's done, he folds it up and gives it to me. "Those are the ones I remember. Not all of them might still be active but you hang around that area enough, you'll find plenty of people to talk to. I put my phone number on there, too, in case you need anything."

"That's really helpful. Thank you."

Timmy shrugs. "Kills me to think this kid's parents are out there and don't know where he is. It'd be nice to help somebody. Maybe all this shit might end up actually counting for something."

He smiles when he says that and I see a little of the old Timmy.

COULD PROBABLY WALK to Bombay's from here—it's a little over two miles, but Timmy offers to drive. Five minutes later we're pulling up in front of Bombay's building. I reach across and shake his hand.

"I appreciate the offer for help," I tell him.

"And I appreciate the burger. A word of advice?"

"Sure."

"Be careful fucking around with Brick. Last guy I heard about who crossed him? Gone. Disappeared from the face of the earth. He doesn't fuck around."

"Yeah, well, the ones who last the longest usually don't," I tell him. "Thanks for this. For putting yourself out there."

"Hey, sending you out to a few addresses doesn't infringe on his shit," he says. "I'll help you when I can, but anything that's going to cause trouble for him, you're on your own, you know?"

"Fair enough." We shake hands again. "Take care, okay?"

"You, too."

I get out of the car, watch it speed off. Feels like I'm skirting the edge of something bigger than I thought. I think back to last year, when Bombay's apartment got trashed because I was staying with him. Someone was looking for something they thought I had. It's adding some urgency to finding my own place. I've got to limit his exposure.

I try. I really do. And yet, here we go again.

EIGHT

BOMBAY ISN'T HOME. I don't feel like being inside and I've got that feeling of electricity under my skin. No chance of sleeping anytime soon. Used to be, the way I handled this was: drink until I passed out. That option is pretty well off the table so I get dressed and walk down the block and wait for the next ferry to Manhattan. Figure I could do with a walk. Check the old spots. See if they're still around.

It's a thin crowd in the terminal. Most people are coming the other way, headed home from Manhattan. But still there are a couple of wide-eyed nerds excited to be making a jaunt into "the city" for the evening.

That's what Staten Islander's call it. The city. Like a different country, even though the island is a borough. All part of the same organism. But that's the island's lot. Left in the cold. It's why a group of politicians here got together and tried to secede in the early '90s.

The boat doors open and the crowd shuffles over the dual ramps. I'm no longer drinking myself into a stupor but it'd be nice to have something to take the edge off. I order a Bud tallboy at the snack bar and find a quiet spot, watch the dying glow of the sun fade below the horizon. Sip the beer and feel a mix of anticipation.

And something else.

Fear. Should just come out and say it.

I'm afraid of what I'll find on the other side.

After the boat docks, I wander to the R train, take that up to Prince Street. Make the long walk east and cross-town to Alphabet City. It's two weeks to Christmas and it shows. Dead trees strung up with glittering lights, storefronts filled with pleas to come in and shop. On Houston, I pass a man in a skimpy Santa suit and a woman in one-third of an elf suit. It's far too cold for the amount of skin they're showing, but from the way they're stumbling and slurring, I doubt they feel it much.

My phone buzzes. Take it out, and the number associated with the text is all zeroes, but I know who it is.

Status report?

Nothing worth discussing.

Do hurry, darling.

Doing my best.

I stash my phone, keep walking. Let my feet carry me. Cut up and down streets where I used to stumble and rage.

On East Third, I stop. Stand outside the boarded-up storefront that used to be Apocalypse Lounge. When it felt like the world was going to shit, I could always take refuge in Apocalypse. It was a bar that looked assembled from the remainders of a warehouse fire, the walls covered with haphazard graffiti. Dave, one of our crew, was the bartender, and the owner was a no-show, so we had run of the place.

It closed last year. Became a restaurant. I guess that didn't work out because now there's plywood over the windows, everything else stripped away, a sign offering it as a rental property. The street is quiet. One of those sleepy little corners of New York where it feels like the world fell away.

I consider pulling the plywood off the door, or picking the lock on the sidewalk grate. I'm sure whatever was left of Apocalypse was torn away, but I wonder if the secret room is still there. Down in the basement, in the bathroom under the stairs, behind the bookshelf. A dingy little room with two couches and a coffee table. An office for me, a place to do illicit shit for a lot of people. Ultimately, for all of us, a little piece of something we felt like we owned, even though we never did.

Once I can't take it anymore, I turn and walk north to St. Dymphna's. Step inside, a burst of warm air enveloping me like a hug. Walk up to the bar. It's crowded. I don't recognize the bartender. She's in the weeds, struggling to make four drinks at once, doesn't even acknowledge me. I look around, don't recognize anyone else. Walk to the back. Find the smoking patio is still locked. The neighbors upstairs had complained about it so the bar manager closed it. Well, then don't live above a bar, assholes.

I leave. Wander. Find more bars. Don't find anyone I know. The city feels so different. I recognize it, but it feels like an old friend. Grown taller, lost weight, different hair. That image you had of them slightly skewed.

The people here seem younger. More hopeful.

Maybe I'm less angry.

Even after the burger with Timmy, I'm still hungry, so I head down to Milon. That's still there, at least. One of four Indian restaurants grouped around a stone staircase. Two at the top of the staircase, two at the bottom. As I make my way up the stairs, waiters of all four restaurants come out and try to hustle me into theirs, but I always go to Milon. Up and to the left. I've always understood it to be the best of the four, even though I have nothing to base it on.

It looks the same. Exactly the same. Christmas lights hanging from the ceiling so low I have to stoop, but not because it's the season, it's always that way. The seat right by the window is open so I sit and the waiter appears with a plate of papadum and dips. He hands me a menu but I hand it back and ask for meat samosas and lamb kori and garlic paratha. Probably more than I should eat in one sitting but I don't care.

I chew on the thin, crisp shards of papadum and stare out the window. Watch people scurry by, collars pulled up, hands jammed into coats, going from one warm place to another, Indian techno playing softly on the speakers.

"**E**ARTH TO ASHLEY."

I looked up. I had been rubbing the side of my head where Samson threw his elbow during the pimp job. It was tender. Sometimes I pressed on it hard to make it hurt, because when it hurt enough, it distracted me from stuff I didn't want to think about.

The first thing I noticed when I looked at Chell all those years ago was her left eye. The discoloration in the white part that made it look like there was smoke billowing around the iris. A birthmark, she told me once. Then her red hair, a shade somewhere between a fire truck and the flames it was rushing to put out.

Finally, the smile like she had a secret and would never, ever share it.

"Where'd you go?" she asked.

Someone opened the door of the restaurant. With the air conditioning pumping and the heat wave currently pressing a boot into the city's neck, it was like standing in front of an oven door. Outside, the sidewalk radiated sunlight. A woman walked by topless, her sweaty shirt draped around her neck. Some men hooted and hollered. She didn't seem to care, but I considered going out and hitting them because hitting people made me feel good.

"I'm right here," I said.

Chell grimaced. "No, you're not."

"It's been a hard few weeks."

"More than a month, Ashley. You haven't even spoken to Bombay."

"How do you know that?"

"He told me. He's worried. We're all worried."

It was a dance. We both knew why we hadn't talked. I had—once again—gotten slightly more drunk than necessary and told her I loved her, that she should give me a chance, that maybe a relationship between us could work. She rebuffed me, again, told me she loved me, but not like that, and we were better as friends. It made me feel lousy and I drank to cover it up and that sent me into a spiral.

Funny thing about a city of eight million people: it's real easy to be alone if you want to be.

The waiter arrived and put down our food—a shared plate of rice, lamb kori for me, chicken tandoori for Chell, an order of garlic paratha to split. The little cast iron bowl the kori was served in, set atop a wooden block, still sputtering. I picked up the plate of rice, dumped some of it onto the empty plate in front of me, and offered the plate to Chell. She waved it off like she always did.

"I'm sorry," I said.

"What are you apologizing for?" she asked.

Shrug. "I dunno. Stuff."

"It doesn't count as an apology if you don't know what it's for."

I piled some lamb onto the rice, ate even though it was too hot. Washed it down with the beer we bought in the bodega downstairs. The bottle said it was made with rice and it had a pink tint. "I'm sorry. I'm a fucking mess."

Chell's eyes went soft. The way they did when I gave her a peek behind the curtain I spent far too much time and effort trying to hide behind. She was the only person I ever let see me like that. Not even Bombay.

"Ashley…" she started. The way she said it made it clear she didn't really have a destination in mind.

I shrugged. "Forget it. We've had this conversation too many times. You know how I feel, and I know how you feel. You know the things I carry, and I know the things you carry. Just the way it is. I want you in my life and I accept that it won't be the way I want it. That's on me. I get it. It's a cycle. We do the same things, over and over, expecting a different outcome, but there never is."

"Well, you talk a good game," Chell said as she speared a piece of chicken, chewed on it while gazing out the window. Turned back to me. "So, how long until you think we'll end up having this conversation again?"

The words dripped with something viscous and caustic. I didn't know how to respond.

Part of the reason I loved Chell is that, because of the way my dad died, people always wanted to talk about it. They were always saying they were sorry. And I hated it. One, because I don't want to talk about it with every fucking person I come across, but two, because I hate that someone would apologize as though it was their fault.

Chell never told me she was sorry. Never pushed when she felt me pull back. Just gave me the space to do what I needed. Sometimes I needed to cry, and it felt safe to do that in front of her.

But I could see it on her face. The way she squinted, heaviness to her brow. She was getting tired of this dance.

"Why do you do it?" I asked.

"What?"

"Put up with me."

My voice cracked when I said it. I didn't mean for it to, but it did.

The intensity in her eyes disappeared. I was in the process of stabbing a piece of lamb and she reached across the table and put her hand on mine. Her skin was cold from being inside the air conditioning for so long. When she took my hand, I kept staring at the plate, at the piece of lamb on the end of my fork.

She said, "Ashley."

I looked up at her. That smoke billowing around her eye.

"I do not 'put up with you,'" she said. "Please don't ever say that again."

"I'm sorry."

"See," she said, smiling. "That one actually counts."

We ate the rest of the meal in silence. Nothing between us settled. And I think we'd accepted it wouldn't be. We could find a way to co-exist in that. It was important that we had each other in our lives. That much, we were able to realize.

At the end of the meal, she waved over the waiter and said, "You know it's his birthday, right?"

It wasn't.

But it was always one of our birthdays when we ate there.

Two months later, Chell was dead.

THE WAITER CLEARS my empty plates and puts down a small tin bowl with a scoop of mango ice cream.

There's commotion from the other end of the restaurant. One of the waiters goes over to the light switch, another to the ancient boom box hanging from the wall in the back. The waiter at the stereo blasts the volume and plays an Indian happy birthday song, while the waiter at the switch flicks it on and off, over and over. A third waiter comes out of the kitchen with two tins of mango ice cream. One of the scoops has a small birthday candle sticking out of it, the flame dancing in the dim light.

He places the tins in front of a middle-aged married couple. It's the woman's birthday. Supposedly. The waiters clap. The lights flick on and off. I can't help but smile. I don't think I've ever been here, not once, that this didn't happen. I wonder how many are lies and how many are actual birthdays. I'm willing to bet more of the former.

And then it's over. The waiters return to their post. I leave a wad of cash on the table, way more than the bill because I love this place and never want to see it close. Head for the door, back into the cold. Pick a direction and walk. It doesn't take long before I'm in front of my old place.

The building looks the same. Old, red brick, standing strong. A lot of apartment buildings are getting pulled down. The architectural flourishes that used to be so common, disappearing in favor of flat gray boxes. I test the door but it's locked. Probably for the best. What am I going to do? Knock on my old door?

It's not my place anymore.

I'm not as sad as I thought I would be about that.

The fear I felt on the ferry ride over has dissipated. I think it's because I expected this to be way more depressing. That I'd mourn my old life slipping away.

Instead, it just is.

I will never live in this neighborhood again. Not unless I win the lottery, or go back working full time for Ginny. Winning the lottery is more likely. This job is a one-shot deal.

Leaving for more than a year was the hardest thing I ever had to do. There were plenty of nights, especially in those first few months, where I nearly came back. I can see now the good it did for me. It was like a hard reset on my life. A new perspective that let me look at this place as it is, not as I think it's supposed to be.

Here's the thing about living in New York City: There are people stretched around the block ready to tell you what the thing is about living in New York City. But those people don't live here. They live in an idea of what they want the city to be. It ends up defining them, rather than allowing them to define their own experience.

I'm not like that anymore. I'm happy about that. I turn away from the building, walk away.

Put it behind me.

As I make my way down the block, I hear a scratch on the pavement.

Glance over my shoulder, on instinct, and see nothing.

Keep walking.

Hear it again.

This time I turn quick, and I see a flash of something ducking behind a white van.

Could be a rat.

In my experience, it's never a rat.

I'm in the middle of a side street, the streetlights blocked by a large tree so that this whole section is cast in a scatter of shadow and yellow light. There's no one out. It's a bad spot to be caught in a worse spot. Second Avenue is in sight, alive with traffic and people. Safety in light and numbers.

The smart thing would be to keep walking.

But I am never good at doing the smart thing.

I walk in the direction of the van.

The night is quiet, air still. I hold my breath for a second and listen, in case I pick anything up. Only the wind rustling the branches of the trees, dead leaves scraping the pavement, that electric hum of the city that never turns off.

I try to walk quietly, though at this point, whoever's hiding behind the van has to know I'm not retreating. It dawns on me that whoever's there could have a weapon, so I glance around, see if there's anything I can pick up. Find nothing, so I step out on the sidewalk, cut a wide arc around the back.

Those last few feet, my heart pounding, I leap forward.

There's no one.

I look up and down the block again. At the far end is someone turning a corner, but that could be anyone. Maybe I'm being paranoid. I've been up for too long. I should go home. Get some sleep.

But then I smell it.

Cigarette smoke.

I crouch down, find a butt dropped on the pavement. Pick it up.

The tip is still smoldering.

NINE

THE SUN INTERRUPTS a rotten night of sleep. I can't stop thinking about the cigarette.

Could be nothing. I'm working a case and that makes me jump at shadows. But that's the thing about jumping at shadows. Sometimes it's better to jump than not jump, in case there really is a monster around the corner.

The safest thing to do is assume I'm being followed. It could be Ginny keeping tabs on me, making sure I'm doing the work. More likely it's related to Brick. The guy at Sanctuary already knows I was asking around about him, and then I had to go wandering around Park Hill. Someone might have seen me and put it together.

I'm putting the odds at 70/30 it's Brick over Ginny. There can't be anyone else. At least, I don't think so. I only just got back. I haven't had time to piss off that many people.

I climb out of bed, a little stiff and achy, stutter-step into the kitchen. Bombay nods at me from the counter where he's pouring a fresh cup of coffee. I smile and take it from him. He grumbles and goes into the cabinet for another mug.

We sit on the couch and wait for the coffee to wake us from our morning stupor. He puts on a home renovation show. The premise is that a couple is looking for a home, but can't afford a new one, so this goofy husband and wife team help them to find a fixer-upper. There are many trials and tribulations related to things like budget overruns and knob-and-tube wiring and the need for open concept floor plans. I find myself oddly engrossed by it, and by the end I'm happy to find that they were able to get the kitchen of their dreams and still complete the guest room despite needing to pay to replace a broken waste pipe. Then I hate myself a little.

"I want to watch this all day," I say to Bombay. "Does that make me a bad person?"

"Yes. But also, I do too."

"Is this what becoming an adult is like?"

"A few nights ago, I went to dinner at five because I knew the restaurant would be empty. And you know what? It was fucking wonderful, bro."

The next episode starts. I get up, pour myself another cup of coffee, and sit back on the couch. Same series, except this time it's a gay couple who insist they need a space in the suburbs that's also close to their jobs in the city, which doesn't seem to make a lot of sense.

"Speaking of food, what happened to Thai last night?" Bombay asks.

"Got tied up on some stuff. Remember Timmy, from high school?"

Bombay takes a sip of coffee. Thinks about it.

"Math class," I tell him.

He nods. "Right, right. Nice guy. Parents died, I think?"

"I ran into him. He's having a rough go. Turns out he's using, which sucks for him, but is good for me, because it might give me a little entree into that community."

"Still working on Ginny's thing, then?" he asks, making sure to brush on a heavy glaze of disdain.

"How did you know about that?"

"Lunette told me," he says.

Well fuck. Wish she hadn't done that. She did it for the right reason—she's worried about me—so it's hard to be upset. Still.

"She paid me," I tell him. "To find someone who's missing. What else am I going to do? Sit around all day?"

"You could do a lot of things," Bombay says.

"You're in a mood."

"Just want to make sure you're not sliding."

"What does that mean?"

He throws me a sideways glance and a raised eyebrow. "No disrespect. But c'mon. Sometimes things were good with you and sometimes they were bad. And I want to make sure they don't get bad."

A little flame of anger ignites in my chest but I blow it out. I get what he means, even though I think he's off base. Even though I'm a little annoyed he doesn't realize what the past year has done for me.

"It's different now," I tell him.

He nods. Chooses his words cautiously. "Saying and demonstrating are two different things."

I knock back a big gulp of coffee. "Fine. You want demonstration? Here's demonstration." I get up, place the coffee cup on the kitchen counter, and head toward the bathroom.

"What does that even mean?" Bombay asks.

"I'm getting a grown-up job," I tell him.

JAY GUNNER'S OFFICE is a few blocks away, in an office building off Richmond Terrace. I take the elevator up to the fifth floor and find the door for AAA Advanced Investigations. Locked, which is a little annoying, but then again, it's not like I had an appointment.

I figure the best thing I can do is utilize the direct approach. Show him I'm passionate, I'm energetic, I want to be put to work. As I stand in the hallway and wait, I consider whether I should have brought a resume, but then realize, what the hell would I even put on it? Years of odd jobs, for which I either have no references, or references I can't trust, or references who would straight up incriminate me.

After fifteen minutes of me fucking around on my phone, a young girl, college age, comes down the hall from the elevator. Dark hair tied back in a tight ponytail, glasses with purple plastic frames that match her long coat, skin the color of milk. She's balancing a cup of coffee and a pile of folders. She tries to keep everything upright and unlock the door at the same time so I step over and ask, "Need a hand?"

"Thanks," she says, handing me the folders.

She gets the door open and takes the folders back, steps into the office before stopping and turning. "Are you waiting for us?"

"I am."

"Do you have an appointment?"

"I do not."

"Come on and we'll see what we can do," she says, stepping inside.

The office is a small, cramped room, with not much more than a desk, a filing cabinet, and one chair against the wall. No windows. There's another door, presumably Gunner's office.

"I'm Sarah," she says, extending a small hand. We shake. "What can we help you with today?"

I'm suddenly struck by how silly this entire endeavor is, but I'm here. May as well see it through. "I want to be a private investigator. And to do that, I need experience. So I wanted to see if Mr. Gunner was looking for an apprentice or an intern."

"Intern?" she asks, like it's a word in a language she doesn't understand.

"I'm not too proud to make copies and fetch coffee."

Sarah nods, slowly. "This is a new one."

"Sorry."

"Don't apologize," she says, gesturing toward the chair. "Why don't you have a seat? Jay will be here in a couple of minutes and we have a light morning, so I think I can get you in for five minutes."

"Thanks for that." I take off my coat, drop it on the chair, and sit. The chair is perpendicular to the desk, so I'm facing the filing cabinet on the far wall. Sarah sits at her desk and types at her computer. I feel inclined to chat but don't want to interrupt her so I sit there in silence.

After a couple of minutes, she says, "Do you live around here?"

"Right now, up the block. Looking for a new place."

"Good luck with that."

A few more minutes of silence.

"What does the triple-A stand for?" I ask.

"So we're first in the phone book." She looks up at me. "Not that I think it matters. I don't think people even use phone books anymore. But I guess it's good to be the first one alphabetically?"

"What kind of guy is Mr. Gunner?"

"He's my uncle," she says. "And he's a pretty nice guy. But he's also pretty serious. I honestly have no idea how he's going to react to you. The reason I'm even letting you meet with him is because I want to see how this plays out."

"That's not encouraging."

She gives me a tight smile and goes back to her computer.

The smile isn't encouraging either.

I'm reassessing my game plan when the door swings open and Gunner walks in. He's a little grayer than in his photo, but still, he looks like the kind of guy you want standing behind you if you're about to do something challenging, like buy a car or shush someone at the movies. He's dressed in a white button-down shirt and a pair of slacks with dark, comfortable shoes. He has his cell phone pressed to his ear. He comes in, looks at Sarah, looks at me, then looks back at Sarah, asks, "Appointment?"

"Walk-in," she says.

He looks back at me. "Two minutes."

As he hustles into his office, a flock of butterflies puke in my stomach. I rehearse what I want to say in my head but keep on getting the words tangled. This was a bad idea. But I have to start somewhere. Ten minutes later, Gunner pokes his head out of his office and says, "Come on in."

His office is as cramped as the front room. There's the desk with a laptop and a couple of neat stacks of paper and some framed photos, facing him. A few fancy-pants papers in gold frames on the wall, the content in fancy script. Diplomas or commendations. There are two comfy chairs sitting in front of the desk, and behind it is the window looking out over the bay. The view isn't nearly as good as the view in the picture on his website.

We shake, and his hand nearly crushes mine. "Jay Gunner," he says.

"Ash McKenna."

He gestures toward the seat. I take it as he asks, "What can I do for you?"

"This is going to sound a little weird, maybe, but I've been thinking about becoming a private investigator, and I know you need experience to do that…"

Gunner puts up his hand. "Let me stop you right there. How old are you, kid?"

"Twenty-five."

"And what do you do? What's your background?"

My cheeks are flushing. Thinking about that makes them flush more. "Well, I mean, I don't have an official background. I've been working as an amateur private investigator. Finding people, helping people out, stuff like that…"

"Amateur," he says, leaning back in his chair. "So, without a license. You know what that is?"

"Class B misdemeanor?"

He pauses, like he wants to laugh, but also thinks I don't deserve that reaction. "Yes. But I was going to say it's a little ridiculous."

It's right about here my heart climbs into my throat.

"There are two things you need to know from the jump, kiddo," he says, putting so much emphasis on the final word I feel like I'm shrinking in my seat. "First and foremost, this job is probably nothing like you imagine it. I spend most of my day tailing men cheating on their wives and people trying to put one over on worker's comp.

"Second, and most importantly, this is not a goddamn game, but your tone and your cavalier attitude make it sound like that's what you think it is. And that right there means you're not right for it. You think I woke up one day and decided, 'Oh, I'm going to be the next Sam Spade'? No, I did not. I spent twenty years getting my ass kicked in the NYPD. I paid my dues. You want to fight bad guys? Go sign up for the force. You're young enough you can put in your twenty, get yourself a good pension, and then you'll be ready to do this kind of work. That little piece of wisdom is so goddamn good I ought to charge you for it, but I won't because I'm in a good mood. So, take your little fantasy elsewhere, okay, kiddo? It's time to grow up."

He leans back in his chair, gives me a minute to absorb the shot on the chin and find my feet again.

"You have yourself a nice day," he says with a solemn nod, in a way that sounds like a forced-polite version of "fuck off."

I get up, take my jacket, my face flushing, palms sweating. "Sorry to have bothered you."

As I step into the front office, I try to avoid Sarah's gaze, but I can't. Her eyes are big and soft, her lips pursed, like she just saw a kid get slapped by his mom in public. She mouths "sorry". I nod at her and leave before I get any redder with shame. Hit the button for the elevator, but when it doesn't magically appear, take the stairs down to the ground floor, leave the office, walk until I find a bus shelter, which has a bench, and sit.

Look out over the harbor, at Manhattan glinting in the sunlight, ferries and tankers drifting across, leaving foam in their wake.

Wish I had a cigarette.

A girl walks by sucking down a Newport and I consider asking her for one. Instead, I take out the to-do list.

Find a place to live

Get a job

Find Spencer Chavez

See my mom

Check on Crystal

Next to "get a job" I put a question mark. Because now I'm wondering if I need to reevaluate. I guess I should have anticipated that. It was kind of silly. Doesn't make it sting any less. Not that I need Gunner to like me. Whether or not he does is immaterial. The problem is, I knew what I was going to do with my life. I *knew* it.

And after a year of being completely untethered, that felt good.

Now, I don't know.

Maybe this is a fantasy.

I pull out my phone to check the time. Find I have a text I must have missed while I was getting kicked in the teeth. It's from Timmy.

Think I found a lead on the guy you're looking for.

That's something.

IT TAKES A lot of buses and a lot of walking to find the block where Timmy wants to meet, where, apparently, he ran into someone who said they knew Spencer. The whole ride I feel like everyone is staring at me. Like Gunner called each and every person on the bus and now they're asking, "Why is he still at it with this bullshit?"

I do my best to ignore it, which means I can't, really.

South Beach is mostly suburban with shades of beach community. During the warmer months there's the smell of salt in the air. Along the beach there's a boardwalk. Not much to do—it's not like Coney Island, with rides and food and stuff. This is more parkland, with wide open parking lots and vacant space. A good place for families to play during the day, and for teens to get high and drunk in the evenings.

The street where Timmy wants to meet is empty, so I stand at the corner and wait. Take in the surroundings. I wasn't here when Sandy hit but I followed the news. I know a lot of the island got spared but this area was devastated, with it being so close to the water and absorbing the brunt of the surge. Along one side is a row of houses, most of them boarded up. Damage from the hurricane still showing on the exteriors—rotted wood, broken windows, torn-up landscaping. On the right side of the street is one big construction site. Whatever was there—probably more houses—has been yanked down. Everything is fenced in by a big green plywood wall, a backhoe visible over the top. The block feels abandoned, and could very easily stand in as the backdrop in a movie where people are trying to eat each other.

Every broken house makes me think of a family that's no doubt been broken by City Hall's inability to get its shit together and make things right. Exhibit A for why I don't want to be a cop. I'm not a big believer in systems of government.

There's a crunching sound behind me and I turn to find Timmy. He's not looking great. Much worse than yesterday. He's shaking a little, I don't think from the cold, hugging himself. He nods and smiles when he sees me, fighting through it.

"You're here," he says.

"I am."

"Follow me."

We walk down the block. Timmy walks ahead of me, head jerking from side to side, not saying anything. I've seen Lunette like this, back when she was using. It's not a fun place to be.

"So what happened, exactly?" I ask.

Timmy turns and glances at me. "Saw a guy I know who gets around. I asked him if he knew a guy named Spencer who also does drag. He said he just saw him at a shooting gallery down here."

"Thank you for this," I tell him.

"Don't thank me yet," he says. He trails off for a second, and then says, "We haven't found him yet, and we might not."

"Still," I tell him. "This is better than the nothing I have so far."

And it's going to make me feel a lot better about the ass-kicking I got from Gunner. The shame is dissipating. Now I want to solve this, put together a PowerPoint presentation about it, and then sit his ass down and explain to him that, no, I'm not a kid, and yes, I do fucking know what I'm doing.

We stop in front of a brick home, still under construction, high off the sidewalk. The top of the front porch feels like the second floor. Post-flood build. There's a tarp hanging over the living room window, but the top floor looks finished.

"This is it?" I ask.

"This is it," Timmy says "There are some more we can check out, but we'll start here."

I climb the stairs, grab the fancy handle on the door, give it a squeeze. The door pops open. Step inside the foyer, everything raw wood and insulation. In the living room and kitchen beyond I can see the guts of piping and electrical. These folks did not go with open concept.

There's a sound from upstairs, so I make my way up, footsteps echoing off the wood. Find a long hallway with a series of doors, no light. It takes a second for my eyes to adjust.

I turn to Timmy. "Is there some kind of decorum I should practice here?"

"Yes, you have to knock three times, bow, and spin. C'mon, go."

I head down the hall, peek into rooms. There are mattresses, old food wrappers, used condoms, discarded clothing. No people. Pass another door and hear music playing behind it. Underneath that, people arguing? I can't really tell. Try to open it but it's locked. There's a bathroom. I check inside and immediately regret that, try to erase the sight and smell from my mind.

There's one last door at the end of the hallway. It's ajar. I nudge it open, step into a blank room. Probably a master bedroom. It has a vaulted ceiling but, again, everything is exposed.

Well, this one is a dead end. I'm about to turn, to retrace my steps and try to get into the locked room before we move on to the next place, when I hear Timmy say, "I'm sorry, Ash."

And then something slams into my back and knocks me to the floor.

TEN

I HIT THE FLOOR hard. Pain jolts through my bruised ribs and snatches my breath away. I try to stand but something presses into my spine. A knee, I think. My hands are lashed together behind me, hard plastic biting into my skin. Then my ankles are bound.

Stupid. So stupid.

I should have known something was off.

Timmy may be jonesing, but it was more than that.

He was scared. Maybe a little guilty.

The pressure comes off my back. I give my hands and legs a tug but they're completely restrained. Roll onto my back and find Timmy, standing in the corner, head down. Looming over me are two black women.

The one on the right is tall and thick. She's got a shock of dark hair, large gold hoop earrings, and a look on her face like she's about to open a Christmas present. The one on the left is short, thin, body like a dancer, wearing a red wool hat. Her head looks shaved under the hat. She's glaring at me like I smell bad.

The two of them each grab me under an arm and pull me to the wall, get me in a sitting position. Timmy shakes his head and rushes out of the room, leaving me alone with them.

"So let me get this right," the big woman says. "Your name is Ashley. You do know that's a girl's name?"

"I'm the modern day boy named Sue."

She laughs, looks at her partner. "The fuck is that supposed to mean?"

"Doesn't matter, I guess."

"Well, my name is Athena," she says, bending down toward me a little. "And my silent partner over here is Paris."

"And you're, what, hired thugs? Nice to see Brick is an equal opportunity kind of guy."

Athena's face goes cold when I say this. It was probably not a smart thing to say. My time in Prague, around two women who handed me my ass a few times over, taught me not to underestimate people based on gender.

Athena says, "We ain't his thugs. We his bodyguards. Like the Dora Milaje."

"I don't know what that is."

"You don't read comic books?"

Now that's an insult. 'Course I read comic books. I mean, not a lot lately."

"You a Marvel or DC boy?"

"Marvel."

She huffs. "Then you should fucking know. Dora Milaje are the bodyguards for T'Challa. Black Panther. Motherfucking king of Wakanda. But I guess I shouldn't be surprised you don't know him. White boys don't read Black Panther."

"I don't have anything against Black Panther…"

"No, you don't, but you didn't read him either, because you can't see yourself *as* him" She looks at Paris. "See, this is the problem. Why Black Panther gets canceled. White boys ruin comics 'cause they ain't open-minded."

Paris nods. "Mm-hm."

"I feel like we're getting off track here," I tell them.

Athena snaps out of it. Looks down at me. "Yeah, I guess we are. We have some questions for you. Which you are going to answer, or I'm going to lay my fucking boot into your face. The one we start with is, why the fuck are you looking for Brick?"

"I'm not looking for him," I tell her. "I'm looking for a kid named Spencer. I heard Brick ran the show out here and I thought if I found him, I would find some users, and I could take things from there. In retrospect, it probably wasn't the best plan."

"You damn right it wasn't," she says. "Brick don't fuck around. Especially not when it come to his business. Which is why you're going to tell me the whole motherfucking truth. Because we both know there's more to it."

"What do you mean?"

"What do I mean?" she asks, her voice taking on a high mocking tone. She looks to Paris and says, "He wants to know what I mean."

Paris shrugs. Without looking at me, Athena steps forward and places the toe of her foot on my balls. Presses down. Pressure builds until a dull ache radiates through my stomach. I've got another inch or two before we hit the danger zone. I try to back away but there's no place to move.

"What I mean is, you work for that faggot on the Lower East Side, don't you?"

Ah fuck.

I'm starting to think Ginny hasn't been entirely honest about the reason he has me looking for Spencer. A year ago, she was at war with other district leaders from around the city. I figured that had been settled, but this might be the start of something else. If they know I'm associated with her, there's no use in lying.

"I do, but honestly, I don't give a fuck about Ginny or her agenda. All I know is there's a kid missing, and he might be in trouble, and he has a family that's looking for him. My loyalty begins and ends with them."

Athena takes her foot off my balls and nods. I think maybe I've gotten through to them, so I push my luck.

"Was it one of you following me in Manhattan last night?" I ask.

Athena nods toward Paris. "My girl is usually light on her feet. I'm a little surprised you made her."

"I've got some experience with that kind of thing."

Athena sighs, looks to Paris. "You think he telling the truth?"

Paris shrugs. "I'm not psychic."

"Neither am I." Athena leans down to me. "I'm not a psychic either. What I am is very protective of my man and his business. We can't have some cop-looking motherfucker coming around our neighborhood and bothering people and asking questions that shouldn't be asked. Plus, I heard all about what went down in Port Richmond. Brother wants to ask you a few questions, you got to take his gun away? Fuck is wrong with you?"

"What the fuck is wrong with him?" I ask. "All he had to do was ask. He didn't have to draw down on me."

She puts a finger in the air. "Excuse me. Did he remove his motherfucking gun from his motherfucking pants? Or did he just show it to you?"

"He just showed it to me."

"Then nobody drew down on nobody. Christ, you are a jumpy motherfucker. And that's the kind of thing that makes Brick nervous." She spreads her hands. "And we can't have that."

There's a finality to the way she says "we can't have that" that I really do not like. It sounds like the period at the end of the sentence. I realize something very disconcerting: they told me their names and let me see their faces. Could be they're careless, but I don't think so. Could be they expect me to be too scared to contact law enforcement or seek retribution, but they already know I was willing to snatch a gun out of someone's belt.

More likely they don't expect me to be make it out of this room alive.

"Look, I don't want to cause anyone any trouble," I tell them. "I'm not a narc and I'm not going to fuck things up for any of you. I tried something and it didn't work. I'm sorry. So how about we call this one a draw, okay? I'll stay off the hill. You won't see me again."

Athena purses her lips. Thinks about it. Then says, "No, no, we're well past that. Stupid people take chances. We ain't stupid." She turns over her shoulder. "Tim, you got the thing?"

After a few seconds, Timmy comes back in, holding something in his hands. He won't look at me. Takes a few steps forward and keeps his hands down. Athena gives him a hard smack on the arm.

He holds up a needle.

Paris takes it from him, holds it up to the light, and nods.

"Enough to drop an elephant," she says. Glances at Timmy. "Ain't that right?"

Timmy looks away from me. My body surges with panic. I yank and jerk at the bindings, but they're tight and I don't have good leverage. Next, I try to kick at Athena's knee, thinking that'll buy me a second, but she sees it coming, steps out of the way and slams her boot into my stomach. I double over, cough, try to breathe.

"You…motherfucker," I tell Timmy.

"I'm sorry, Ash, I really am. They said if I helped, they would carry me for the next year." He pauses. "And if not, they'd cut me off. Not just from them, from everyone. You don't know what it's like. I can't live like that. I'm sorry."

Paris kneels down with the needle and I jerk away, throwing myself toward the corner of the room, trying to come up with something, anything. But Athena climbs on top of me, holds me down as Paris pulls up the sleeve of my coat. The weight on me increases so that I can't move. A strong hand grips my forearm. There's a slap against my skin and a little sting as the needle goes in.

Liquid gold blooms through my body.

IT FEELS LIKE a cold winter day. But winter is outside where it can't reach me. Like I'm in a warm bed under a heavy down blanket, frost on the windows and sunlight barely filtering through the blinds. I've got nowhere to be in the world but under this blanket. I'm not tired, not hungry.

I drift.

When do we ever just drift anymore? When do we even have the time?

Those moments you wish you could disappear down.

Except better.

Because I know I'm about to die and even that doesn't bother me too much.

Life is the leading cause of death. Why get so worked up over an inevitability? That's like being upset the sun is going to rise.

I'm sad, briefly, for my mom. Someone's going to find me and the last thing she'll know is I came home and didn't bother to see her, but did find the time to overdose in some half-built home in a broken neighborhood.

I wonder if anyone will be surprised.

All told, it's a pretty clever way to do me in. I'm an addict. Always have been. Drugs and alcohol. Pain and violence.

Why do I do it? I tell myself because it's the right thing, because someone needs to do it, but in the end, isn't it also pretty nice when someone is thankful for a thing you did? Doesn't matter how altruistic your motives, sooner or later, it's going to pay off.

Acceptance is the first step.

I close my eyes.

The pain in my ribs is gone.

Take a deep breath.

Hear breathing.

The bed I'm in. I'm not alone.

There's a bundle of blankets, pulsing gently. Heat radiating. I slide my hand across the smooth surface of the sheets and feel skin, warm and soft. The bundle turns, and I expect that, given this is the last sparks of consciousness granting me something pleasant before I die, it'll be Chell.

But it's not. It's Crystal.

Those blue-green tempered glass eyes. Black hair fanned out on the pillow. One half of her head shaved. She smiles at me and that smile looks like all I ever wanted in this world.

She opens her mouth to say something but I can't make it out.

I ask her to repeat it.

Her voice is muted, stretched, like it's coming from another room.

"What the hell is wrong with you?"

A pulse travels through me.

She's right.

Giving up is easy.

There's a way out of this. I know there is. I know there is.

Because I remembered something. Put it in my pocket before I left Bombay's.

Thoughts slip through my fingers like they're coated in oil.

The naloxone. I remembered the naloxone.

I'm not in a bed.

I'm on the floor of a house.

A house in South Beach. My mother a few miles away. My friends, the people I love, all around me.

Slide my hand across to the inside of my coat pocket.

Stop the overdose in its tracks.

Try to work my hands inside.

Find I can't.

The feeling of being in a bed is replaced by the feeling of falling.

Everything warm and soft.

Peaceful.

I can't reach it. Too far gone.

This is it, then.

Sorry, Chell.

Sorry, dad.

Sorry, mom.

I tried.

And I let you down.

As per usual.

THE FALLING STOPS and I hit the ground. My sinus cavity blazing. That feeling of serenity and comfort is replaced by the polar opposite—pain. Throbbing, angry pain that comes at me in waves. The hardness of the floor feels amplified, the cold on my skin hard and metallic. Sunlight through the window stabbing me in the eyes.

I struggle to get into a sitting position, and in the process, heave my guts onto the floor. Cough and sputter and cry and something plastic drops and rattles next to me.

A spent naloxone injector.

There's someone else in the room with me.

Athena calls out. Her voice muffled. Downstairs.

"Spencer! Clean out this motherfucker's wallet and let's go. He's taking us to Wendy's."

Spencer?

Above me. His face a mix of fear and relief. He's nervous, shaking, holding the other naloxone injectors in his hands, which he places on the floor. His face is dirty, left eye bruised, hair greasy. He looks thinner than he did in his pictures. He pauses, like he's going to say something. I want to speak to him but am concentrating on not throwing up again. He reaches into my pocket, pulls out my wallet, takes a little cash but not all of it, and drops it on my lap.

"Wait…" Feels like I have a mouth full of clay.

He turns and hurries out of the room.

"Wait…" I tell him.

He doesn't.

I'm alone.

I consider getting up, but instead, I puke on the floor again. Wonder how it is my body can expand to make room for so much pain. Wish more than anything in the world I can go back to that bed built by a needle.

ELEVEN

BOMBAY ISN'T IN the apartment when I get back. Small mercies. I drag myself to my bedroom, strip, grab a clean pair of clothes, and hit the bathroom. Turn on the shower full blast, let the small room fill with steam. Look in the mirror.

It's like I've got the flu but my head's not stuffy. My body aches and I'm tired. My brain feels like it got stuck in a mosh pit and stomped on for hours. I look worse than I feel. My skin is waxy, my eyes heavy. It's a relief when there's enough condensation on the mirror I can't see myself anymore.

I spend a little time checking the structural integrity of my ribs. Every little stab of pain is a blessing and a curse. It reminds me I'm alive—that's the closest I've ever come to death, one foot dangling over the precipice—but it also makes me think of not having that pain.

Even knowing I was dying, I want back in.

For years I crammed my head full of drugs. Coke, prescriptions, sometimes ecstasy. Stuff that blew out my serotonin and made me feel happy and shiny and chatty. Like the entire world was one big party and everyone was a new best friend waiting to be made.

Stuff that made me feel not so alone.

The thing about uppers is they're psychologically addictive. You want them because they make you feel good. You come to think you can't feel good without them. It's a feedback loop, but one you can break if you try hard enough. I was a heavy drinker, too, enough that at one point I went through alcohol withdrawal. Even then, I didn't feel like I couldn't live without it.

Heroin, though. It's a whole new universe. And not the feeling of need that's gnawing at me, like how sometimes I want a cigarette and I can feel a little tug in my body. That tug is there, amplified so that my skin aches.

But more than that, it's what the heroin gave me.

Oblivion.

I get it. Intellectually, I know heroin is pure destruction. That the first high is the best and you'll never match it, but you will end your life trying.

And knowing these things, all I want is another taste. Just a little.

Best thing I can do is distract myself.

Because there's something else I want right now.

Answers.

RING THE BUZZER for the penthouse in Ginny's building. No answer. Try the door for the lobby and it doesn't budge. I call the number she gave me—again—but it just rings. I go to the bodega on the corner, get myself a cup of coffee. It has the taste and consistency of motor oil. I go back, sit on the steps. The cold serves to keep me awake. I wonder if I should see a doctor after getting pumped full of heroin and then naloxone.

My head spins when I think about the needle. I hope it was clean. But they had no reason to use a clean needle.

All of this is bad.

All of this is very bad.

My stomach threatens to empty itself for the fifth time. I don't know if that's from the drugs in my system or the fear in my chest, thrashing around like a wild animal. Maybe a mix of both.

Maybe it's the shitty coffee.

A black SUV pulls to the curb. I know it's Samson before he rolls down the window. He glares at me through his sunglasses, even though the sun is going down and he doesn't need them. We sit there like that for a minute, me sipping my coffee. He looks at me like he wants to hit me.

"So, how 'bout them Yankees?" I ask, practically yelling.

"Season's over, motherfucker," he says. "Get in the car."

THE SUV PULLS up to a restaurant in Little Italy. As I climb out, I say, "Thanks, pal" to Samson. He doesn't say anything.

The place is old, classic. Red checkerboard tablecloths, candles on tables, olive oil instead of butter for the bread. I know I should eat, I know I need the calories, but my stomach isn't having that. The sight of food makes me nauseous.

The place is busy and I don't see Ginny. After a moment of standing awkwardly at the front, a short Mexican man in a white shirt and black slacks comes up to me, beckons for me to follow. He leads me first into the kitchen, a cramped, hot space where men move around each other in choreographed routines. There's a door at the back. He nods toward it.

I squeeze through and find a small room, decorated much like the front: red paint, wood paneling, gold accents, tin ceiling. There's a table that seats four, and Ginny, sitting alone amongst the remnants of dinner. Empty glasses and empty plates. Three chairs are pulled out like they were vacated in a hurry.

Ginny is done up slightly more than normal. Her wig is brunette and ornate and there's a trace of glitter in her eyeliner. She's wearing a dark, sequined dress with spaghetti straps that show off her bony shoulders. Sitting on the table in front of her is a martini.

I sit across from her and we stare at each other for a second. Then I point to her drink. "Always figured you for a gin and tonic girl. Would you call this ironic? I don't know if that's the right word."

"What in the sweet lord happened to you, darling?" she asks.

We run through it. My path to Brick, or at least, Brick's people. That I saw Spencer. That they know all about Ginny. That they loaded me up with a hot dose of heroin. When I get to the end, Ginny nods, a look of concern cast over her face. She takes out her phone. Taps away at it for a few moments, then looks up at me.

"You need to be seen by a doctor," she says. "I have someone. Samson will bring you there straight after this. No charge, of course."

"Ginny."

"Ash?"

"What the fuck is going on?"

Ginny sighs. Takes a long sip of her martini. Looks around the room and her eyes settle on me. "Drink?"

"Holy fucking shit."

"Okay, okay. Look, I wasn't lying about Spencer. I wasn't lying about the fact that his parents want to know where he is. But, yes, I did hold some things back. He didn't go to Staten Island for the fun of it." She pauses, purses her lips. "I sent him."

"For?"

"There's a new player on the board," she says. "Not Brick. Someone else. Someone who's amassing a great deal of power, very quickly. Enough that people are noticing. Brick has the biggest operation on the island, but it seems like this new player is angling to take over. Do you follow me? It's a turf war. As you can imagine, the isle of Staten is a very valuable market right now."

"And what's your interest in this?"

"Things like that have a way of encroaching on my business," she says. "I wanted to learn more. That's it. So I sent Spencer. He was supposed to work his way into Brick's crew and see what he could see. And then he stopped responding to me. I figured he was dead, or else they had him locked away somewhere and were keeping him fed on heroin. It's so hard to find loyalty among users."

"Tell me about it. Remember Timmy, from high school?"

She pauses, thinks. Smiles. "I do."

"Yeah, he's the one sold me out to Brick."

"Well, that wasn't very nice."

"So where does this leave us?"

Ginny throws back the rest of her martini, places the glass down with a great deal of care. "Well, it leaves you in a bad spot. They'll probably want to kill you after they find out it didn't work the first time. But from what I hear, all you have to do is wait. This new player wants to take Brick off the board. In the meantime, just try to keep a low profile as you try to find Spencer. We know he's alive now. You've actually made a good bit of progress."

"Nope. No fucking way. I'm done with this bullshit."

"Don't you want a little revenge?"

"Not worth it."

Ginny smirks. "That's new. Used to be you would have given the money back for the pleasure of putting some hurt on them."

"That's not me anymore."

"Fine. I'll double your fee."

"What?"

"Forty thousand. Find Spencer for me. Forty thousand."

"This isn't about the money."

Ginny stands, brushes her hands down her dress to smooth it out. "Yes, it is. Everyone needs money. And more than that, you need to protect yourself. Your friends. Your family. Yes, Brick is close to being deposed, but until then, he's a problem. So you can run and hide from it, or you can confront it."

I don't bother getting up. "Is that a threat, Ginny?"

"No, it's a warning. The smartest thing you can do is see this through."

"It really feels like that's not the case."

Ginny raises her hand, gestures for me to stand, and leads me toward the door. "Sleep on it. See the doctor first. I suspect a good night's sleep will help you put this into perspective."

"Yeah, I really fucking doubt that," I tell her.

"This new player," she says. "He's dangerous. Nobody moves that quickly that fast unless they're willing to hurt a lot of people. There's something bigger at play here, Ash."

"What's his name? Do you know?"

"Not his real name. He goes by Kid Vicious."

I sigh. "Fucking Christ."

SAMSON DROPS ME off outside an apartment building in Chinatown. He rolls down the window, says "Number four" and rolls the window back up. Doesn't pull away. Must be waiting to give me a ride home.

There's a metal panel next to the door, rounded buttons next to numbers. I hit four and the door buzzes. Climb the stairs to the fourth landing, and there's an apartment door sitting open a crack. Inside is a small living room area with comfortable seating and a stack of magazines on a coffee table. The room smells of vanilla.

I go to take a seat when a tall and lanky Asian man steps out from the hallway in baby blue medical scrubs. He's model-handsome, with a mop of black hair. Bones tattooed on his arms, like they're meant to be an x-ray of what's under his skin.

"Are you Ash?" he asks.

"Indeed. And you are?"

He raises an eyebrow, frowns a bit. "You can call me Doctor Feelgood."

I guess it was rude to ask. Real names don't go over well in this business. "All right then."

"Come on back."

The doctor leads me to what I figure would be a bedroom, but there's a massage table covered with white paper, a small sink, cabinets, medical supplies. Everything pristine and gleaming, which is a good sign. I sit on the table, the paper crinkling beneath me. The doctor remains standing.

"Needle prick?" he asks.

"Little more than that. Got shot with a lethal load of heroin, then some naloxone."

"First time using heroin?"

"Yeah."

He doesn't let on that this is surprising or uncommon. "Show me the injection site."

I pull up my sleeve and go hunting in the crook of my arm but can't find it. He takes my arm, runs a gloved hand over the skin until he locates a tiny red mark. "Doesn't look too bad. That's the first good sign."

"Good how?"

He looks toward the neat stacks of supplies. "Puncture this clean, they probably used a new needle. I deal with a lot of junkies and they tend to be pretty fastidious with swapping out for clean works. Whoever prepared the dose for you probably used a new one out of habit. I'd bet money on that. But there's a big difference between betting money on a hypothetical, and contracting hepatitis or HIV."

"Yeah, not something I want to gamble on."

"Take off your shirt."

I strip down. The doctor presses his fingers lightly into the bruising on my torso. "I'd ask if they beat you up before hand, but none of this looks new…"

"Yeah, unrelated. Everyone's got a talent."

He runs his hands over my ribs, pressing in the odd spot. "Nothing broken."

"Lovely."

He swabs my arm with an alcohol pad and gives me a shot. Then he hands me a small paper cup with some pills, and another small cup with water. I throw them back. "What is all this?"

"Dirty needle puts you at risk for HIV, as well as Hep B and C," he says. "This is all a cocktail that might help prevent that from happening. I'm going to give you a course of these—you're going to have to take them at regular intervals for the next few weeks. I'll draw everything up, make it nice and simple to follow. Do not miss a dose. I'm not even going to tell you what to do if you miss a dose. Because you cannot miss a dose. Understood?"

"Yes."

He goes to the drawer, pulls out some more vials. "I'm going to take some blood now, and again when you follow up with me in a month. Like I said, you'll probably be fine."

"The more you say it, the less I feel like it's true."

He turns. Gives me a smile like someone died.

"Sorry," he says, and I believe that he is.

As he portions out pills and makes notes on a yellow legal pad, I ask him, "So how do you get into this line of work, anyway?"

He turns, gives me a withering look over his shoulder. The kind of look that makes me think I shouldn't have asked. He turns back to his notes and writes some more. Says, "You ever find yourself in a place where you felt like you didn't have a choice?"

And I understand why he's upset by the question.

"I get it," I tell him. "I really, really do."

SAMSON PULLS THE SUV to the curb outside Bombay's apartment. I sit there and clutch the bag of pills. Sit in the warmth of the car's heater, not wanting to get out. Because getting out will make all of this real. That in the course of a single day I've pretty much walked back every little bit of progress I've made in the past year.

My job prospects are suddenly fucked. All my talk about walking a straighter path, and I picked a fight with people who have actively tried to kill me, and might want to do it again. And, oh, I could have a virus ready to lay waste to my immune system.

"You going to get the fuck out of my car or what?" Samson asks.

"Why do you hate me so much?"

"I told you…"

"No, I want a real answer. Not some smartass bullshit. What

the fuck did I ever do to you? I've never raised my hands to you. I've said some smart shit, but nothing that bad. I know that whole thing with the pimp went a little sideways, but c'mon, you act like I killed your fucking cat or something."

Samson sits there for a couple of seconds. I wonder if he's not going to answer.

Then he does. "Two reasons. First is, you're a thug. But you don't know that. You think you're better than that. And you're not."

"I'm not a thug."

"You mean not like me."

"Yeah, you could say that."

He laughs. "See? You look down on me. What I do doesn't live up to your lofty standards. Problem is, we both do the same shit. At least I'm honest about it."

"What's the second thing?"

"What second thing?"

"You said there were two reasons."

He thinks. "Right. Yeah. It's what you do to my boss. You start trouble for her."

"Has she ever told you how the two of us met?"

He doesn't respond.

"Ask her sometime. Ask her about the big guy that tried to choke her to death. Ask her if she'd even be here without me."

He doesn't say anything and I don't care to argue anymore so I climb out of the car.

The SUV lingers for a second and I half suspect the window is going to come buzzing down, but then it speeds off, and I contemplate how to hide the paper bag of pills in my coat so I don't have to explain them to Bombay.

But before I do that, I walk up and down the block. Peek into the parked cars. Make sure there's no one watching. No one waiting. No smoldering cigarettes.

As I make my way into the building, I check my phone and find a text from Lunette.

Ready to look at some apartments tomorrow?

The thought of tomorrow is exhausting but I write back: *Sure.*

TWELVE

THE APARTMENT IS nice enough—the walls are freshly painted and the floor is hardwood. The faux shitty kind, but at least it looks nice. It's not what I expected from the crumbling façade and the fifteen-minute walk from the subway.

But it looks barely big enough to fit a bed and a couch together. There's a small kitchenette in the corner, featuring a mini-fridge and a stove with only two burners. Not that I cook much, but that feels cheap. We're facing the rear of another building so the view is chipped brick. Also, something smells funny. It smells like a dank basement even though we're three floors up.

Lunette's lady friend Dee paces the apartment, cell phone pressed to her ear, making affirmative noises every few seconds. She's a pro. Handshake like a vise, intense eye contact, hair cut short in a way that's more efficient than stylish. She wears a checkered bow tie that has her neck in a death grip.

"Fine, do it," she says, lowering the phone and turning to me. "Well?"

"What neighborhood did you say this was again?"

"Woodside," she says. "I like to call this part the used-tire district."

Lunette pops out of the bathroom. "You have to see this."

I step inside. It's cramped but manageable. I figure she wants to show me the shower stall. The showerhead comes up to my chest and there's enough room to turn around, but maybe not enough to bend over and reach my feet. Then I realize she's looking at the toilet. There's a little wall in front of it. Anyone but a very small child would have to sit on it sideways.

"Fuck this," I tell her. "I hope you're showing me the shittiest one first."

"Actually, no," Dee says. "I'm showing you this so you can see what you're up against. This is two grand a month. Utilities not included. For what you want to pay, if you want to stay in the city, you're looking at getting a roommate or going to Staten Island. Otherwise, you're headed for Jersey City or up to Yonkers."

"There's got to be something…"

"There isn't."

"But…"

"There isn't."

"Well, fuck."

"I know it sucks," Dee says. "Lunette told me about your old place. I hope you enjoyed it while you had it. We'll have better luck finding a unicorn than we will another one of those."

I walk to the window, look out into the dirty alleyway below. I take out my list:

Find a place to live
Get a job?
Find Spencer Chavez
See my mom
Check on Crystal

Pull a pen out of my pocket and add a question mark next to "find a place to live." Stare at it for a second, then I write "again" next to "find Spencer Chavez." Fold the paper up and put it back in my pocket. Turn to Dee and Lunette.

"So you took me all the way up to Queens to teach me a lesson?"

"It's like one of those HGTV shows," Lunette says. "Where they show you the house you can't afford before making you settle for a fixer-upper. You've got to learn to settle."

Dee nods knowingly, like this is a very good comparison.

"So everyone watches these shows now?" I ask.

Dee says, "My favorite is where the husband and wife who hate each other flip homes in Reno. Because everything they do is obviously staged. Also, I'm pretty sure the husband is gay."

"I like that one, too," Lunette says.

"So I imagine you have no more places to show me?" I ask.

Dee nods. "I will have more for you. Soon as you tell me what you're willing to settle for."

"Let's get some coffee and discuss," I tell them.

They move toward the door but I step into the bathroom to take a sideways piss. Finish up and wash my hands and look in the mirror. The bruises are almost gone but I look like I didn't sleep at all last night. Which was actually the case. I know the doctor said I shouldn't get too worked up, but my blood feels hot. Like there's something wrong in my body. I can't help but think about what might be growing inside.

I'm still not sure what I'm going to do about Spencer. I need the money. I run the math through my head. If I can find a place for two grand a month and Ginny pays me forty, that floats me for more than a year. I can live cheap while I find a job. I stopped smoking and cut down on drinking. Those were my biggest expenses besides eating. I don't need cable. Bombay would flip me a computer.

Maybe I could make all that work.

It remains contingent on finishing this job.

I join Dee and Lunette in the hallway outside the apartment. As Dee looks up, I ask, "Say I could do a ceiling of two grand a month. Think you could find a decent one bedroom for that? Even a studio? Somewhere in Brooklyn, at least, so it doesn't feel like I'm going through fucking Mordor to get home at night?"

Dee sighs a bit. "I can try."

"That's all I ask."

DON'T KNOW THE bartender at St. Dymphna's. Some guy. At least it's not crowded. Lunette orders a glass of cabernet, and when he asks me what I want, I hesitate. Ever since my little bout with alcohol withdrawal, I've set some new rules for myself: beer only, limited intake, no hard stuff. Beer is like water. Barely touches me. Whiskey is a coping mechanism.

And yet, this fucking week.

"Jameson rocks," I tell the bartender.

I deserve it, all things considered.

I'm not slipping.

Lunette doesn't know any better, so when the bartender puts down the small rocks glass filled to the top with amber liquid, she raises her glass and we clink them together. I take a small sip. It fills my mouth and then my head. Memories come rushing back. Most of them not very good. I don't care. At least they're familiar.

"So what's wrong with you?" Lunette asks.

"Today didn't go great."

"No, it's not that. Something bigger. You've had this look on your face all day."

"Maybe that's the way my face looks."

"Stop it."

I take another sip. What can it hurt? It's only liquid in a glass.

Nothing compared to what got pumped into me yesterday.

I tip the glass to the ceiling, drain it. Flag down the bartender, ask for another. I know I'm crossing a line. I know this won't be it. Two will turn into three will turn into the bottle. But I can't get over the sense memory. The feel of it. The woodsy sting of the whiskey bringing me back to a previous time. I can already feel the tickle of drunkenness at the back of my brain. My old life shining through the cracks.

I tell Lunette about everything that's happened so far.

It feels good to get it out to someone, and I can't talk to Bombay because I can't bear how he would react. Lunette has always been far less judgmental, and we haven't been friends long enough that I worry about hurting us. Not that I don't value having her in my life, but for some reason, this stuff—being myself—comes so much easier with her.

When I'm done, she realizes her wine glass is empty. She asks for another.

"That all sucks," she says.

"Succinct."

"And you saw a doctor?"

"He didn't seem terribly worried, but gave me a bunch of stuff to take, to be safe."

"Should you be drinking?"

I wave down the bartender for a third. My words taking slightly more effort to form. I am out of practice. Used to be I didn't get this way until my sixth. Then again, I skipped lunch. "Alcohol is a disinfectant."

"Stop that."

"Stop what?"

The bartender puts down my third and Lunette says, "He's cut off after this."

"I'll decide that…" I tell her.

"Shut up," she says. She turns to the bartender. "Got it?"

He puts his hands up and backs away.

"The fuck is wrong with you?" she asks.

"Nothing."

"Except there is something wrong. You just explained to me all the things that are wrong. And now you're being evasive. Do you know how fucking proud of you I was, to see you've got your shit together and you didn't feel the need to tie one on in the afternoon? 'Cause a year ago, you and me would have gone out for a drink and you would have been fucking blotto by the time we left. These are good things."

"I know."

"Then why are you doing it?"

"Because."

"That's not an answer."

I take a sip. "You're not an answer."

"You're acting like a child."

I take the third whiskey. Contemplate it. I'm about the down it when Lunette snatches it out of my hand and drinks it herself. Then she tosses a pile of cash on the bar.

"Let's get something to eat," she says, pulling her purse onto her shoulder.

We step outside to find a light snow falling. Not enough to stick, but enough to reflect the light as it falls in lazy spirals to the ground. Lunette leads us to the pizza place at the end of the block, orders four plain slices, and sits at a table in the corner. I sit across from her. My head swimming in whiskey, afraid to make eye contact with her because I feel like a child who's just been scolded by a parent, and more than that, justifiably.

After a few moments, the man behind the counter calls her over. She fetches the slices, two each on two trays, and proceeds to cover hers with red pepper flakes. I leave mine as is, watch as the oil pools, turning the paper plate underneath transparent. When they're a little cooler, we eat in silence. I finish before her and sit there while she works on her second slice. I feel better with food in my stomach.

"Thank you," I tell her.

"We do what we do," she says. "What are you going to do about all this?"

"For as stupid as it sounds, I think I should keep looking for Spencer. I need the money. Forty K is not insignificant."

"Is it worth dying over?"

"I'm going to do a better job of keeping my head down. The mistake I made was trusting a junkie. No offense."

She cringes. "I hate that fucking word."

"Junkie?"

She puts down the crust of her remaining slice. "Junk implies garbage. I did heroin for a very long time. Do you consider me to be garbage?"

"Absolutely not. I don't think that's even how it works. Junk is slang for heroin, right? I mean, it's not about the person, it's about the substance…"

She puts her hand up. "Doesn't matter. A lot of people look at heroin users and they think we're all pieces of shit. Subhuman. I could tell you stories about things people did to me or said to me while I was using, and you would get up right now and find every one of those people and beat the shit out of them. Heroin isn't an indulgence. It's not pie and you're eating too much pie. It rewires you. It twists your body so you need it to function. We all know what it does and we all do it anyway, and that's on us, sure, but that word? It's a slur. It's a slur against people who need help."

"I'm sorry."

She shrugs. "Just don't use that word."

"I never respected you any less."

"I know that. Though…" She looks down. Twists her hands together in her lap. "I've been meaning to tell you something."

"Shoot."

"I used to sneak cash out of your wallet. When you were drunk."

"Are you kidding?"

Her face softens. "I've been wanting to tell you. It's why I paid for the pizza. I probably owe you a few pizzas, in the grand scheme. I never got into the whole twelve-step thing but I still feel like I need to make amends for some stuff. And that's one of them. So, I'm sorry."

"Huh."

She frowns, tenses up. Like maybe I'm pissed. But I'm not. Instead, I laugh. Quietly at first, but then I lose control. Lunette smiles and joins me, and within a few moments the two of us are laughing so hard people are staring.

It feels good to laugh like that, even if it's hell on my ribs.

After we've calmed down and caught our breath, she asks,

"You're not mad?"

"Of course not. Just, you know, I would have given it to you if you asked."

"I know. But I couldn't ask."

"Yeah, I get that."

I laugh a little more, then slide out of the booth, grab my tray and Lunette's, dump the empty plates into the trash, and put the trays back on the countertop. As we exit the restaurant, the alarm on my phone goes off. I reach into my pocket for the pill bottles, dry swallow the two I need to take.

"For the needle thing?" she asks.

"It's going to be at least a month before I know."

"You know there's a pretty simple solution to that?"

"Which is?"

"Find that guy. Timmy. Find him and ask him."

Yeah. I think it's about time to do that.

NORMALLY, WHEN I'VE got computer work to do, I ask Bombay for help. But besides not wanting to get him involved, I figure it's time I start learning this stuff for myself.

Not that this was a tough one. I never met Timmy's parents, but I remember how things were in high school. He wasn't one of the rich kids, but he was well off enough that I can assume his parents were homeowners. When his parents died, there's a good chance he inherited the house. A lot of things could have happened between now and then, but it's a start.

It didn't take much effort on Google to find the stories about the crash—hit head-on by a drunk driver traveling the wrong way on the expressway. That gives me his parents' names. Using those, I'm able to play around in White Page listings until I find their address.

Twenty minutes on a bus and I find myself on a quiet block off the main drag of Forest Avenue. The houses are old, modest, and neat. I wander down the sidewalk, hands in pockets. Catch a blind drawn aside and then falling back. Someone wondering who the figure in the dark jacket is this late at night.

I probably could have guessed which house belonged to Timmy. It's tan with green accents, the windows dirty, the lawn dead and not kept. There's a small pile of supermarket circulars by the front door. Timmy's car is parked in the driveway.

No lights. No movement. I give the block a good look, make sure no one is watching, and head into the gloom around the side of the house. There's a little snow on the ground now, stuck to the grass, so I make sure to stick to the paved areas so I don't leave any footprints.

At the back of the house is a small deck leading to a door. I climb the stairs, slide the lock pick set out of my coat, and get to work. It takes a few minutes, and it's a little louder than I would like, but I manage to get the bottom lock undone. The deadbolt isn't engaged, I suspect because of the Corona bucket outside the door that's overflowing with cigarette butts.

The door opens onto a large, outdated kitchen. I expect the house to be in a state of disarray but it's actually quite tidy. That stems from the kitchen not being used much. The sink is dry and there are no dishes in the dish rack. The open dishwasher is empty. There's a pile of delivery menus on the counter and a couple of garbage bags in the corner. Even in the darkness and through the murky bags I can tell they're stuffed with takeout containers.

I move through the house quietly, pressed along the edges of the walls, where the floorboards are less likely to creak. Make my way to the front. Living room is empty. There's a soft sound coming from the stairs. I stop and listen.

Music on the second floor.

The staircase groans under me. No sense in being quiet now. If he's up, he heard me.

At the top of the landing there are a series of doors, all of them ajar except one. The one that's closed has a crack of light coming out from underneath. I choose that one.

It's a kid's bedroom. Lots of bright, primary colors. Posters on the wall for movies and video games. A TV and a series of video game consoles crammed in the corner, controller cords spilling across the floor. Elliott Smith is playing from a clunker of a stereo on the dresser.

Timmy is lying on the bed, face up, a needle sticking out his arm.

I kneel on the bed next to him, give him a slap. He doesn't stir. Press my fingers to his throat. Can't find a pulse but that doesn't mean anything. I'm not trained in this shit. I'm also furious at myself, for not hailing a cab, not getting here sooner.

Next to him is a piece of paper on which he's scribbled, *I'm sorry.*

I touch his face again. He's not cold yet.

"No you don't, motherfucker," I tell him. I pull a naloxone injector out of my pocket, shove it into his nostril, press the plunger. There's a hissing sound as the drugs shoot into his sinus cavity.

Nothing happens.

My heart drops in my chest and bottoms out somewhere around my intestines. I want to cry. Not because the answer to my potential medical condition is suddenly out of reach. Because as much as I want to be angry, as much as I don't want to feel bad for him—I do. I knew Timmy well enough to know he wasn't the kind of person who'd sell me out lightly. And it was wearing on him.

Heavy enough to do this.

I wonder if I should call an ambulance, perform CPR.

If I should even be here.

His eyes flutter open and he breathes in. He squeezes his eyes shut and presses his palm to his face as I stand back from the bed. Then he opens his eyes, looks around, and when his eyes settle on me, the tiny bit of color left in his face drains.

"Oh shit," he says.

"Hey, dickhead," I tell him.

THIRTEEN

TIMMY SITS AT the kitchen table, a fresh cup of coffee in front of him. He stares into it like he might be able to divine something from the steam curling off the top. He won't lift his eyes to meet mine.

I brewed the coffee for his benefit but I pour myself a mug, too. It's getting late and I still feel like my thoughts are dragging a half-second behind my body. I sit across from him and rap my knuckles against the table. He jerks a little, looks at the coffee again.

"The needle they shot me up with. Was it clean?" I ask.

"Huh?"

"Was it a new needle?"

He raises his eyes. They look like a shattered mirror. Like I can see parts of myself reflected, and it makes me wish he had kept looking at the coffee. After a moment, he lifts his chin and drops it back down. Every muscle in my body unfurls and I lean forward, laugh a little, like air releasing from an over-filled balloon. Okay, one issue down.

Timmy takes a little sip of the coffee. "How are you here?"

"Spencer. I had a bunch of naloxone in my pocket. He used one on me. I used one on you just now."

Timmy pauses, thinks. "Not the first time I got dosed." He puts his fingers on the bridge of his nose, massaging, trying to soothe his roaring sinus cavity. "It's not a nice feeling."

"I can venture a guess," I tell him, "but do you want to tell me exactly what you were sorry for, that you figured an OD was the price you had to pay?"

His looks at me and his eyes mist. "I never thought they'd take it that far. The most I figured they would do was smack you around a bit. Not to say I was endorsing that, you know? But, man, things have been tight. My parents left me some money but most of it is gone. I don't want to lose the house. They offered me all-you-can-eat for a year."

"How did you even know you could sell me out to them?"

And Timmy walks me through it. Apparently, everyone in Brick's crew is on high alert, given the climate. Some white kid—me—poked around the business, in relation to Spencer, who they knew was working for Ginny. They went straight to DEFCON 1. Eliminate the threat.

Timmy heard someone talking about the white kid, he put it together. He swears up and down he didn't offer the info but they smelled it on him and said if he flipped, he'd be taken care of. Hold back and he'd be cut off.

"What's the deal with Spencer?" I ask. "He's with them now?"

"Yes and no," Timmy says. "He's there, but he's not with them. I don't think he's there entirely of his own free will, you know?"

That accounts for the way his face was all banged up.

"Do you actually know this Ginny person?" Timmy asks. "I've been hearing about her."

I stifle a laugh. "You don't know?"

"Know what?"

"Remember Paul? I think the three of us were in a math class together. Sophomore year? We had the teacher with the glass eye?"

He thinks about it, nods. "Yeah, Paul. I remember Paul."

"He goes by 'her' now."

"Wait…so this badass drag queen crime lord everyone seems so afraid of is Paul? That Paul? That guy weighed like a hundred pounds."

"People change."

Timmy leans back in his seat. "So you're not going to kill me?"

"Not how I roll." I put a little emphasis on the words, hoping they'll sting. He winces, which means I did my job.

The doorbell rings.

Timmy tenses up, eyes so wide I can see white all the way around his irises. He jerks his head toward the door.

"Oh fuck…" he says, barely audible.

I drop my voice to a whisper. "Who's that?"

"Probably Paris and Athena."

Panic nearly splits my forehead. "Are you fucking kidding me?"

"They promised to keep me flush, you know? Honestly, I suspect they're trying to give me more than I need in the hope I overdose and they don't have to pay out what they promised."

"Can we wait them out?"

"My car is in the driveway, and…"

I see it. The thirst. The way his eyes short out, the way his muscles twist under his skin. The thing about naloxone is it doesn't just stop the overdose. It stops the high. The entire weight of this shit world—all that weight you forgot even existed—comes crashing down in an instant. The first thing I wanted when I got dosed was to go back. I'm sure he feels the same way. Except he's much further into this than me, which means his ability to control himself is pretty much nil.

Which is confirmed when he bolts toward the door.

Fuck. Can't go through the back door. It's in line of sight of the front.

I root around the kitchen for something, anything, I can use to defend myself. There's a knife block on the counter. I pull the biggest one out. Blade nearly as long as my forearm. A little grisly and not really my style, but beggars can't be all high and mighty about the method that keeps them breathing.

There are two doors off the kitchen: a small doorway that leads to a hallway that goes to the front, and an archway that goes into the living room. I pick the archway. The lights are off and the floor is carpeted, which muffles my footsteps. Between the foyer and the living room there's a little wall separating the two, so I post up behind it. Figure if Timmy rats me out, they'll go straight past him to get to the kitchen, and then I have the element of surprise.

Timmy says, "Hey…" Trying to sound nonchalant, doing a shitty job.

"As promised." Paris. Crinkle of a paper bag.

"Thanks."

"This was a courtesy. We had business in the neighborhood. Next time, you come to the hill."

"Sure thing."

"I have to pee."

"What?"

"You got a bathroom, don't you?"

"Oh, sure…"

I press myself against the wall. Listen to Paris clomping down the hallway in heavy boots. The bathroom door closes and I see Timmy looking frantically around the kitchen for me. He finally finds me in the gloom of the living room. He waves at me to get down and I hit the floor, climb around the couch as the toilet flushes. Listen to Paris's footsteps going down the hall.

Maybe he was lulling me into a false sense of security. Maybe he's whispering to her that I'm here. Maybe she's about to pounce. I get on my knees and clutch the knife, ready to dive if I see her. My heart slamming so hard into my ribs I fear she can hear it.

The front door opens, slams closed.

I listen for a moment. A car engine engages and roars off.

When I stand, Timmy is looking at the paper bag on the coffee table. I give him a second and then clear my throat. He looks up at me and gives me a weak smile.

"I hope this shows you can trust me," he says. "I want to make up for what I did."

"This is a start, yeah," I tell him. "I still want to beat the shit out of you, but I'll hold off. Now you need to give me something I can use. Where can I find Spencer?"

He's not listening. He's undoing the top of the bag, unfolding it, searching for the prize inside.

I snap my fingers. "Hey."

He looks up but doesn't let go of the bag. "When we went to Wendy's afterward, they were talking about some stuff. Not all of it I understand, but it feeds into some rumors I heard. Like, context clues, you know? They have a waypoint. Place the stuff gets held before it goes to processing. A bodega off Richmond Terrance. They bring it in off the water, right across the street, boom."

"Right. Forgot you guys jacked me to get fast food." I add that to the mental list of grievances. "There are dozens of bodegas on the terrace."

Timmy raises his shoulders, lets them fall, goes back to the bag. "Best I got."

I replace the knife in the kitchen, return to the living room. Peek into the paper bag on the coffee table. It's stuffed with dime bags, each one of them holding a kiss of white powder. I take a couple of them out.

"What are you doing?"

"For bargaining purposes," I tell him. "Just in case."

It's a lie. He knows it's a lie, the way he looks at me. But he doesn't stop me either.

BOMBAY IS ASLEEP when I come in. I grab my laptop from my room, set it up at the kitchen table, search the fridge for something to eat and find leftover Chinese. Dump pork fried rice and beef chow fun onto a plate and stick it in the microwave.

As the microwave whirs, I check my e-mail and find a note from my mom. She's getting worried. Wants to know when I'm getting in. I write back that I'm tied up with a flight cancellation and a customs issue and that I'll be home in a couple of days.

Apologize profusely.

Hate myself.

The food finishes. I pour myself a glass of water and dig in while doing a search of Richmond Terrance.

It's six miles, running along the northern edge of the island. As with most urban waterfront neighborhoods, it's not the nicest area, especially as you approach the western shore. Lots of vacant lots, industrial buildings, ancient homes in various states of disrepair. The kind of place you don't want to break down or wander around at night.

There are a dozen bodegas that I can find on Google Maps street view. I rule out the ones closest to the ferry terminal. The foot traffic is too high. Too many people. There's a police precinct not too far from there.

The terrace runs close to the water, except in the middle, where there's a marina and a water processing plant. Too risky to bring stuff onto shore there. Probably eyes around the clock. Cameras. I strike out that area, too.

If it's true that product comes in from New Jersey, which is what a lot of the news coverage indicates, the western end would make sense. You could throw it in a kayak and go from shore to shore. There are plenty of leisure vessels in the bay. Probably less so during the winter, but under cover of darkness? It stands to reason.

That narrows it down to four possibilities. At least on my list. I might be missing a few, but it's a start.

There are two close to each other, past the Bayonne Bridge. Both located in places without a lot of nearby businesses, probably don't have a lot of foot traffic. The kind of places that might need a little extra help staying open. I'll start with those. Surveillance first. See what I can see.

There's a shuffling sound behind me. I jump up, immediately fall into fighting stance.

Bombay is standing at the entrance of the kitchen, bleary-eyed, squinting. Bare-chested, in a pair of boxer shorts and big gray socks with red trim.

"You're a little jumpy," he says.

"Who wears socks to sleep?"

"My feet get cold," he says, opening the fridge. Then, "Fuck."

"What?"

"I was saving that beef chow fun, bro."

"For two in the morning?"

"It's best at two in the morning."

"I didn't eat all of it."

"You ate enough of it."

There's still some left on my plate. I offer it to him. He waves it off. "It's fine."

He prepares his own plate, sits down to eat it cold. As he stabs at the wide rice noodles with his fork, he asks, "What are you working on?"

I explain to him about the mysterious bodega, the search for Spencer. Leaving out the part about the attempted murder by OD. When I'm done, I eat some more of the food that's on my plate. Our forks screech on the ceramic. Bombay gets up from the table, removes a beer for the fridge. Offers me one but I shake my head. He sits down with his own and cracks it.

"You know what you can do," he says. "If you've got a couple you think might be prospects. Go inside. You have to figure if they're storing it, they probably need space. So if the building is, like, a hundred feet long but the bodega only goes back fifty, that could be something." He takes a long pull of beer. "Unless they're in a basement or an apartment above the store."

"Not a bad idea," I tell him.

Seeing him pull on the beer makes me wish I had one, except I don't really want a drink. What I want to do is take a little taste of that heroin in the pocket of my coat.

I could cook it, I guess. I don't have any needles but I could get some easy enough. You can get them at pharmacies. There's got to be an all-night pharmacy somewhere close. As for the cooking, I know the gist: mix it with a little water on a spoon, heat it up, toss in a bit of cotton to filter it. Draw it up, knock out the bubbles, send it home. I don't know how to hit a vein. It seems hard, but a lot of people manage.

I'm sure there's more to it. That's what Google is for.

I could snort it. That's supposed to work, too. Less efficient, but who fucking cares. I could do that right now rather than having to worry about going out to get a bunch of gear.

"Ash?"

"What?"

"You okay?"

No. Not even a little.

"Yeah, I'm fine."

THE THIRD BODEGA is a real possibility.

The first one I walked into this morning seemed to take up the entire footprint of the bottom of the building. There were a lot of cameras and the place felt too clean. Too put together. At the second, a pair of cops were waiting for breakfast sandwiches as the owner chatted them up like they were all best buds. It really didn't strike me as a "keep your enemies closer" kind of thing.

The third bodega seems like someone came in and set up a fake store in an old one that had been abandoned.

A small, cramped space, despite the fact that it looked like there was plenty more room in the back to spread out. The shelves half full and the refrigerator case keeping drinks lukewarm at best. The place needed a good dusting and mopping and for someone to run it who actually gives a shit.

The owner eyes me as I walk to the counter with my bottle of water. The sunglasses and newsboy cap pulled down tight over my face make me feel a little better—I wasn't wearing either when I ran into Paris and Athena or the dude at Sanctuary—but still, it's a little nerve-wracking. I keep things brief, get my water, get out.

This may not be the right one, but it feels like a good contender.

I walk across the street, sit down in the bus shelter, which blocks the wind coming off the water. A bus just went by and it's after rush hour so there won't be one for a little while longer. That gives me a bit of time to sit here and watch and not look like I'm sitting here and watching.

Check my phone. Text from Bombay: *Sorry to ask bro, but you got some cash lying around? Ordered delivery and forgot to put it on my card.*

I respond: *In my bag. Take what you need.*

After a little while, a car pulls up. It's a blank car. The kind of inoffensive, cookie-cutter sedan that if you were looking for it in a big parking lot, you'd get lost.

A short, stout black woman climbs out. Older, hair in cornrows that wrap around into a bun on the top of her head. Long black coat. Thousand-yard stare. She glances at me and heads inside. She smells like a cop. I consider getting up and leaving but I don't want to give up so easy. I yank the cap down a little more over my eyes.

After a few moments, she comes outside. Looks around. Settles on me.

The neighborhood looks deserted. No cars. No one out in the cold. She crosses the street to me and reaches into her pocket. I get up, preparing to run.

"Excuse me, sir…"

The bus shelter has me blocked from one end and she's looping around on the other, boxing me in. On purpose? My only good move is to run diagonally past her. I'm setting my feet and preparing to do it when she pulls a photo out of her pocket.

Even from a distance, even at an angle, it looks familiar.

When she's within a few feet of me, she holds it up.

"Sir, I was wondering if you'd seen this young man."

The picture is of Spencer Chavez.

FOURTEEN

FOR A HOT second I think of playing it cool, like maybe I don't know who she's talking about. But she's got this thing with her eyes. The way she looks at you makes you feel like you have something to apologize for. She smirks nearly as soon as the words have left her mouth because she sees I know something.

"Who are you?" I ask.

She holds my gaze for a moment, slides the picture into a pocket on the inside of her jacket, and removes a small leather billfold from another. Holds it up so I can see it. "Turquoise Reese," she says. "I'm a private investigator."

"And why are you looking for Spencer?" I ask.

"Usually, this works the other way around," she says. "You are?"

"Ashley McKenna," I tell her. "I'm uh…actually looking for Spencer myself."

She cocks an eyebrow. "You a friend?"

"Not really."

"Then why are you looking for him?"

"A mutual acquaintance hired me."

She narrows her eyes. "You on the job, too?"

"No. I'm more of an amateur, I guess."

At this, she chuckles. I'm a good head taller than her, but the tone of it makes me feel six inches shorter. Like a kid, right back to Jay Gunner's office.

"All right, all right," she says in a flat, even way. Her emotions on this are completely indecipherable. "You drink coffee?"

"I do."

"How do you take it?"

"Black."

She turns and walks toward the bodega, shoes clicking against the pavement, and she disappears inside. After a few minutes, she comes out with two cardboard cups. Nods toward her car and climbs into the driver's seat. I get into the passenger side. The inside smells like a chemical forest. She turns on the car and launches the heat full blast, hands me one of the cups.

"Turquoise Reese," I tell her. "I dig it. Kinda like Cleopatra Jones."

She throws me a side-eye that says it's not the first time she heard something like that, but she damn well wants it to be the last.

"So now I bought you a cup of coffee, and in return you are going to tell me what in the world you are doing," she says.

Part of me feels like I should hold back, like I should keep what I've learned to myself. But truthfully, the longer Spencer is out there, the more likely he's going to get killed or hurt or OD, so I'm not doing him any favors by playing coy.

That, and I'm hoping she'll be impressed.

I tell her most of it, leaving out some details. Tell her how I tracked down Brick, that it led me to Spencer, that he got away, now I'm staking out bodegas that might be drug mills in the vague hope I'll see someone or something useful. She listens, taking the occasional sip of her coffee, not removing her eyes from the front of the store. When I'm done, she lets the silence hang for a bit.

"You said you're an amateur," she says.

"I guess."

"You guess?"

"Yeah," I tell her, trying to be bold, failing. "It's just…a thing. I help find people or find stuff or learn things about people. You know, word of mouth gets around." The explanation is a ball of twine in my mouth.

"You understand you can't just be a PI, right? That's not something you pick up and do."

"No, I got that," I tell her. "You know Jay Gunner?"

She nods her head slowly. "He works up in St. George, right? Does a lot of business with the white shoes." She sees my confusion. "The fancier law firms."

"I went in there the other day trying to get an internship or apprenticeship and he chased me out the door. I know I need those things if I want to do this real. And I do. I don't know how."

"Why?" she asks.

Again, the words get tangled on the way out. Because it's not enough to say it. I need it to be right.

I'm still fishing for something to say when she takes her eyes off the bodega, twisting in her seat to look at me. "Why this? Why not go into the department and get your twenty and your pension, and then come around to it? You're young enough."

I sit back in the seat. Sip my coffee. I can feel anger trickling up my spine. She's pushing me, trying to get me frustrated. Testing me, I think? I take a deep breath. "Gunner said the same thing.

But I don't do well with rules. I don't do well with authority. That's not for me. I know I'm young and I know I have a lot to learn but I'd rather be governed by my own moral compass than someone else's."

She nods. Takes it in.

"Okay."

The way she says it, she sounds a little disappointed.

My answer wasn't good enough.

After a few more uncomfortable ticks of the clock, she says, "I got hired by the family. I've mostly been asking around law enforcement, hearing the same thing as you." She points up to a three-story apartment building next to the bodega. "Narcotics has this place under surveillance but I know the guy running the op. He said I could come poke around a little. Because he knows I can keep it discreet."

That last bit was a jab. She glances at me to make sure it landed.

"You know what's not discreet?" she asks.

"Me?"

She smiles, points her finger. "Bingo."

"So you want me to go, I guess?"

"Look," she says. "You've got half a brain in your head. That much is clear. You made it this far, and without any of the tools or contacts a real, actual, legal private investigator would have access to. But you've been at this for, what, how many days now?"

I have to think about it. "Three."

"Right. I started this morning. I want you to know that because I don't want you to give yourself too much credit."

That's enough to make my ribs ache. "Okay."

"Here's what's going to happen," she tells me, both hands gripped around her cup of coffee, like she's warming them. "You can consider that coffee a thank you for the work you've done so far. I would put work in air quotes but as you can see both of my hands are occupied. And you're going to stop screwing around on this. All you're going to do is get in my way. You understand me?"

I don't answer right away, which prompts her to repeat herself, her voice cracking like a whip.

"Do you understand?"

"Thanks for the coffee," I tell her, getting out of the car. I make sure she's looking and I dump it, three-quarters full, into a wastebasket on the corner. It's childish but it feels good to do anyway. It's four miles back to Bombay's. I start walking.

I DON'T REMEMBER HOW old I was. Young enough I was still a sponge.

It was late. I had trouble sleeping when I was a kid. That hasn't really changed much. When I was a kid, I would stay in my room and read comics, but this night I was thirsty, so I went to the kitchen for a glass of water.

I could hear my dad watching television in the living room, so I came down the stairs carefully, cut a sharp turn at the bannister to make it down the hallway and stay out of sight. My dad heard me anyway, said, "That you, kiddo?"

I poked my head out. He was sitting on the couch in sweatpants and a white t-shirt, bare feet propped up on the beaten ottoman, four drained beers next to him, though if you hadn't seen them you wouldn't have been able to tell he was drinking. Gray light from the TV danced across his face and the wall behind him.

"Need a glass of water."

He nodded. "Go get it and come here."

I grabbed one of the yellow plastic cups with the logo of his firehouse on the side—a freebie from the annual company beach picnic. The house was full of them. Got my water and went into the living room and he patted the empty cushion next to him. "Get on up here, kiddo."

That smell. I can remember that smell all this time later. Beer and aftershave and that vague odor of black smoke that never seemed to go away.

He was watching a black-and-white movie. A man with a sharp haircut and a sharper face, a cigarette dangling from his lip, traded pointed barbs with a beautiful woman.

"This right here," my dad said, cracking another beer that had grown wet with condensation from sitting out. "This right here is a classic. *The Maltese Falcon*. One of the best movies ever made."

I asked if the man was a cop. The way he was talking, the air of authority he carried, I thought he was a cop.

"No, he's a private eye," my dad said. "That's Sam Spade. Spade gets hired by the woman, Ruth, to find her sister."

"What's a private eye do?" I asked.

"Private eye is like a cop," my dad said. "Except people hire them for specific jobs. Like if someone goes missing."

"Why not go to the cops?"

"Because sometimes the cops can't help. Sometimes you need someone who's going to bend the rules a little, you know? Someone who only has to focus on one job at a time. I'll tell you, I almost thought about being a cop before I got into the fire department, but it just wasn't for me."

"Really?"

"I got some time until I retire, but when I do, I think I might hook up with some agency that does fire investigations." He took a swig of beer, paused like he was thinking of offering me some, but ultimately didn't. "I won't be no Sam Spade, but it might be a good use of my time. I like it. Figuring stuff out."

I asked him why he didn't become a cop.

My dad shrugged. "I'm not the biggest fan of people telling me what to do. You get that in the fire department, but not as much. But PIs, they do the right thing, too, but there's a purity to it, you know?" He was drifting a little, the beer finally soaking into his head. "They do it for money, sure, but they do it because they want to, because it's right. Not because someone told them to do it. Not because they're working toward some arbitrary retirement date. They do it because they want to do it. They do it because they want to help."

He put his hand on my shoulder, got this look in his eyes, the same way he got when he told me his mother, my grandma, had died, which made me a little scared at first.

"This world is a tough place," he said. "There are good people and there are bad people. And the good people, they've got to stick up for each other. Because sometimes no one else will. I want you to remember that, okay, kiddo?"

"I will."

"Promise me."

"I promise."

He ruffled my hair. Smiled. "It's late. Go on up to bed, okay?"

"Can I finish the movie with you?"

"It's halfway through."

"I don't mind."

He looked side to side, said, "Don't tell your mother."

Then he wrapped his arm around me, pulled me close, and caught me up on the plot. Even though I was finally feeling the call of sleep tugging at me, even though I didn't totally understand what was happening, I stayed up to the end to watch it, because I knew it would make him happy.

ALMOST AT BOMBAY'S. My phone buzzes. Unknown number. I don't answer it.

Considering how long I've been outside, stepping into the building is like being wrapped in a warm blanket. My muscles feel tight so I opt for the stairs over the elevator. Make it up to Bombay's floor and see a bundle of something outside his front door.

As I get closer, I realize it's my bag.

Sitting on top are the bags of heroin. Empty, rinsed clean.

I don't need a note to tell me the message Bombay is sending.

For fuck's sake. I let him go into my shit for cash. I should have remembered.

I bang my fist on the door. No answer.

Try the key, but the deadbolt is engaged so the door won't open. That one takes a second key I don't have. Bombay must have been leaving it undone for me.

I take out my phone, text him: *Dude, I know this doesn't look good, but I can explain.*

Send it. Sit and wait. Get nothing back.

Call him. I don't hear his phone inside the apartment.

Well, fuck.

Now I don't have a place to sleep. I consider picking the lock, but that's going to invite some odd looks and maybe the cops if someone pokes their head out the door. And anyway, I'm going to need to handle Bombay with kid gloves after this. Not that I can even offer to take a piss test. It'll come up dirty. I can't even prove I'm not actively using.

I take my bag outside and sit on the ledge over the sidewalk. Take out my phone as I'm crafting the text message in my head. Something to get the ball rolling. Before I can open up the text message app, my phone rings again. Unknown number. Probably Ginny. Fuck it. I watch the phone until the call goes to voicemail.

What do I do now?

My best friend thinks I'm on heroin. I kinda maybe sort of wish I was.

And now two private investigators essentially told me to fuck off.

Maybe they're right.

Who am I to be doing this, anyway? I'm like a kid in a costume. Me and Reese may have gotten to the same point but it took me three days and nearly dying. She made it sound like a morning stroll through the park.

I run through the last year in my head. When Chell died, I lost my shit, and I picked fights with anyone who was breathing. Nearly got myself killed a couple of times. In Portland, I took a fight too far. Killed a guy who I then had to bury in the woods. In Georgia, I was nearly poisoned, nearly shot, nearly drank myself to death. And in Prague, I managed to pick a fight with a former Spetsnaz hitter. I walked away. Mostly due to dumb luck, with a concussion and enough body trauma I probably have some kind of permanent damage.

That's before my run-in with Paris and Athena.

Maybe I'm not good at this.

Maybe the mark of being good at this is to find people and solve cases without leaving so much damage in my wake. Without hurting so many people.

Without hurting myself.

What if Samson is right? Maybe I am a thug with delusions of morality.

My phone rings again. I ignore it. I don't want to talk to Ginny right now. Because if there's a real private investigator on this, I should back off. Let her do her job. Ginny mentioned something about paying me even if I didn't turn anything up. Hopefully, she

153

sticks to that. At least I have the original ten grand. But that puts a big damper on my housing plans. Ten grand and I am fucked.

I make a list in my head. Stuff I can do. Bartender, waiter. Stuff I can start right now so I can put together a little money and figure out what comes next.

I get up, sling my bag over my shoulder, and walk. Down at the bottom of the block are some run-down motels that look like a great place to score crack or get sexually assaulted. They're not pretty, but they're close. As I'm walking besides the parked cars running along my right, a horn blares so loud and so close I jump and yell out. Turn and find a dark SUV with tinted windows, engine softly purring.

Ah fuck.

The window rolls down.

"The fuck aren't you answering you phone for?" Samson asks.

I stare at him for a second. "Go away."

"Get in the car."

"I say again, go away. I'm tired."

He takes off his sunglasses, his eyes ablaze. I think this is the first time I've seen him with his sunglasses off. I never knew what to expect from his eyes. They're a light, light brown. Like cappuccino. "I'm not asking, motherfucker."

"What are you going to do, get out of the car and fight me?"

"You gonna make me do that?" There's maybe some excitement in his voice, so I figure the answer is yes.

"Why are you here?" I ask.

He sighs. Evens out his voice. "Get the fuck in and I will explain. You think I'd be here if it wasn't important?"

I shouldn't do it. I should go back inside.

Call my mom.

Find an apartment.

Get a real job.

Track down Crystal.

Do anything but get in the car, so, of course, what I do is get in the car. Before I've even got the door all the way closed, Samson jerks away from the curb, cutting someone off, inviting a barrage of horn blows and, presumably, profanities.

"The fuck is the rush?" I ask.

"It's Ginny," Samson says. "She's gone."

FIFTEEN

"WHAT DO YOU mean, she's gone?"

Samson ignores me, weaving through traffic, clearly with a destination in mind.

"Hey, answer me," I tell him. "What the hell does this have to do with me?"

"Shut the fuck up," he says. "You'll know when you need to know."

We roll up on a red light. I pop the door and climb out. He yells at me but I cut him off when I slam the door closed. I turn around and walk up the hill, against traffic. There are cars behind him so he can't back up. He's got nowhere to go but forward.

I walk for two blocks before the SUV comes roaring at me and leaps onto the curb, slamming to a stop about a foot from my knee. I step around it, ready to keep walking to Bombay's. The window rolls down.

And Samson says a word I've never heard from him.

A word I never expected to hear from him.

"Please."

That word stops me dead where I'm standing. It's not that he says it. It's how he says it. There's something else there, under the usual about-to-hit-a-boil pot of anger. Can't put my finger on it. But it chills me.

I stare him down for another few seconds and climb into the car. Tell him, "No more bullshit. I want to know what's going on or else I get out, and then I'm going to make you work to get me back in."

Samson sighs. "Ginny went to a meet. Didn't come back. I know where she is and I need someone good with their hands. Helps that you're white. I'm a little conspicuous where we're headed."

"Why couldn't you have just said that?" I ask. "Why did you have to be such a dick?"

He doesn't say anything. Pulls away from the curb. Drives. Back to the status quo.

"Some more details would help," I tell him.

"Open the glove box. All the details you need."

"Do we really have to do this dance again? You really want me to get out?"

No answer.

"Who was she meeting?"

Samson swings the car around a light, cutting someone off, horns blaring. He says, "She insisted on going alone. I knew it was a mistake but she didn't want to hear it. Told me she could handle herself. Hour ago, I got a ransom demand. A million flat to get her back alive."

"I'm assuming we aren't rolling with a briefcase full of money in the back, are we?"

Samson shakes his head. "We don't have that much liquid. Best I can do on short notice is maybe a few hundred grand, and even then, fuck 'em. We go in, we get her out. Her phone broadcasts her location, even if it's turned off. Safety feature. They should have destroyed it. That's how I know we aren't dealing with pros."

"Have you thought maybe they aren't amateurs? And they left the phone on to draw you in?"

He nods toward the glove box. "Hence."

"Which you already know I am not carrying."

"Fuck you aren't."

"I'll get out."

"Goddamnit," he says, smashing his palm against the steering wheel. "One motherfucking time I need you, you're going to get all fucking high and mighty on me? It's not enough I'm paying you a goddamn compliment? You think I didn't have my pick of people on this?"

"You know, this is funny."

"What?"

"This is the most we've ever talked, I think."

He huffs. We drive in silence for a bit. He merges onto the Staten Island Expressway. Still no idea where we're going. Traffic is light, and that much is a kindness. I consider turning on the radio but Samson is like an old stick of dynamite. Best to sit still and be careful rather than risk something that might set him off.

We turn onto the West Shore Expressway. Headed south then. Immediately slam into a wall of traffic. To the right, wetlands dotted with snow. Beyond them, the Arthur Kill and the industrial shores of New Jersey. I consider the situation. I've never seen Samson charged up like this. Angry, yes. That's his primary level of functionality.

But I know what that thing is, the thing underneath in his

voice that gave me chills.

He's desperate.

I always considered Samson to be strictly a driver and bodyguard. Maybe there's something more to the relationship. I give him a look. He's focused on the road, eyes behind his sunglasses, hands gripped around the wheel so tight it's a wonder he hasn't yanked it off. I consider pushing the issue but figure that's a good way to get shoved out of the car once we get back up to speed.

Still, we should attempt to do a little planning.

"If I'm going to help you, I need to know what's going on," I tell him.

He breathes in deep through his mouth, hard out his nose.

"Quit with the bullshit," I tell him. "We're not going to accomplish a goddamn thing if you go in there looking to rip out someone's throat. Believe me, I know. You have to control your anger. Right now, your anger is controlling you."

"I don't need a lecture from you."

"Yes, you do."

He breathes again, in through his mouth, out through his nose. A little burst of air. He does it again, and by the third time, I recognize it as a coping mechanism. I give him a minute and ask, "What's the deal?"

"Ginny tell you about Kid Vicious?"

"Yeah."

"He's about to go to war with Brick. Or they're at war already, I don't really know. Point is, Ginny's been putting out feelers to see if there's anything in there for her. Someone sent up a balloon, made it sound like Kid Fuckface was open to talk. Ginny wanted me to stay behind because she said I don't create an 'amenable environment.'"

159

"Well, you are scary as fuck," I tell him. "And where exactly are we rolling to?"

"Someplace down in the burbs. We get in quiet and get out the same way."

"Guns aren't quiet. How do we get in quiet?"

"We'll figure something out."

"This is the time in which we figure it out. What's the address?"

He rattles it off. I plug it into my phone and pull up the street view. Spin the camera around. It's a quiet street. Cookie-cutter homes. An entire block of them, in various states of new construction. It's not replacing anything, like with Sandy. It's just that the rest of the city is running out of room and the growth is pushing for the borders. There's a lot of empty land on the south shore, and a lot of people looking for something comfortably between city living and the suburban experience.

The construction gives me an idea. As we approach the Victory Boulevard exit, I tell Samson, "Get off here."

"We're not even close to where we're going."

"I know. We're making a stop."

SAMSON UNLOADS ME around the corner from the house. He goes off to look for a spot the next block over, and then he'll circle around to the back of the property, while I walk down the street in my brand-new olive-green coveralls.

They don't fit great—too tight around the ass and too loose around the chest, somehow—and the fabric is so stiff it's chafing, but it'll do.

To the coveralls I added tan work boots, a baseball cap pulled down low over my eyes, and some heavy-duty zip ties crammed into my pocket. Plus a clipboard with some credit card forms on it, which I swiped from an unmanned booth in the mall. I felt bad stealing it, but Samson was pretty pissed about paying for the coveralls and the new boots, and I didn't want to spend my own money on props.

Figure anyone else walks up to the house, the people inside go red alert. But someone in coveralls carrying a clipboard would be wallpaper in a neighborhood with new construction. I could be from any number of agencies or crews with business around here.

The street looks about the same as the street view, except the construction is a little more finished. There are three houses at the end that are still being built, but the rest of the homes are done, and some of them even look lived in, shiny SUVs and luxury cars parked in the driveways.

Samson was right about one thing: this is the kind of neighborhood where if someone peeked out the window and saw him moseying around, they'd put a call in to the cops just in case. Report a suspicious character. *Suspicious* being the polite word for *black*.

So, yes, bringing me was pretty clever, except for the fact that now I'm here, and I'm probably about to get in a fight, and I don't want to be in a fight. I shouldn't have gotten back in the car. I should have told him to fuck off, let things land where they may.

But if this is who I am, if this is what I do, maybe I should embrace it. Maybe I'm no better than a thug. I'm good at it. I'm sure I could work for Ginny full time. That would make a lot of my problems go away. All I would need to do is compromise my newfound morals.

What are morals, anyway? They're self-developed systems. They can be whatever you want them to be.

I climb the brick staircase to the front of the house. Knock on the door. Feel my heart squeeze out a little extra blood. The house

161

is painted gray to remind you of a sad, cloudy day. Like concrete but with less personality. I hear footsteps beyond the door, then some scuffling, like someone is looking at me from the peephole.

I look around like I'm bored, then check my watch. Act inconspicuous. The door opens a crack. In the darkness of the foyer I make out a white kid wearing a hoodie and sweatpants, barefoot. He's young and high. Given the size of his pupils, the slack in his jaw muscles, I could probably tell him I'm from Mars and he'd be cool with it.

"Gas company," I tell him. "Getting some funky readings in the neighborhood. Okay if I pop down your basement, check your connection? Make sure there's not any kind of leak?"

"Uh…what?"

Like I said: High. As. Fuck.

"Two minutes," I tell him. "Basement. Just making sure your house doesn't explode."

"Explode?"

"Yes. It is a thing we like to avoid when we can."

His eyes dart back and forth. He's thinking about it. Trying to process it. He looks toward the second floor. Either that's where they have Ginny, or that's where the person is who can grant permission.

"Two minutes, in and out," I tell him. "Easy peasy."

"Real quick?" he asks.

Jesus Christ. "Yes."

He nods, opens the door. I step into the foyer. The living room is to the right, dining room to the left, kitchen in the back. Everything tidy and barely lived-in. Almost no furniture. No open concept. There's a vague chemical smell but otherwise the house is silent. It looks more like a home staged to sell rather than a home that people live in.

The kid points toward the kitchen. "Basement door is over there."

"Thanks, buddy."

I head that way, figuring Samson has worked around. I can pop open the back door and let him in and the two of us can get to work. All without having to shoot anyone. Seems like this will be an easy one, until I start walking, and I regret my new construction boots because they echo on the hardwood floor, the sound reverberating through the house.

That incites more footsteps from upstairs.

Someone comes down the stairs fast. Hits the floor and turns into the hallway.

Another white kid. Tall, dark hair, solid muscle. He doesn't skip leg day. Lots of tattoos, but tough-guy lame and generic— Chinese characters and barbed-wire. He's got a heavy tan despite the season and his dark hair is slicked back with a tanker-disaster amount of grease.

He sees me and his hand flicks toward the back of his pants. He freezes when his eyes settle on the clipboard.

"Who the fuck are you?" he asks, accent so thick it sounds like he's doing a bit.

"Gas company," I tell him. "Like I told your buddy here, there are some wonky readings in the neighborhood. Gotta check the connection. Make sure your house isn't going to get blown to kingdom come. Takes two minutes."

He nods. His hand relaxes, no longer reaching for the back of his pants. I try not to make the tension disappearing from my shoulders so obvious.

"Go ahead, then," he says.

I move toward the door, make sure to keep him in my peripheral vision. Try to pull the door. Can't, because it's a pocket door. I push it aside, feel for the light switch. Flick it on. There's a staircase and, at the bottom, a concrete floor. I step into the basement, now wondering how the hell I'm going to play this. Maybe there's a weapon down there. Maybe I can subdue him.

"Why don't you come on down," I tell him. "Case I can't find it."

"Sure."

I get halfway down the stairs and turn. Look up.

He's got his foot on the first step and he's holding a gun, pointed down, vaguely in my direction.

"No gas line on this street," he says. "Developers cheaped out and wouldn't put one in. We have to get oil delivered. Which is crazy, right? It's like, we live in New York City, not fucking Appalachia. So why don't you tell me who *the fuck* you are and why *the fuck* you're here?" He punctuates his profanities by stabbing the air in front of him with the gun.

"Um…" is all I manage to get out before Samson comes flying into view, throwing his weight into the guy as he cracks him across the jaw. I throw myself down the stairs as the gun fires. Bullets smash into the wall above me, raining dust. Look up and the stairway is empty. I climb up to find Samson holding the gun on him. The guy is on the floor, blood streaming from his mangled nose, doing a crab walk toward the front door.

I grab the barrel of the gun and yank it up. It fires into the ceiling, kicking out dust and plaster. Another stab in the ears. I yank the gun away from Samson. He grabs me by the throat and slams me into the wall, the cheap sheetrock giving under my weight.

"The fuck is it with you and this bullshit?" he screams, his eyes raging.

I drop my weight and twist out of his grasp. I take a few steps back, not pointing the gun at him, but making sure he knows I have it. "Calm the fuck down."

There's a scratching sound from the front. The guy is reaching up from the floor, trying to get the knob. Samson loses interest in me, stalks across the room, and kicks the guy in the stomach. He leans over and groans.

"Where is she?" he yells.

More footsteps from upstairs.

The other kid. The one who opened the door. I lost track of him. I pull some zip ties out of my coveralls and toss them at Samson and run up the stairs, into the hallway. There are four doors, one of which is open.

I hold the gun in front of me, not terribly thrilled to have it, but I may as well use what I've got, and nudge the door open with my foot. Find the kid in the corner of a sparse bedroom, floorboards pulled up, stuffing something into a gym bag.

"Hey," I tell him.

He doesn't stop.

"Hey," I say again, louder.

He keeps packing. I come up behind him, find some loose money and a few plastic packages the size and shape of a brick, filled with white powder. Not too hard to guess what that is.

"Hey, dummy," I tell him.

He stops, turns, looks at me.

Reaches into the bag and comes out with a shotgun.

I kick it, hard, before he can even get his finger into the trigger. It flies across the room and hits the wall. I pick up the kid, throw him out the door. Push him toward the stairs. Find Samson, still yelling at the guy, who is now tied up, his face a little more mangled. I go back into the bedroom, toss the gun onto the bed, then untuck the blanket and rub it hard on both sides to take off my prints.

165

I push the scrawny kid down the stairs. Samson goes to work tying him up as I peek out the front window. No cop cars. No one outside. That's good. Don't know how long that's going to last. Two gunshots should serve to attract some attention. But it's early enough that most people are probably still at work.

Samson leans down to the guy with the slicked hair and asks, "Where's Ginny?"

The guy smiles. "Fuck you, you fucking Canadian."

Samson squints, looks up at me, shrugs. Balls up his fist and jabs the guy in the mouth.

Jesus, this is not good. Samson reaches back to swing again but I lock my arm in his, tell him: "Check upstairs."

Samson pulls away, I think considers hitting me. Then he clomps up the stairs. There's a crash. Good. Let him work out the anger some other way.

I look down at the guy. "Canadians?"

"It's what we call the nigs. Less racist." He says this like he is very proud.

"I think that's actually more racist."

"Well, fuck you, and fuck him, and fuck that crossdresser, whatever the fuck his name is." The guy tries to work himself into a sitting position. "You are so fucked. You have no idea who you're fucking with. Kid Vicious is going to run this island. That tranny thought he was hot shit. Acting like Kid should bow down to him. He had no idea. Just like you have no idea."

"No idea about what?" I ask.

"The storm that's coming," the guy says.

"Oh, give me a break," I tell him. "You know, I'm probably the only thing standing between you and that big motherfucker. The more you talk, the more I want to let him go to town on you."

In response, he smiles, his teeth stained with blood.

I'm considering a response when Samson comes down the stairs.

"Nothing," he says.

I now care way less about protecting this guy, so I tell Samson to watch them and head into the basement. Find a bare concrete space with a washer and dryer and slop sink. Some shelves and cleaning supplies. And a door, leading to another room. I put my ear to it. Can't hear anything. Try the handle and it's locked. Figure on going upstairs to find a key it, but then realize I don't want to be in this house a second longer than I have to be.

I stop at the door, rear back, slam my foot into the wood next to the knob.

The door buckles but doesn't budge.

Try it again.

Pain shoots up my leg. Something inside the door splinters.

The third kick does it. It flies open, making a sharp crack on the wall.

Inside, there's a chair.

The chair is empty, save for a phone.

I pick it up. Purple-pink glitter case that catches the light and sparkles. Ginny's.

That's when I hear the sirens.

At the top of the stairs I hold up the phone. "Not here."

"Fuck," Samson says. He snatches the phone out of my hand, drops it to the floor, and drives his heel into it, hard. He stomps on it a few more times, then looks back up. "Let's go."

The two guys are still zip-tied by the door. I figure it's best to leave them. I follow Samson, duck out the sliding glass door onto a deck, then go down the stairs onto the grass, across the narrow backyard to the fence. Samson vaults himself over. Given his size it's almost shocking to see how agile he is, but then I remember the cops, and pull myself up after him.

We end up in another yard, this one full of kid toys. Samson nearly wipes out on one of those red-and-yellow smiley-face cars, but he rights himself and tears ass down the empty driveway alongside the house that leads to the street. I follow behind. The SUV beeps but before Samson can even get all the way around to the driver's side door I hear: "Police!"

Stop. Turn. There's an Impala with tinted windows blocking the road, the doors swung upon, a little electronic dinging sound coming from inside the car, the keys still in the ignition. There are two cops holding us at gunpoint. A petite Latina and an older guy with a bald head and a bushy mustache.

Samson and I stop. Put our hands up.

"You know the drill," Samson says, soft enough I can hear it, not loud enough they can.

I don't answer. Of course I know the drill. Shut my mouth. I'm slightly less concerned about that, and more concerned about what I might have touched in the house. At least I wiped the gun.

The cops move in on us.

"Against the car, now," the woman says.

We assume the position. I watch in the reflection of the SUV's tinted windows as the cops move in on us. The older one takes me, pats me down like he's trying to put out a fire on my clothes. Takes my wallet.

The woman finished patting down Samson and doesn't come up with a gun. That's a little surprising. I figured he was carrying.

The woman proceeds to read our Miranda rights to us while the cop fiddles with my wallet, looks at my ID, and walks back to the cruiser. He comes back a few moments later, as the woman is cuffing us. He's nodding his head and smiling.

"Got us a big one," he says to the woman, nodding toward me.

I have no idea what he means, but I know better than to ask.

"Ashley McKenna," he says. "You are under arrest for the murder of Brian Marks."

SIXTEEN

HIS NAME IS Detective Perry. Under different circumstances, I would like him. Probably former military, from the way he carries himself, the caution of his diction. He wears a light pink dress shirt, which you'd think a guy like him would avoid, but I think he wears it because he doesn't care what people think.

The way he talks to me is like we're pals. Like I'm in a jam and he can help me.

Even though I know it's not true, he's almost sincere enough I believe it.

"Tell me what happened," he says.

I look around the room. Walls painted sky blue. The table is heavy duty and scuffed. It has a little metal loop screwed into it. They uncuffed my right wrist and attached the handcuff to that. With my free hand I can sip at the small Styrofoam cup of coffee that must have come from a pod or a packet. It's supposed to be

French vanilla but it tastes like a chemical spill.

"This guy Marks was not a good guy," Perry says, his voice low, like he doesn't want anyone to overhear us. Which seems like a charade because I can feel the mirror across the room vibrating. Someone standing on the other side, watching.

Perry sits back in his seat.

"What he did to that neighborhood. The lives he ruined. I mean, you have no idea. You probably think you have an idea. You have no idea. I'm not saying what you did was okay, but you might have had a reason. And if it's a good enough reason, I might be able to help. So level with me, okay, kid? Tell me what happened. How did it go down?"

I repeat the phrase I've said a dozen times already: "Lawyer, please and thank you."

He sighs. Shoulders slump. "Fine," he says. He stands up, walks around the table to me, leans down close. "Remember this moment. This is your last chance. We could have done this the easy way. I get it. It's fine. But remember this moment. Because at some point, things are going to get really tough and you are going to wish you had played ball. There are no do-overs here."

I attempt to smile. The smile is meant to cover up the feeling like I want to cry. He can tell, because he lingers for a second like he thinks I might finally crack. Too bad for him I'm too smart to do that. Or else, I'm too dumb. At this point, I can't even tell anymore.

He nods and leaves the room, letting the door slam behind him.

Well, this sucks.

Best I can figure is that Brick's real name is Brian Marks, and someone killed him, and they think that someone is me. They kept mentioning "prints on the gun." Mine, specifically.

But, what gun?

I know how the cops have my prints. All those years ago, that fight I had to pick in Esperanto. Had I been smart enough to sit back down, to listen to Bombay, to ignore it, to *walk away*, I might not be in this mess right now. They would have had me on something, but not murder.

I run through the events of the past couple of days in my head. Try to remember. Maybe Paris and Athena pressed a gun in my hand after they dosed me. Insurance? A frame job? Maybe it's the cops. The guy we smacked around in the stash house made some noise about there being something bigger at play with Kid Vicious. It's a little heavy to think a heroin ring might stretch into the NYPD, but hey, you never know.

Otherwise, what is there?

And then I remember.

The guy outside Sanctuary.

I took his gun. Threw it in some bushes. Of course he went looking for it after I left. But I touched it. I left my prints on it.

I guess I could explain all that, but then what?

Would that even help?

I'm trying to figure out how to play that when the door opens. An older Italian guy built like a linebacker strides in and sits across from me, slapping a briefcase on the table. He's wearing a carefully tailored charcoal suit. His gray hair is slicked back with so much grease it shines. What is it with Italians and this goddamn hairstyle?

"I'm your attorney, Anthony Moretti," he says.

I glance at the gold cufflinks and the watch I think might be a Rolex. "You look a little high class for a court-appointed attorney."

He laughs. "I look like some public schlub defender to you? No, an associate of a mutual friend asked me come over."

He doesn't have to explain it any more than that.

Ginny.

He leans forward. "Here's the deal. A little before noon, a man named Brian Marks was shot and killed in an apartment in Park Hill. He's a known heroin dealer who goes by the street name Brick. After he was shot and killed, his apartment was cleared out and then torched. A gun was recovered at the scene with your fingerprints. So first things first. Do you have an alibi for this morning for around that time?"

I laugh. "I do, actually. I was having a conversation with a private detective. Turquoise Reese. We sat in her car on Richmond Terrace."

Moretti smiles. "That's Turk. I know Turk a little. That's good, kid. It's good to have an alibi. Makes my job a lot easier if I don't have to find one for you. Now, want to tell me how your prints got on that gun?"

I explain the altercation. Taking the gun, tossing it away. I don't explain why it happened and he doesn't ask.

"Easier and easier," he says. "That takes care of the murder charge. Turk is law enforcement. She vouches for you, it goes a long way. All that leaves is why you were on the block where they picked you up. We're not even going to bother coming up with an answer for that one. I hear the kids they found inside are clammed up. Your prints inside?"

"On one of the doors, maybe."

He sighs. "I'm going to talk to the cops. You are not going to say a word from now until we walk out the front door. We are going to knock this out toot-fucking-sweet. You got me?"

"I got you."

Moretti disappears. He's gone for a little while. I sweat a bit. The coffee bubbles like acid in my stomach. I wonder if all of this is going to work.

I've completely lost track of how much time has passed by the time Moretti returns with Perry, who is in a sour mood. He undoes the cuffs and tells me, "You're free to go. Don't stray too far. I expect we'll be talking again soon."

Like Moretti told me, I say nothing. I rub my wrist and exit the room, heading toward the front of the precinct. As we near the doors, I stop at a desk to retrieve my coat, and, luckily, my bag, which the cops pulled out of Samson's car. I give a quick peek and the money is still there. As I'm getting everything situated, Moretti looks around, makes sure we're alone, and says, "You're lucky. We got Turk on the phone. She verified she was with you. I explained why the prints were on the gun. They're not thrilled, but they can't come up with a better explanation. Beyond that, they got nothing. Best they could do would be to hold you on a minor trespassing charge for being on someone else's property, but that's stretching, and I made that clear."

He roots around in the front pocket of his suit and hands me a card.

"He's not lying. This won't be the end of it. Call me if you need me. All covered by our friend."

"Okay."

"And in the meantime, keep your fucking nose clean, you hear?"

"Okay."

"And stop saying okay like a goddamn parrot."

"Okay."

He smiles, smacks me on the arm. "Attaboy. Get out of here. I have some cleanup to do."

He disappears into the bowels of the precinct. I wonder if by cleanup he means Samson. Or maybe he cleared things up with Samson first.

I step outside. It's evening now, orange light sinking in the sky. It's snowing again.

Is this what rock bottom feels like?

The fall to the bottom hurts so much more when you've managed to climb out of the hole and see some sunlight.

All I can think about is that little taste of oblivion. I could go to Timmy's. He could show me how to shoot. I could spend the night on the couch drifting away from all of this. It sounds like a very workable plan.

But then I see it.

I hadn't hit rock bottom.

Because standing at the curb, her face twisted into a frown of epic proportion, is my mother.

There is nothing lower than this moment.

She's wearing a tan coat. Her short gray hair collecting snow. Her arms are wrapped around herself, like she's trying to shrink away from me. Like she's trying to protect herself.

We stare at each other for a few moments. She looks so much older than when I saw her last. I think it has less to do with it being a year and more to do with the circumstances of our reunion.

"Get in the car," she says, her voice a few degrees colder than the air.

NEITHER OF US looks at each other. Neither of us speaks. The console between us is like a demilitarized zone. Two opposing factions waiting for the other one to surrender. We make it most of the way home before she opens her mouth.

"How long have you been home?" she asks.

"Couple of days."

She winces.

"What happened to your face?"

"Got in a fight."

"Are you hurt?"

"I'm alive."

She nods. Sniffs. Still won't look at me. Not even a glance. I feel sick. Sicker than I did after the naloxone. Sicker than when I was detoxing in a broken down bus in the middle of the woods. Sicker than all those times I was pretty sure I was about to die.

This is worse than all of that.

"Ma..."

"Why did the police come to my house this morning looking for you?" she asks. "They came and said they wanted to speak to you about a murder investigation. Then I get a call that you're at the station and to come pick you up. Tell me what's going on, Ashley."

"It's a long story..."

She yanks the wheel, throwing us to the curb outside a coffee shop. A man walking along the sidewalk jumps from the sudden appearance of the car, even though he's a safe distance away. She puts the car in park and places both hands on the wheel, staring out. The man comes to the window to say something, but gets a good look at the both of us and backs off.

"What is happening, Ashley?"

No sense in lying.

She can tell when I'm lying.

So I tell her, starting with when I left: saving Crystal and her daughter. Saving some innocent people from being hurt by a militant environmental group. Getting wrapped up in a political conflict in Prague. And then trying to find someone who was missing, which put me on a path that made me, very briefly, a murder suspect.

After I'm done, there's no sound but the whirring of the

engine and the dull thud of the wiper blades, flicking snow off the windshield. Those two sounds combine until they're deafening. A car coming in the other direction illuminates her face. I can only see a small sliver of it but there's a reflective streak on her cheek. She's crying.

I'm past rock bottom. I'm digging furiously into the ground, hoping I'll find a place to hide, but I can't. My throat gets thick. I try to swallow, but I can't.

Nothing in this world has ever hurt me as much as making my mother cry.

"Why?" she asks, her voice fragile, like glass.

"Because I wanted to help."

Her voice drops to barely a whisper. "Your father died because he wanted to help."

"I know."

"Then why are you doing this to me?"

She finally looks at me, not trying to hide it anymore. She's crying, which gets me going, my vision blurring and burning. I look down at my hands in my lap. Try to come up with an answer that's going to be right, that's going to make sense, that's going to fix this.

But I don't have one.

There is no correct answer here other than to tell the truth.

"When dad died," I start. Rip off the scab. Breathe deep. Collect myself. "I wanted so much to be like him. Even though sometimes he got hurt. He saved people. He protected them. He was my hero. And heroes aren't supposed to die. After it happened, I kept thinking about what he said. That there are good guys and bad guys, and the good guys had to stick up for each other. I felt like…he left this void in the world. And I had to carry on with it. I know this all sounds really childish. In a lot of ways, it is,

because I was a child when he died, and I think part of me just…
froze in that moment. I fell into helping people. Stopping bullies.
Protecting people. It felt right to do those things. And I kept doing
those things until it seemed like the only thing I could do. People
started to joke that I was like an amateur private investigator. And
I began to believe it. So I thought it was something I could do with
my life. But the whole time I've been…I don't know, a kid playing
pretend."

I interlace my fingers, squeeze my hands.

"But now I know. This is what I'm supposed to do. I'm here to
help. Because I can take it. I can live with it."

I look at my mom, who is back to not looking at me.

"But I can't live with hurting you. I can't. Nothing is worth
that. If you tell me to stop, I will. I'll go get an office job. Something
safe. Wear a suit. Whatever you want. Say the word."

She turns like she's going to look at me, but then she doesn't.
She puts her hand on the gearshift, pulls the car so it's parallel to
the curb, and turns off the engine. Opens the door, the interior
illuminating, snuffing out when she closes it. She heads toward
the coffee shop and I wonder if I should follow, or if she doesn't
want me to. But then she turns and waves at me, annoyed, like I'm
making her late for something.

I climb out of the car and head inside. The place is half full,
people eating waffles covered with sauces and candy. The smell
of ground coffee and fried dough. My mom goes to the counter
and orders two large black coffees and a glass of ice water, hands
the girl behind the counter a ten. Without waiting for change she
carries the coffees to the front window, where there's a table and
two worn wingback chairs.

She places the coffee down and we sit. She opens the cups and
tips in some ice to cool them. The folly of drinking coffee black:

you have to wait longer for it to be an acceptable temperature. But like she told me, years ago, when she wants coffee, she wants coffee, not a milkshake.

Once she's put the tops back on, she takes a sip, makes a face, like it's still a little too hot, and settles into her seat. Stares out the window. I wonder if I should start talking but I think I've said enough.

"You wouldn't know this," she says. "You were just a baby. But your father said almost the exact same thing to me when he got the call. You know, you take the exam and sometimes you wait years for a spot to open up. He had been driving oil trucks at the time. The day before he went to the academy, he took me out to dinner and he told me that if I didn't want him to do it, to say the word, and he wouldn't."

She looks at me. Her lip quivers but she forces it into a smile.

"How could I say no?" she asks. "That's who he was. It was his dream. It wasn't a fair question because if I told him not to do it, he would have resented me. But the truth is, I didn't want to say no. I admired that about him. Your father was such a good man." She squeezes her eyes, pushing out some tears. "And so are you. Even if you can be a bit of a dunce."

I laugh to keep from crying. "Ma..."

"Just because I didn't say no to your father doesn't mean I wasn't afraid," she says. "I was afraid all the time. Every time he left the house, I was worried it might be the last time I saw him. And then one day..." She puts her hand to her face, hides her eyes from me. Takes a second. "Then one day, it was."

She takes a sip of coffee, looks back out the window.

"I'm not going to say no to you," she says. "I admire that you want to help people. Even if I'm afraid. Even if I think this is a little...stranger than the path your father chose. I'm not going to say no. I can come around. But I need you to make me a promise, right here, right now. Promise me you will be careful. And you will pursue this like a real job. No more of this amateur nonsense. And, damn it, you will stop lying to me."

"Yeah, Ma," I tell her. "Of course. I promise. And I'm sorry…I wish I had told you all this sooner…"

She takes a long sip of her coffee, peering at me over the top. She puts down the cup and smirks. "I have a surprise for you, you know. Not even sure you deserve it."

"Oh yeah?"

"Come to the house," she says. "Maybe I'll be in a better mood after dinner."

WHEN I STEP onto the back deck, I feel fifty pounds heavier in my gut from lasagna and garlic bread and salad, and about a hundred pounds lighter in the region of my conscience. Not that my mom is all the way there yet, but by the end of dinner we were talking the way we used to.

The snow has stopped. There's a dusting on the deck. As we walk across it to the garage, my mom asks, "So what happened to the girl in Portland? Ruby? Sapphire?"

"Crystal."

"I knew it was a stripper name."

I turn to throw an eyebrow at her and she smiles. She remembered it was Crystal. Her memory is relentless. She just wanted to make the joke.

"It didn't work out," I tell her.

"That's too bad," my mom says. "I could tell from the way you talked about her, you really liked her."

The garage door is an ancient, heavy monstrosity. I have to

wiggle the key to get it to unlock, and then nearly throw my back out getting it open. It's a wonder my mom even gets inside. The door slams into place and I flip the light switch.

My dad's old Chrysler LeBaron convertible sits in the light like a dull brown slab on wheels. It doesn't really show its age. Still in pretty good shape. His first car, and he never wanted to part with it. Since he died, my mom and I have pretended it wasn't here.

Because right now, looking at it, I'm smacked with memories of driving out to Coney Island, out to Long Island, up to the Catskills. Summer with top down, wind in our hair, my dad blasting Springsteen and Led Zeppelin and Guns N' Roses. I can smell the saltwater, the mountain air. I can get lost in moments like that.

"Does this even still run?" I ask.

"Just had it looked at," my mom says, standing behind me, holding up the keys. "Needed a new battery and had to do a little work on the engine."

"You're sure?"

"He'd have wanted you to have it. But when you were living in Manhattan, there was never a reason to give it to you."

I take the keys. I don't know what to say. I'm so tired of taking buses everywhere. It'll be nice to have something I can drive around.

More than that, it's nice to have something of my father's.

I pull my mom into a hug.

She feels so fragile.

After a moment, I realize that's actually me.

I kiss her on the cheek, say, "Thank you."

"I love you, Ashley. You're so much like your father. For better and worse."

"I'll take that," I tell her.

181

MY OLD ROOM is untouched. The door has been closed so long there isn't even really much dust. Frozen in time. Wood paneling, a twin bed bowed a little in the middle. A dresser stuffed with some old t-shirts. A small television and an Xbox, the controllers sitting in front of it, the cords carefully wound up. I suspect that was my mom. I wouldn't have left them like that.

All the clothes in my bag are dirty. I root around in the dresser, find an old pair of jeans and a t-shirt. They're musty but they'll do.

In the corner of the room is a small green plastic box. On the top is my name, painted like a cartoon. A gift from my aunt. I open it up, find the detritus of my life. Random odds and ends I didn't want to throw away but didn't have any use for.

My first cell phone. A set of darts. A few dollar chips from a casino in Atlantic City. A USB drive. Who knows what the hell is on that.

There's a pile of pictures. Me and my friends acting like idiots. Our features washed out by the cheap, harsh flashes of disposable cameras. My face is slimmer, facial hair lighter. I almost don't recognize myself. I look happy in a way I don't ever remember being happy, and after a few minutes of flipping through them, I'm surprised to realize that many of them are from when after dad died.

There are pictures of him, too. I kept a few with me, while I was traveling, but here are more: in the back yard, building the deck, barbecuing. For a long time now I've felt like he was getting lost in a fog. Like I could still see him but his features were growing dimmer with time. Seeing these makes it all come rushing back. The way he used to smoke cigars but never around me because he didn't want to set a bad influence, but I could always tell, because he would smell like them. The way he would ruffle my hair when he was proud of me. He never said it. The ruffle said it.

The way he loved me like I was the best thing he ever did.

I put the pictures away. When I find a new place, I'll bring them. They'll be nice to have.

Time for bed. Tomorrow, I get to work fixing things.

I glance at my phone, to check the time, and realize it's off. Turn it on and I have three voicemails.

One from Bombay. One from an unknown number. One from Timmy.

The one from Bombay is a hang-up. My heart dips.

The unknown number is Reese.

"Got an interesting call about you today. Come by my office tomorrow. I'd like to have a chat."

Then:

"Ash, man, listen. Can you come by tomorrow? We need to talk. Look, I fucked up. I know that. But, you know, I've made a fucking wreck of my life…I want to make good. I want to make it up to you. I know I can barely do that, but I found something out. Something important. You really need to hear this."

There's a pause. I think the call has been disconnected.

But then it comes back.

"A lot of people are going to die," he says. "Come by tomorrow, okay?"

SEVENTEEN

AFTER TWO HOURS of not sleeping, I get in the car, wince as
I start the engine, afraid it'll wake my mom. But my cell doesn't
light up by the end of the block so I figure I'm in the clear.

The roads are empty and I make quick work to the middle of
the island. I park the car on an abandoned service road running
alongside the expressway.

I wanted to come sooner. I didn't because it's hard to get to
without a car. That's what I tell myself. It's probably not the whole
truth. I feel a little bad coming here without my mom, but I'm sure
we'll come here together in the near future. Right now, I want to
be alone.

The car locked up, I start walking. Sprawling before me are
the rolling hills of the former Fresh Kills landfill. The only thing
people outside of Staten Island seem to know about it. That we've
got the biggest dump in the world. When I was a kid, you'd come

out to the mall in the middle of summer and you would have to run from your car to get inside, the smell was so overwhelming. Great masses of seagulls feeding on the trash seemed to blot out the sun. People said it was one of the only man-made structures besides the Great Wall of China you could see from space, though I'm not sure I believe that.

Not that it's still active—Giuliani closed it back in the '90s as a gift to the local Republican lawmakers who got him elected. One of the only positive things that rat-faced fuck ever did for this city.

When the landfill was slated to be closed, someone decided to turn it into a park. Supposedly, it's going to be three times bigger than Central Park when it's done. The mounds of garbage will be capped and vented. The area will be remediated so that people who visit it won't even know they're standing on old diapers and rotting takeout and the corpses of buried mobsters.

It sounds crazy, but a lot of this city is built on trash. Ellis Island was constructed on top of debris dug out for the subway system. The FDR Drive was built on the rubble of European cities bombed during World War II, which ships crossing the Atlantic used as ballast. Battery Park City was built with dirt excavated from the site of the original World Trade Center.

None of this city is new.

The dump was supposed to stay closed, but after 9/11, the city carted debris here to sift through. Not the most dignified thing, but there were sorting facilities and plenty of space.

The question is, the question always is, what to do with the remains?

Workers sifted for anything down to a quarter of an inch. But mixed in with the dirt and the rubble were microscopic pieces of people, vaporized when the planes slammed into the buildings, when the buildings fell.

They're still here.

My dad is still here.

I find a hole in the fence. Climb through. Set off toward the top of the hill. I know where I'm going. I'll know it when I find it. I visited it with my mom a few years ago.

My dad is here. But maybe he's not. I have no idea where he is. They never found his body. One of his buddies speculated it could be he got too high up in the building, where he was assisting with the evacuation. So when the tower collapsed, he turned to dust.

Here, but not here.

A woman sued the city over this. Her son died. She thought it unfitting that a landfill be his final resting place. She said the city should sift through the rest of dirt and move everything over to the memorial down by the new Freedom Tower. The city refused to do it. Said it was too much money to spend on something you couldn't see.

I'm not sure how I feel. Looking at it dispassionately, I see their point. It's a few metric tons of dirt with microscopic particles.

But it's a woman's son, her family, and how the fuck am I supposed to argue with that?

How can anyone?

Besides City Hall.

I stop at the crest. This doesn't look right. Nearly right, but not right enough. I keep walking. Down one hill, up another, the wind pelting me in the wide-open space, threatening to send me tumbling down. I move slow, careful of my footing, trying not to trip in the dark.

Probably would have been smarter to do this during the day.

I stop. Rolling hills and trees beyond, snow lit blue by the moon, the Manhattan skyline sparkling in the distance. A cold, clear night. The way the city glows, so sharp and so precious.

This is it.

I wipe my nose on the back of my sleeve and stick my hands in my pockets, fall into a sitting position on the hard earth. Take my hand out of my pocket and press it to the ground. Dead grass brittle underneath my fingertips. I would push my fingers into the soil if I could, but I can't because the ground is frozen. It's all I can do to press my hand down hard until my palm is flat against the earth. As close to it as I can get.

"Hey, Dad," I say, the words snatched from my mouth by the wind, barely audible, but still, it doesn't feel like I'm saying them to myself.

I SEE MORNING COMING from a mile away, peering through the venetian blinds and white lace curtain. A few hours of sleep and a little time to think, during which I reached a couple of conclusions.

The big one is, no more lying to my mom. No matter if it hurts, no matter if it's painful. No more lying.

Next: I have to see this thing through.

Not just because Timmy said the magic words, that people will die. The way he said it felt too damn ominous for me to sit on the sidelines. And anyway, with the current interest the NYPD has in me, I get the sense none of this is going to end for me until it's over anyway. May as well lean into that.

Plus, now Ginny is missing. For all the shit that's gone down between us, she's my friend. And I won't abandon her. So, now I've got two people to look for.

My jeans are lying in a bundle on the floor. I fish the now-crumpled list out of the pocket and cross off the first item I've actually been able to accomplish.

Find a place to live?
Get a job?
Find Spencer Chavez again
~~See my mom~~
Check on Crystal

That feels nice. Not that I foresee a whole lot of progress on the rest. Still no idea where I'm going to live, or how I'm going to make a living. I doubt Reese has had a change of heart given I ended up a suspect in a murder investigation. But she did ask to see me today. Maybe there's something to be hopeful for. More likely she's going to yell at me.

I take a shower. Find my clothes are cleaned and folded, lying in a laundry basket on the living room couch. Get dressed and go into the kitchen where I give my mom a kiss on the head as she reads the newspaper, her hair smelling like Pert shampoo. That smell so entwined with this house, like my childhood in microcosm. Funny the way a smell can do that. Make the past into a set of clothes you can slip on and off.

As I'm leaving, she looks up at me. "Don't do anything stupid."

"I promise I will never lie to you again."

"That's good," she says. But then she gets what I mean, and she frowns.

"Don't worry," I tell her. "I've made it through worse."

I give her a smug little smile. She rolls her eyes in response.

The car feels good, even with a little bit of snow on the ground. It's not fast and it's not flashy—even with the top down it's not that much to look at, like an electric razor from the '70s—but it's nice to have a car.

It takes forever to find a spot around Bombay's apartment. After I do, I consider calling ahead, but even if he's not there, fuck it, I'll risk it and pick the lock. Hang out until he gets here. It's not like I actually did the heroin. I fucked up a little, not a whole lot.

I slap my palm against his door. There's a shuffle, then the sound of the little metal disc being lifted off the eyehole.

"Fuck off, bro."

"Let me explain."

"Nothing to explain."

"Goddammit, for all we've been through, can you spare me two fucking minutes to tell you what happened?"

Silence on the other end.

I'm reaching for my lock pick kit when the door swings open. I expect Bombay to be furious, but he's not. He's hurt, his eyes wide and wet and sad, and that's even worse.

"You told me you were clean," he says.

"I am. Technically. Two minutes."

He stands aside. Lets me in.

"Sit," I tell him.

He sits on the couch. I remain standing.

I tell him what happened. The forced OD. That feeling like I wanted more. The stupid decision to bring it into his house. I apologize at various points. He listens, his face a blank expanse of stone. After I'm done, he nods slowly.

Says, "Good."

"Are we friends again?"

"You shouldn't have brought it here."

"I know. I fucked up. Again, I'm sorry."

I fall into the couch next to him. We stare at the wall for a few seconds.

"So what the hell happened to you yesterday?" he asks. "You got arrested?"

"Let me guess," I tell him. "My mom called you."

"Soon as the cops showed up. She didn't have your new number but thought I might have been in contact with you."

"What did you tell her?"

"I didn't answer. She left a voicemail. You know I can't lie to your mom."

I run him through the interrogation. When I'm finished, he laughs. "How the fuck do you get tied up shit like this, bro?"

"Everyone's got a talent."

"You've got, like, the worst fucking talent. Ever."

"I know."

"What's on the docket for today?"

"This private eye wants to see me," I tell him. "Not sure why. But I figure I'll swing by, see what's what. Then I'm going to see Timmy."

"Oh shit, man, Timmy." He trails off for a second, then nods. "Can I come with?"

"You know, yeah. That might do Timmy some good. Sure. I'll go see the detective, then come get you?"

"Got it." He looks at his watch. "Also, I've got a surprise for you. I mean, I was already in the process of doing it, and after I found the heroin, I wasn't going to fucking give it to you. But knowing what I know now…you got a second?"

I laugh. He doesn't realize I'm laughing because my mom gifted me a fucking car, like somehow I deserve people being nice to me. "Sure."

He gets up, slides his bare feet into a pair of slippers, and takes me to the front of the apartment. Grabs his keys off a hook on the wall and steps into the carpeted hallway. Bombay's apartment is at the end of the hall in an angled alcove with two doors. He steps to the other door, opens it, and pushes inside.

The apartment is dim and a little dusty. There's some cast-off furniture. A couch and a small table. A bookshelf. The kitchen looks a little older than Bombay's. But it's generally the same shape. Two bedrooms. It's a nice space, with a view of the bay through the living room windows.

"I get it," he says. "You don't want to live on Staten Island. But honestly, why?"

I walk through the apartment. It's warm. The way old brick building hold the heat during winter. But more than that.

"Just, think about it, maybe?" Bombay asks. "The landlord here loves me. If I recommend you, you're in. This is a good building, Ash. There are roaches sometimes, but other than that?"

I walk around the living room, my boots echoing on the hardwood floor. Walk through the galley kitchen, check the cabinets. Peek into the bathroom and bedrooms. I try to come up with a good reason about why I shouldn't live here.

And I can't.

There are two types of people who grow up on Staten Island. The ones who look around and see a nowhere town and dream of a bigger life. And the ones who live and die here, who think trips on the ferry are some grand occasion. I fall hard into the first category, but I guess that was the problem.

Assuming there needed to be categories.

Doesn't matter where you live. It only matters how.

Being close to my mom, the people I love—that's a life. This is the thing I've been waiting for. I didn't realize I was waiting for it. It's easy for me to fall down black holes, but in reality, I am way luckier than I have any right to be.

"Set it up," I tell Bombay.

He smiles, gives me a hug, slaps my back hard. "You serious?"

"Yeah," I tell him. "I'm tired of not having any roots. Time to lay some down."

"Got it. I'll get everything taken care of. They might want to see some credit and employment history and shit…"

"I've got cash."

"All right, man, I'm going to go down to the office right now." He hands me the key. "Lock up when you're done. This is going to be so fucking cool. Living right next to each other, bro."

"I'm already crashing with you."

"Yeah, but now there's less of a chance I'll grow to resent you."

"Fair."

Bombay smiles and rushes out the door. I take the list out of my pocket.

~~Find a place to live?~~

Get a job?

Find Spencer Chavez again

~~See my mom~~

Check on Crystal

Today is turning out to be not so bad. Time to go make it worse.

THE SKY OUTSIDE Reese's office looks like a cauldron. The DJ on the classic rock station says there's a bit of snow coming today, but a lot more on tap for tomorrow. Up to a foot, possibly two. Lovely. This car will be basically useless.

Reese's office is a converted apartment on the second floor of a building on Forest Avenue. On the first floor, there's an optometrist. I ring the bell and the door buzzes. I climb the heavily carpeted steps and knock on the door on the first landing, which has her name on it.

Turquoise Reese. I swear. Coolest name ever.

A voice inside: "Come in."

The front is a converted living room. There's a couch and a few chairs. Nothing matches but it's all very neat. There's a young girl sitting on the couch, preteen, pink sneakers, hair pulled back into a ponytail. She's reading a book.

"You the secretary?" I ask.

That earns me a laugh. "It's my mom's office. She said you can go back."

"How does she know I'm here?"

"She said you were coming. The white boy who looked like he'd been beat up."

"What are you reading?"

She tilts the book up at me. *To Kill a Mockingbird*.

"For school," she says.

"That's a good one," I tell her, heading toward the back. I pass a room that's full of filing cabinets, and a pristine bathroom, and make it to the room at the rear, which used to be a bedroom but now is an office. There's a desk, some maps on the wall, lots of pictures: Reese in uniform. Reese with another man—husband?— and the little girl out front, at various life events. Graduations, plays, beaches.

Reese is seated behind the desk, reading a thick stack of paperwork, peering down through a pair of glasses. When she sees me, she pulls the glasses and lets them fall against her chest, kept in place by a small chain looped around the back of her neck.

"You're here," she says.

"You asked me to stop by."

"You didn't have to."

"You scare me a little bit."

She laughs. Nods toward the open chair in front of the desk.

"So, would you like to explain to me why I got a phone call from a crook like Moretti to alibi you yesterday?"

"Moretti is a crook?"

"He's a great lawyer if you're guilty and you have money. I'm a little surprised to hear about the company you keep."

"Yesterday was the first I met him. He's employed by a mutual acquaintance."

She gives me a terse smile. "Again, the company you keep."

"Childhood friend. Our paths diverged a long time ago. But he's the one, asked me to look for Spencer."

Reese tosses the bundle of paper onto the desk, sits back. Takes a deep breath. "Here's where I'm at. This is a big heroin market. I'm sure you know that. Which means territory here is valuable. There's a lot of money to make. Best I can figure it, we're in the middle of a coup." She picks up a copy of the *Post*, tosses it at me. On the front page is Brian Marks. He's posing with a woman in a club or a bar. He's dressed neatly, in a polo shirt, smiling wide.

Brian Marks.

Brick.

The guy I took the gun from outside Sanctuary.

Mother-fuck. Biggest dealer on the island working in a treatment center. Was he scoping new customers? Keeping his ear to the ground? I don't know. But the hell that seemed to come down on me out of nowhere suddenly makes a lot of sense. It wasn't that I was skirting the edges. I fucked with the man himself.

"He was the king," Reese says. "Now someone else wants the crown."

"Kid Vicious."

She stops. "What?"

"The new guy. Probably the guy who killed Brick, or had him killed. Kid Vicious. It's a very dumb name and I'm almost ashamed to say it out loud."

"Huh," she says, more to herself than to me. "I did not know that. Not even my contacts in the PD knew that."

It happens so briefly, like a bolt of lightning on the horizon that I can't be sure I saw, but I think I see her smile.

"Here's what I'm trying to figure out," she says. "How the hell do you fit in all this?"

"The person who hired me, Spencer works for her," I tell her.

"And what does this person do?"

"Nothing good." Reese frowns, so I add, "I'm not doing it for her. I'm doing it for Spencer."

She searches my face for a minute, says, "No, that's not entirely accurate, is it?"

After a moment. "No, I guess it's not. She offered me a lot of money."

She nods. "If you're the kind of person who trucks with dealers, that puts us on opposite sides of this fight. I was born in this city. I saw crack pull it apart in the '80s and now it's happening again. Same song, different verse. I will not sit by and do nothing. This job is getting a lot heavier than finding a missing kid."

My turn to smile.

I like her a lot.

"I want to help," I tell her.

"Okay."

"That's my answer. In the car, you asked me why I wanted to do this kind of work. It's because I want to help."

She nods. Maybe not the right answer, but close enough. Closer than last time, at least.

"How'd you find out about…what was that dumb name again?"

"Kid Vicious. Heard it dropped a few times. I've got a lead on something else, too. Guy I know said he heard something big.

Something that's going to end up getting a lot of people dead. That's my next stop after this."

"Will you share with me what you learned?"

"Are we negotiating?"

She breathes in through her nose. Stares at me, through me, to the back of the room, and then out the building, before returning her attention to me.

"You're persistent," she says. "I like that. You're resourceful. And you seem suited for a lot of the work I'm tired of doing. Those are all things that count in your favor. There's a lot counting against. You're hotheaded. That's written all over your face. You don't grasp the intricacies of this job. You think it's a chance to be Batman without being rich or having to put on tights."

She trails off. Returns to it.

"But sometimes it can be a little like that," she says.

"So what does that mean?"

"Find out the thing you're going to find out. Share it with me. Share with me anything else you find. And I will think about having a conversation where I consider bringing you on as an intern. I might still say no. The only reason I'm even taking it this far is that you walked in here and told me something I didn't know. And that's not nothing."

I stand up. Extend my hand.

She gets up, shakes it.

"Does this mean I get to call you Turk?"

Her grip goes tight, eyes cold.

"You call me that again..." she says.

She doesn't need to finish the sentence. I put my hands up and back away.

"Sorry," I tell her, and get the hell out of her office before she can change her mind. So high I feel like I'm floating.

THE SNOW IS falling steadily by the time Bombay gets in the car. As I'm waiting for an opening in traffic, he says, "I think we're good to go on the apartment, bro."

"Went well?"

"Yours if you want it."

I pull away from the curb, the roadway piling with a mixture of gray sludge and snow and salt. We used to have a term for that. New Yorked. How the snow was so pristine on its way down but within moments of landing soaked up the filth of the city.

Still. There will always be clean snow to replace it.

"So Timmy isn't doing great?" Bombay asks.

"He wants to make good on selling me out. Are you sure you want to come with me? I can drop you at a bar down the block or something. I don't want to put you in a bad spot."

"No, I'd like to see Timmy. I remember thinking of reaching out after his folks died and I didn't. Not that it probably would have changed anything. But I wish I did. And I don't mind pitching in every now and again. I mean, you barely understand how to use a computer. You need me in your life."

"I know how to use a computer."

"Not nearly well enough."

"Congratulations on being a nerd."

We drive a little more.

I reach across and smack Bombay on the thigh.

"Thank you," I tell him.

"No problem, bro," he says.

TIMMY'S CAR IS in the driveway. I park my car on the street and our boots crunch in the snow on the way up the walkway. There are no lights on inside. I ring the bell. Wait a minute. Take out my phone and call Timmy. It goes to voicemail. Bombay stands on the walkway, bunched up in his coat, hands in his pockets, stamping his feet.

I do not like this.

He could be sleeping.

It could be worse than that.

"C'mon," I tell him.

We walk down the driveway. I keep an eye on the windows of the house next door, make sure no one is watching.

"What are we doing?" Bombay asks.

"Checking the back door."

"I don't really feel comfortable with this."

"It'll be fine."

We get to the back door, find it's locked. I take out my lock pick set, make sure no one can see us from where we're standing, and go to work.

"Now I really don't feel comfortable with this," Bombay says.

"I do this shit all the time."

"Yeah, and look where it gets you. Plus, you're white. This shit is a little different when you're brown, bro."

"You're with me. I'll vouch for you."

"Doesn't work like that."

The door clicks. I push it open. The house is tomb quiet. I call out, "Timmy."

Nothing.

Fuck.

We move through the kitchen, into the living room. Nothing out of order. I go back to the kitchen, grab the biggest knife in the block. This time I know where it is.

"Whoa," Bombay says.

"We're probably alone. Stay down here."

Bombay nods as I climb the stairs. Smelling the air. Listening. Anything that might spell ambush. See the door to Timmy's room is open. Nudge it with my foot.

I can smell him before I see him. Lying on the bed, arms and legs spread wide, needle sticking out of his arm. My hand goes to my pocket, to the naloxone, but it doesn't matter. That stopped being an option hours ago.

EIGHTEEN

WHEN I TELL Bombay, his mouth falls open. He wants to say something, but instead of saying anything, he sits on the corner of the couch and folds his hands, then presses them against his face.

His first dead body. And he hasn't even seen it. I forget how many this is for me. I feel bad about that. But also a whole bunch of people died in Prague so it's hard to keep track. Give me a dark room and I remember all their faces.

"We should probably go, right?" Bombay asks though his fingers.

Used to be I would agree with that. And maybe it's not the smartest thing to call the police for a dead body when I'm a person of interest in a major crimes investigation. But the reality is that Timmy doesn't have anyone in this world. Which means no one's going to find him. He's going to sit here and rot until the neighbors notice the utility bills piling up. There's no dignity in that.

I could call it in anonymously, from a payphone down the street, or wherever there are still payphones left in this city, but there's no dignity in that for me.

"No," I tell him. "I'm going to call the cops. You can go if you want. Take my car."

"I don't want to bail on you."

"You're clearly not comfortable with this."

He shrugs but doesn't move from the couch.

"People are going to die," I say.

Bombay looks up. "What?"

"That's what Timmy said. A lot of people are going to die. Now we don't know how."

That makes me wonder about the circumstances of Timmy's death. I know he tried to OD a few days ago, but that's when he thought he killed me. Or, at least, lent a helping hand. But he seemed much more optimistic, more ready to help. Maybe that needle sticking out his arm upstairs was an accident. Maybe it wasn't.

I check the front and back door. No signs of forced entry. It'd been snowing and there were no other footprints besides ours. I would have noticed that.

In the kitchen is a laptop, plugged into the wall, the little green power indicator glowing green. I call Bombay and he comes in slowly, stepping like there might be a wild animal crouching out of sight, waiting to pounce.

"What do you think?" I ask, gesturing toward the laptop.

"Dude, I don't want to fuck around with that. What if the cops lift prints off it?"

I pick up a kitchen towel and open drawers. After a few, I find what I'm looking for: freezer bags. I pull out two and toss them on the counter.

"Gloves," I tell him.

"This is getting into the realm of too much, bro."

"This could be important," I tell him. "I wouldn't ask if it wasn't."

He closes his eyes, nods his head, and pulls the bags over his hands. Wiggles his fingers to make sure he can type, and pulls a USB stick out of his pocket.

"You always travel with those?" I ask.

"I have, like, four on me right now."

"Get to work. I'm going to check the rest of the house."

First stop is the basement, to make sure it's clear. No broken windows, no door leading to the outside. Not a point of entry. I come upstairs, past Bombay, who's poking the laptop, then head upstairs. All untouched, like when I was here the other day.

I peek into the bedroom one more time.

The room doesn't turn up much. The covers are undone, sloppy. Could have been jerked around in a struggle, could be Timmy didn't like making his bed. I certainly can't remember the last time I made mine.

Something about the scene is a bit odd.

Something about the way it looks now that doesn't line up with the way it looked a few days ago, when I caught Timmy trying to kill himself.

I look at him lying there, skin slack.

And then it hits me.

Last time, the needle was in his left arm, probably because he's right-handed.

Now it's in his right.

I get a little closer and look at the crook of his left arm. Scattershot of open, scabbed-over, and scarred track marks. Could be he couldn't find a good vein, or he wanted to balance out the wounds. There are a few stray injection points surrounding the needle poking out of his skin. Maybe nothing, maybe something.

On the nightstand there's a pile of clean needles, cotton balls, a bottle of water, a bent and charred spoon. I touch the spoon with the balled-up knuckle of my finger. Cold and dry. Not sure what that means. Maybe he used it recently, maybe he didn't.

There's a small glassine envelope sitting next to the works. Stamped on it in red ink is a slice of pizza.

Dealers like to mark their product. Corporate logos and movie titles and funny little images. Could help lead me to a batch or a dealer.

Other than that, I've got nothing but a thought that someone may or may not have dosed him.

I do know some people who like to do that kind of thing.

Back downstairs, Bombay is shoving the freezer bags deep into the garbage. When he's done, he looks up at me and holds the USB. "I made a virtual copy of his browser. We can check his e-mail and his browsing history. That's about it. Didn't seem to be much else helpful."

"Did you see his phone?"

"Not down here. If his account password was autosaved, I can probably access his records."

I take out my phone, call Timmy's cell. Straight to voicemail. Could be gone, or it could be dead, lost in a couch cushion or up in his pocket.

No sense in waiting any longer. I dial 911, and when the operator answers, I tell them my friend OD'd and the address and that I'll wait. I'm only a little surprised by the use of the word "friend."

T'S QUITE A show. The first to arrive is a fire truck, and I let the firefighters in and explain to them there's not much to be done, so they mill around on the block outside until some cops arrive. By this point there are people standing at their windows, some coming outside to ask what happened. When the cops take my name, I tell them immediately that I was in for questioning and then let go. Figure it's best to be honest. They give me some vicious side-eye but otherwise seem satisfied with my reason for being here: checking on my friend, was worried about him, back door was unlocked, found him dead.

The last to show up is the white medical examiner van. A few people come in and start poking around, taking pictures. A tall, skinny Asian woman, her hair shaped into careful curls, leads me and Bombay into the kitchen. She takes all our information. After she's got it, she takes a deep breath. An ID badge hangs from the lanyard around her neck. Emily Chan.

"How did you know him?" she asks. Her voice is weary, and for a moment I wonder if it's rooted in disinterest, but there's something a little heavier under that. Sadness. Like she's gone on a lot of calls like this lately.

"We went to high school together. I ran into him recently and we reconnected."

"Any next of kin that you know of?"

"Parents are dead. He made some reference to not having anyone."

"Did you notice anything weird or off when you came into the house?"

"No. He invited us over. When he didn't answer, we checked the back door. I didn't notice anything until I got upstairs."

"Did you touch anything?"

"No," I tell her, throwing a quick glance to Bombay. His lips are pressed hard together but it doesn't look like he's going to crack.

Emily nods, jots down some notes.

"What's going to happen to him?" I ask.

She sighs again, her shoulders sagging. "We'll do the best we can to find next of kin. Could be an aunt or uncle floating around somewhere. But if what you say is true, even if we do, I doubt anyone's going to want to take possession of the body or take on the funeral expenses. Chances are he's going to end up on Hart Island."

"What's that?"

She creases an eyebrow, like she's surprised I don't know. "Up between the Bronx and Long Island. The potter's field for New York City. That's where people go when there's no one to claim them." She looks around the house, frowns. "At this rate, we're going to fill that place up pretty soon."

Hearing that is a fist to the chest.

It makes me think of my dad. The dirt that might hold him, or not. Standing in a field and wondering where he went. I know how I feel about it. I hate the idea of that happening to anyone else.

"What if I claimed him?" I ask.

Emily stares at me for a second, maybe to see whether I'm kidding. I don't think I am. I'm not a big believer in the afterlife. I'm not a fan of wakes or funerals. It's not like you're doing it for the deceased. They don't know it's happening. But there's something so repellant about the idea of leaving him in a fucking field.

"Are you serious?" she asks.

"Yes."

"If you're not, I'm on the hook."

"I want to do this."

She nods, fishes out a business card, and hands it to me. "You got eight hundred bucks?"

"I do."

"I know a cremation service. Couple of days, you'll have the cremains. Does that sound amenable to you?"

"It does."

She asks for my number, scribbles it on the clipboard. "You can pick it up in a few days," she says. Her face shifts and she realizes the way that sounded, and she apologizes. I accept even though I don't know that she needed to apologize.

Once she's done, we leave, to find more snow on the ground and a bitter wind. I take it slow on the way back to Bombay's. We don't say a word, and by the time I pull into a spot down the block from the apartment building, I realize the radio isn't on either.

'M NOT HUNGRY anymore but it feels like a sin to leave one uneaten slice of pizza. When Lunette and Bombay both decline, I fold it up and go to town. Wash it down with a beer and sit back on the couch as we continue with our marathon of home renovation shows.

A young couple laments that their fixer-upper has knob-and-tube wiring in the walls, which is, apparently not up to code. Their renovation budget got kicked in the teeth for an additional ten grand. The husband complains that they're spending so much money on renovations they can't even see, and that they might have to surrender their marble countertops to make budget.

"You know what I hate?" Lunette asks. "These assholes are like 'Ooh wah, we have to spend extra money to make sure our house doesn't burn down'. You know what would be nice? Making enough money to live in a house."

"Fucking yuppies," I say.

"Fucking yuppies," she agrees.

I turn to Bombay. "Any headway?"

He nods without taking his eyes off the screen. "Couple of things. I've got a list of all the numbers he called, and he had his text messages synced to the cloud so I was able to review everything. Nothing of real interest in that, or in his e-mail. Different story with his geotagging. I was able to lift location data through one of the apps on his phone. Which is something I'm going to look into because that app isn't supposed to do that. He went to a couple of places on the south shore. I can't get addresses but I can get pretty rough locations. Last thing is, he looked at a bunch of websites that were about fentanyl."

"Huh," Lunette says, sipping her beer.

"Huh what?"

"That's some nasty shit."

"It is," Bombay says, hitting pause on the TV. "Heroin comes from a plant. Fentanyl comes from a lab. It's a synthetic. It's supposed to be an alternative to morphine. So, like, after surgery for people who are opioid-tolerant. But it's also, like, fifty to a hundred times stronger than morphine."

"Real nasty," Lunette says. "Easy to OD. Still, lots of folks like to mix it into their stash."

"So a lot of people are going to die, and maybe that's related to fentanyl." I turn to Lunette. "What do you think? We know there's a new guy on the block and he wants to make a name for himself. But if he's using fentanyl, what, he kills a bunch of his customers? That doesn't make a lot of sense."

Lunette takes a long swig of beer. Finds that the bottle is empty. Puts it down on top of the coffee table. It makes a clacking sound. She sits back, folds her arms over her chest. Almost folding into herself. Shame and guilt sock me in the stomach.

"I'm sorry," I tell her. "I wouldn't if it wasn't important."

207

"Dealers cut their shit," she says. "Powdered milk. Flour. Chalk. I've heard of guys using laundry detergent. Anything to stretch it out. But sometimes dealers will put out pure doses. That can be too much, even for veteran users. Because the more you use it, the more you can tolerate, right? A regular user needs higher and higher doses to get to the same high."

"Okay, but fentanyl is so much stronger."

Lunette's face stretches into a grimace. "That's the point. The point is to make a lot of people OD. Because then everyone's going to want your shit."

"Really?"

Lunette looks away from me. "You have to understand the psychology of this. If someone ODs, that doesn't make you afraid of it, that makes you want it. Because that means it's got to be good. Most of the time, you're dealing with stuff that's been stepped on until there's nothing left. The promise of a better high than the one you've got…"

She trails off. Gets up and goes to the window. Turns on the box fan Bombay set up for her and lights a cigarette. The gray wisps of smoke are sucked away from her, into the night air.

"If this is true, that there's some guy out there trying to make some noise, that's a way to do it," she says. "I mean, it's pretty fucked up, but that doesn't make it not true. A dealer can build himself a dedicated customer base by killing off the first wave of users."

"That is…not good," I tell her.

Bombay looks up from his laptop. "She's right. I'm checking Google now. Found a couple of stories already about dealers cutting with fentanyl for exactly that reason."

Lunette sucks on her cigarette, staring over the glowing tip at me.

Bombay is staring at me, too.

They're waiting for me to say something.

"We can go to the cops," I tell them.

"And say what?" Lunette asks. "Some drug dealer with a dumb name may or may not be planning to kill a bunch of people? You think the cops give a fuck about users? We're vermin to them. No one's going to give a fuck about us."

"I don't think that's true," I tell her. "The detective who questioned me and the PI I've been talking to both seem pretty passionate about ending this."

"Right, but we don't have much in the way of evidence," Bombay says.

I run the scenario through my head. Showing up with a theory and nothing in hand is probably not going to do much, and there's suddenly a ticking clock element. If I were to suss out some more information—something concrete, like more details of Kid Vicious, or when exactly this is supposed to go down—it would give us a little more weight.

Plus, it would look good to Reese. Like I can actually do this kind of work.

Not to be so cavalier as to say this is a great opportunity to advance my career. But it's a great opportunity to advance my career. With the added bonus of stopping a bad guy, saving some lives, and finding some people who've gone missing.

Because this is my home. I know that now. This is where I belong. And I will not tolerate this in my home. Lunette's not wrong—to call them junkies is to pass a judgment we don't have the right to make. Yes, they made their choice. But they weren't helped by dishonest pharmaceutical companies, and politicians who don't care to fund treatment, and police officers who see them as roaches.

It raises the questions of next steps. Knowing what Timmy

found out is only a small part of a larger battle. I need to find out who the fuck Kid Vicious is and where to find him.

"Those locations you pulled up," I ask Bombay. "Is there any way to find out exactly where Timmy went?"

"Not specifically. I could do streets. Maybe a few homes or businesses. But phone GPS isn't as precise as you would think. What are you thinking?"

"That Timmy went somewhere yesterday, got the information, and then he died," I tell him. "Whether he was killed or what, I don't know. But we have to retrace his steps."

"I can tell you generally where he went, and I can tell you roughly how long he was in each place, but we're getting into inexact science territory here, bro," Bombay says. "There's a lot of ground to cover. Would help if we could narrow it down."

I get up, cross over to the fridge. Take out a beer. Consider it. Put it back. Think about asking Lunette for a cigarette. Don't do that either.

Focus on the job.

"Can you put together a list?" I ask Bombay. "As much detail as you can."

"Sure," he says, looking back down at the laptop.

I take out my phone and call up Reese's office. It's well past eleven and I know she won't be in but I'm hoping she stays on top of her messages. When the greeting ends and the recording starts, I say, "This is Ash. I think I've got something but I need your help. Can you meet me tomorrow morning? Let's say ten a.m."

And I give her an address.

NINETEEN

BY 10:08 I'M wondering if Reese didn't get my message, or worse, if she doesn't care. But then I see her car pulling into an empty space down the block from Project Sanctuary.

I had been keeping my car running for the warmth, so I kill the engine and walk over to hers and wave her down. She flicks the switch for the locks and I climb into the passenger seat.

"Usually, I don't even come into the office until eleven," she says.

"It's good that you checked your messages."

"What I mean is, this better be good."

"I think it is."

I explain everything: Timmy being dead, finding out about the fentanyl, the theory of what Kid Vicious might be doing, that I'm worried it's not enough to take to the cops. She listens quietly, nodding along the way.

"Well, it's definitely not enough," she says. "But it's enough for me to shake some branches. So why are we here?"

"Because we know Timmy was rolling around on the south shore. And I've got some rough ideas about the locations, but I don't have time to knock on twenty doors. I'd like to narrow it down." I nod toward Project Sanctuary. "The woman who runs this place might be able to help. Maybe put us in touch with someone who will know if there's anything worth pursuing. I tried to talk to her about Spencer. She wasn't too forthcoming, because who am I? I figure she might be more inclined to talk to you."

Reese laughs a little under her breath. "You really want that job, don't you?"

"Right now, I want to stop a bad guy from doing a bad thing."

"All right, all right," she says, turning the engine off. "Let's go inside and see what we can get."

As we come up on the building, we walk past a group of hard-ass motherfuckers leaning against the wall, smoking cigarettes, shooting the shit. The kind of guys that, if they were walking toward you, even though you might feel bad, you'd cross the street anyway, just in case.

Reese doesn't pay them any attention, but one of them mutters something under his breath at her and she stops dead. Turns. He's two heads taller and maybe a hundred pounds heavier. He's the kind of person I wouldn't want to fuck with and I usually don't feel that way about people. But she marches right over and looks up at him.

"You want to repeat that?"

"I didn't say nothing."

"Don't be a coward on top of being a little shit," she says. As she says it, it's like she's getting taller and he's getting shorter. He looks around to his friends, who all take a step back. He has to deal with the consequences of his actions, they're telling him.

He looks back at Reese. "Didn't mean nothing."

"Yes, you did," she says. "You were showing off for your friends. But you don't talk to women like that. That's not how a man is supposed to act. You understand?"

With his manhood called into question, his face twists. He's ready to say something back to her when Reese puts her hand up.

"Before you say it, shut the fuck up," she says. "Answer the question. Do you understand?"

They hold each other's eyes for a second.

The guy deflates. Reese wins.

"Yeah," he says, looking down and away.

"Yes, ma'am," Reese says. "Respect your elders. Jesus, you're a fucking mess all over, aren't you?"

The guy starts to roll his eyes, catches himself, says, "Yes, ma'am."

Reese smiles. "Good." She looks around, making eye contact with each of the men in turn, and walks away. Some of them look at me. I put my hands up and do a big exaggerated shrug. Slightly more afraid of Reese, but also glad she's on my side.

As we move away, the men taunt their newly-cowed friend. I ask Reese, "What did he say?"

"Not worth repeating," she says. "But when a man thinks he can say something like that to a woman, whether he knows her or not, you shut it right down."

"I knew I liked you," I tell her.

She gives me a little side-eye and a smirk.

The lobby of Project Sanctuary is quiet. No one in the waiting area. No one even behind the desk. But a few seconds after the door closes, a young kid with blue hair and a nose piercing comes out from the back. Reese flashes her ID and asks, "Is Kathryn

Petersen-Wichnovitz around?"

He nods, disappears. A few minutes later, Kathy appears. She looks like she hasn't slept in a week. She glances at Reese with confusion, then me with recognition. She tries to hide the fact that she rolls her eyes. That does not bode well.

"You're back," she says, her voice sharp and impatient. "Did you find your friend?"

"Not yet."

Reese clears her throat. "Ma'am, I'm a private investigator, and I've been hired to find the kid he's looking for. We have something we need to run by you."

Kathy looks back, to what no doubt is a mountain of work on her desk, but gestures to the chairs. We sit and I run through the spiel I gave to Reese in the car.

Her face sinks but she doesn't seem surprised. "What can I do?"

"If there's someone you can point us to who might know a little more about the scene on the south shore, that'd be a big help," I tell her.

Kathy puts her hand to her temple. Presses hard and closes her eyes.

"I'm sorry, I just need to think. It's been a week."

She doesn't know that I know Brick was working here. I'm sure she's figured it out for herself. That's got to be wearing on her. I'm rooting around in my brain for something to say that'll speed things along, get her to focus, when Reese leans forward and takes Kathy's other hand, which is resting on her knee.

"Anything you could tell us would be helpful," she says. Her voice is soft and warm, like the way a mother would reassure a child after a nightmare.

It works. Kathy nods. Smiles, then stops, like she's risking an indulgence.

She says, "I think I know somebody who can help."

BACK IN REESE'S car, the heater roaring, I tell her, "I'll go meet him. See what I can find out."

Reese sits with her hands on the wheel, staring out at the sidewalk. After a moment, she asks, "You parked at a meter?"

"Nope."

"Good," she says, angling the car away from the curb and into traffic. "We'll go together."

"We partners now?"

She throws me a glance hot enough to singe my skin. "No, we are not partners now."

"Cool. Either way."

She taps the CD player in the dash and the car fills with jazzy Latin music. It's good. We drive for a bit. Port Richmond drops away and then we're on the expressway, traffic moving at a steady pace.

"Who is this?" I ask.

"Bronx River Parkway."

"I like them."

She nods like it's a secret of the universe she's cluing me into. "They're good."

"So you used to be a cop?" I ask.

"Used to be."

"Sounds like there's a lot in that 'used to be.'"

"You know the song. Worked twice as hard to get half as much respect. Did my twenty, made it to detective, got burnt, got out."

"Why did you become a PI?"

"Because I like the work, I just couldn't handle the bullshit anymore," she says. "Truth is, part of me wishes I would have stayed. I miss it. I miss the badge. Say what you will about the NYPD. The badge still means something. But I like this job. It's quiet. I get to focus on things. And, usually, it's good things. Finding a missing kid is a good thing."

"That it is."

"Tell me about your face."

"What about it?"

"The bruises. How did you get them?"

"It's a long story."

"It's a long drive."

"Honestly, I don't even know that you'd believe me. But I will say this: I have done some really dumb shit. I've gotten into a lot of fights I shouldn't have. And the older I get, the more I want to live a life of non-violence. But as much as I want to say violence isn't the solution, sometimes it is."

"We can get into the ethical implications of that later," she says. "But I want to point out for the record that you can be a little melodramatic. You know that, right?"

She turns to me and smiles. She's messing with me.

That feels like a step forward.

"Things happen. I keep ending up in situations where things need getting done. The John McClane Paradox of Bullshit."

She laughs. "When he was in the air vent, in the second one. 'How can the same shit happen to the same guy twice'. Or, I guess in McClane's case, five times. Though I don't count the last two movies. They were garbage."

"Oh wow," I tell her. "'I think this is the start of a beautiful friendship.'"

"Okay, okay," she says. "Don't get cute. I'm still not sure about you."

"That's fine. I figure as long as you haven't shoved me out of the car while it's moving, I'm doing okay."

She laughs. I like the way she laughs. It's light and high but also a little defiant. Like no matter how tough the world gets, she's still going to laugh at it.

WE PULL INTO a shopping plaza. This part of the island feels like backwoods Jersey. Trees and homes, suburbs, kids riding bikes even though there's snow on the ground.

The plaza is new construction. Everything smooth and beige. Reese threads the car into a spot outside a pizza place where the guy we're meeting is supposed to work. She shuts off the car and says, "Wait here."

"You're going to make me wait here and you're not even going to leave the engine running?" I ask. "Are you hoping I'll freeze to death?"

She smirks. "That would make my life easier."

"Ha-ha. I'm coming in. Don't worry. I'll sit with my hands folded. Seen and not heard."

She stares at me for a couple of beats, then nods.

We step into the cold. I hitch up my jacket and we make our way inside, where we're overtaken by humid air and the smell of cheese and dough. A few stray diners, and one kid standing behind the counter making pizzas. Short, stocky, with a ruddy Irish complexion, a pristine bright-blue Yankees hat worn backwards on his head.

Reese walks to the counter and asks, "Keith?"

The kid looks up. "Kathy?"

Reese nods as I slide up next to her. She holds out her ID. "My name is Turquoise Reese. This is my…"

217

"Associate," I say. "Ash McKenna."

I don't turn my head to see what kind of look Reese is giving me. I am sure it is withering.

Keith looks around, then at the two of us. "Either of you want a slice?"

Reese shakes her head but I stick a finger in the air, take a few bucks out of my pocket and lay them on the counter. Keith pulls a fresh pie out of the oven, cuts it into eighths, and puts a slice on a paper plate. "Give me two seconds," he says.

I take my slice and we walk toward a table in the back. The pizza is nuclear hot so I let it cool while the two of us wait, sitting on either side of the hard, plastic booth. Keith finishes the pie he's making, sticks it in the oven, and calls a young Hispanic kid out of the back to cover for him, then grabs a soda out of the cooler and comes over to us.

Rather than sit with one of us, he pulls a chair from a table in the center of the restaurant and drags it over to the foot of the booth, the metal legs squealing on the tile floor.

Closer now, I can see his clothes are baggy on him—hand-me-downs, or he lost weight. Under his polo shirt is a long-sleeved white t-shirt that hides his forearms. He's covered in flour and grease, and he carries himself like every movement is a titanic effort. He cracks open the soda, takes a swig, and places it down. He speaks in a calm, quiet voice, but one that's steeped in a lot of emotion.

"If this were for anyone but Kathy, I would say no," he says.

"We appreciate you taking the time," Reese says. "I know this isn't easy. I know this isn't something you particularly want to do. But a lot of people are going to get hurt and we might be able to stop it. And you might be able to help us do that."

He makes eye contact with us each in turn. "You have to

understand something. The only way to turn your life around is to leave all that shit behind. Anything I help you with, I'll do it from here, but I won't go any further than that. I can't go making calls or talking to anybody for you."

"More than fair," Reese says. "Let's start with…"

"The addresses," I cut in.

Reese gives me a look like she wishes she could stab me in the throat. I take the mess of streets and addresses Bombay put together and slide it across the table. Glance at Reese and she nods.

"Anything in here look familiar?" I ask.

Keith picks up the paper, skims it. Puts it back down and pokes at it. "There. Hopper Avenue. There's a shooting gallery on that street. I don't know the number. It's the blue house."

"Anything else?" I ask.

He shakes his head. "Four months sober tomorrow. So four months out. A lot can change in four months."

"We've heard talking about a new player," Reese says. "Goes by the name Kid Vicious."

At this, Keith's eyes go wide. His shoulders bunch up. He stands fast, nearly knocking over the seat. "I have to get back to work."

Reese and I exchange quick glances. It's not hard to see what happened. We both nod.

"Thanks for your help," Reese says.

Keith nearly sprints behind the counter. I pick up my pizza, forgotten during the quick exchange, fold it up, and cram half of it in my mouth.

"You'd better finish that, because you are not bringing it in my car," she says.

I wolf down as much as I can, tossing the crust in the trash as we leave. We get in the car, and before she can turn it on, still with wads of half-chewed dough in my mouth, I tell her, "I'm sorry.

But he seemed cagey, and I was worried that getting into the name game was going to scare him off. So I thought it was best to lead with the addresses."

She starts the car and cranes her neck to check behind us, then backs out of the spot. "Your instincts were right."

"Is that a compliment?"

"Statement of fact."

"So we have an address," she says. "We could roll by there now. But that might draw some unwanted attention."

"I'll go," I tell her. "See what I can see."

She laughs. "What are you going to do? Sneak in? Infiltrate the drug den? That's not how this shit works."

"No, I'm going to go down and take a look and see what I see. If there's an opening, I'll take it. It's better than nothing. Look, you could call your buddies on the force and send them down there. They raid it and everyone clams up. Or you could go down there and everybody clams up. I could try. I speak their language."

She pulls to a red light before the expressway. "What language is that?"

I want to say "thug" but I don't. It sounds silly. But my silence answers the question. The light turns green and she pulls the car onto the expressway. "Okay. But you don't spend too much time down there and you call me immediately if you find anything out. I have to keep some people informed on this. You could get me in a lot of trouble if you go off and try to play Batman."

"Understood."

"Why do I feel like you don't actually understand?"

"Because you are a smart lady," I tell her.

AFTER REESE DROPS me at my car, I stop into a bar to use the bathroom, wash my face, look into the mirror, don't feel shock and revulsion at what I see. The bruises around my eyes are nearly faded, like you'd really have to be looking to notice them. I poke at my ribs. Pain, but not nearly as much.

On the mend.

Ready to rumble.

Because there's only one smart way to play this. I can't sit outside that house and hope something happens. I have to get in there.

I pull brown paper towels out of the dispenser, wipe off my face, and step into the cold. A little bolt of electricity travels up from the base of my spine to my shoulders. It's the feeling I get when I know I'm about to get into a fight.

TWENTY

ON MY FIRST pass down the block, Hopper is like any other suburban block anyone has ever driven down. Lights out at 9 p.m., lawns mowed promptly at 9 a.m. on Saturday mornings.

Closer inspection reveals some cracks around the seams.

The homes are on the larger side, handsome Cape Cod-style, but in disarray. Wooden fences rotting. Sidewalks buckled up by tree roots. Nobody bothering to fight against the entropy, so it sneaks in.

There's one blue house on the block. I drive down twice, not too slow as to attract attention. Try to get a good look at it. There's not much to see. Still daytime. Lights out and shades drawn. No cars in the driveway. I park the car a few blocks away and walk, air stinging the inside of my sinus cavity. By the time I get onto Hopper, big fat snowflakes are drifting from the sky.

The big storm coming in.

The snowflakes makes me anxious, like maybe I don't have time to waste, so rather than dance around this, rather than sit across the street and hope I see something, I take the direct route. Which means climbing the porch, my boots knocking in the hollow underneath it, and trying the door. Locked. I ring the bell. Give it a few minutes. Nothing. Look around to make sure there's no one on the street, no one looking out their windows.

Lots of empty driveways, lots of people at work.

I circle around to the rear and try the back door. It yawns open and I'm smacked in the face by the stench of mildew and rotting food. It physically stops me from going in, like there's an invisible wall between me and the darkness beyond the door. I take a few deep breaths of cold air and step inside.

The kitchen is a wreck. I can't make out much in the dim light with the curtains drawn, but there's a huge pile of dishes in the sink and they've been there a long time. I think I see something scurry away from my presence, a flash across the chipped countertop. Discarded fast food bags and soda bottles everywhere. The floor feels tacky and makes a ripping sound when I take a step. Flies buzz thick in the air, celebrating the buffet of trash.

I pause for a moment, listen. The house is silent. I step through the kitchen and into a dining room/living room combo. Underneath the grime, the house is gorgeous. Hardwood floors and crown molding. Stained glass window in the dining room. It's the kind of home some yuppie couple would scoff at, but the HGTV hosts of whatever-the-fuck show would insist had a lot of potential, and you would want to throttle the yuppie couple for not seeing it.

The living room looks empty—no furniture, just debris—and I'm about to pass it by until I realize the pile of clothes on the floor is a person, and that smell might not entirely be the kitchen.

I don't even need to check to know she's dead. Girl, redhead, maybe my age. Swimming in her sweatshirt, eyes closed like she's sleeping, skin blue, muscles slack. I press the back of my hand against her forehead. Cold. There's a pile of shooting works next to her, as well as a tiny glassine bag with a red pizza stamped on it, like the one at Timmy's.

This might be the heroin with the fentanyl in it. Could be it's out in the world. I'd like to think Timmy wouldn't do that to himself, but I'd also like to think a dealer wouldn't kill a bunch of people to make a name. There's a lot about this I don't understand.

At the same time, maybe I do. After years of doing this shit, Timmy probably built up a big enough tolerance that he needed more to get the job done. The prospect of a strong high might have been too much to ignore, even if it meant gambling with his life.

It's not the same thing, but I certainly remember that feeling from when I was drinking. Those moments when it felt like no matter how much whiskey I got into me, it was never enough to calm the storm raging in my head. That as my tolerance grew, I was drinking quantities that were probably unsafe for bears, let alone people.

Humans can build up a tolerance for anything.

And when we do, it only makes us want more.

There's nothing I can do for her. I say a silent prayer in my head. Not the religious kind of prayer. The kind of prayer when you need to soothe your own soul.

I'll call the police when I leave. At least this way someone will find her before the vermin get to her. I leave the living room and the stench and climb the stairs, find empty bedrooms with holes in the walls and mattresses on the floor.

The last bedroom at the end of the hall is promising, or terrifying. Can't tell which yet, because there's another lump of clothing. I step inside and find a guy on a mattress. He's got a needle in his arm and he's passed out, but his chest looks like it's softly rising and falling. I stick my finger under his nose and feel the faint push of air.

He's a bigger guy. Thick. Maybe not a longtime user because he's still got meat on his bone and his arms aren't all scarred up. He's shirtless and laced with tattoos.

Another glassine envelope on the mattress next to him. Another red pizza stamp.

The guy is gone from this world. I don't know how long until he'll come out of it and I don't have the time to wait. I pull a naloxone vial out of my pocket, say, "Wakey wakey, asshole." Not that he can hear me. I think it's funny. Then I shove the injector into his nostril and push.

I toss the injector into the corner and wait. After a couple of moments, his eyelids flip open. He sits up and groans and puts his head in his hands.

"Sorry to do that, but…"

"You *motherfucker*," he screams, launching himself to his feet, slamming into my mid-section.

He is so much faster than I would have expected. He drives me into the wall and knocks the wind out of me. Balls up his fist and aims it at my head, but he throws it wide, so it's easy to duck. It lands hard on the wall behind me and he screams out in anguish, probably with a handful of broken fingers.

As I step aside, I trip on the corner of the mattress, which absorbs most of my fall, but then he's standing over me, one hand cradled in the other, boot up, eyes on fire. He brings the boot down, trying to stomp the life out of me. He's not doing a great job, but it's good enough to hurt.

I spin so I'm facing him and kick at his knees, not to hurt him, just to keep him away from me, while I reach around the floor for something, anything, that might help. Find a bundle of cloth. A shirt? Throw it at his face. It distracts him long enough for me to roll away and get to my feet, but then he's charging at me.

He throws another punch and I sidestep again, this time pushing him face-first into the wall. There's a wet thunk and a groan. His nose erupts, spilling blood down his bare chest.

"Shit, dude," I tell him, backing up with my hands in the air. "That was not really my intention."

He looks around the room, still not sure what the hell is going on, and falls into a seated position, legs crossed. He throws an arm behind him to keep himself up and asks, "Fuck is going on?" His voice is a mumble, like he's trying to keep gravel from spilling out of his mouth.

"The heroin," I tell him. "Where'd you get it?"

He frowns. "Fuck you."

"Let's try again. Where'd you get it?"

"From a guy."

"Dude. If you really want to make this into a thing, we can. Or we can do this the easy way and you can just tell me."

He looks around the room, finds the works next to the mattress. He picks up the glassine, stares at it for a moment, then grabs the spoon. Looks for more.

"What are you doing?" I ask.

"Fucked up my high, motherfucker," he says.

He looks at the envelope again, slides it open, and peeks inside. "Fucking empty."

Logic isn't getting me anywhere on this. Luckily, I speak addict.

"You know what that means?" I ask. "It means you should get more."

He nods, takes out his phone. "Fucking bullshit." He taps it and presses it to his ear. "Yo, man, I need more of that shit. Yeah, that pizza shit. C'mon. C'mon. I know it's going to snow. C'mon, motherfucker. Please. Fine. Fine, whatever."

He tosses the phone on the floor and falls back onto the mattress.

After a few moments, he's snoring softly, gurgling through the blood.

That's nice. There's a dealer on his way. Now I need to find out where he's coming from. I could beat the living shit out of him until he tells me where he's headed after this, or where he gets his supply, but I'd like to avoid that for now. I could follow him, but with the snow coming down and the roads this far south on the island being generally empty, I don't want to risk it. Too easy to get spotted.

So what, then?

I could track him. But with what? I need something I can follow from my phone.

This guy's phone is sitting on the floor.

Maybe.

I call Bombay. Concern in his voice because we usually only text. A call means it's important. "What's up, bro?"

"Hypothetical for you."

"Here we go."

"Say I wanted to track a phone. Someone else's phone."

"Kind of hard without access to the phone."

"I have access."

"What kind of phone is it?"

I glance down. "Samsung."

"Can you get me the number?"

I pick up the phone, moving slow, not wanting this guy to attack me again. He doesn't stir. Fast asleep. The phone is locked, so

I kneel down next to him and press the fingerprint sensor against the tip of his index finger. The home screen slides into place. A little poking around and I find the number, then pick up my phone and read it off to Bombay.

"Hold on." Computer keys click in the background. They fall silent and a text message pops up with a link. "Click that. Even if the phone is locked I'll be able to find it."

"And what if the battery dies?"

"Then we're out of luck."

The battery meter reads fifty-two percent. Not great. I turn the volume off, turn down the brightness of the screen, anything I can do to get an extra couple of minutes out of it. The guy on the mattress stirs so I back out of the room.

"You'll text me when the phone settles on a location?"

"I will."

"Thanks, man."

THERE'S NO GOOD place to wait, so I crawl under the porch a little, out of view of the driveway and the sidewalk. I can see through the latticework. It's cramped and uncomfortable but it's protected from the wind so it's not too cold. I watch the snow pile up on the lawn. It's really coming down now. I pull the collar up on my coat and wonder if this is a waste of time when a car pulls up and slams into the driveway, jumping up a little on the curb and coming to rest partway on the lawn.

The car turns off. Footsteps crunch in the freshly fallen snow and then echo on the floorboards. Doorbell rings. Same as me, whoever it is gets frustrated and walks around to the back of the house. All I can see is a pair of legs, but as soon as they've rounded the corner, I duck out of my hiding spot and circle around the back of the SUV, careful to cut wide across the neighboring property, and then onto the sidewalk, so there's not a clear path of footprints from the porch to the car.

I drop to a knee by the rear bumper and root around for a spot to stash the phone. Find a depression that seems like it'll hold. Check the battery. Forty-one percent. Goddammit, this thing will not last long. I get the phone into place, do the best I can to make sure it's secure, and hope the fucked-up roads don't send it flying. Then make it back to the sidewalk, stick my hands in my pocket, and head for my car.

"Hey!"

I turn. Not all the way.

It's the guy from the house I visited with Samson. The guy with the fake tan and the casual racism. He's standing by the SUV, eyeing me like I'm trespassing. I've got the newsboy cap on and he's far enough away that maybe he doesn't recognize me. I don't give him more than a profile of my face. Still, I plant my feet, preparing for this to get real bad real fast. The guy inside, I smacked him around pretty good. I don't know how much of it he actually remembers, but I definitely left behind a few physical reminders.

"Hey, man, you good?" he asks.

Takes me a minute to realize what he's doing: I'm near the shooting galley, he wants to know if I'm a potential customer. He's a go-getter.

"I'm good," I tell him, dropping the register of my voice.

He stands there for a moment, staring at me, snow falling on his shoulders. I don't move. Turn toward him too much, he sees more of my face, game over. But if I turn and walk away, he might become suspicious. So I hold his gaze in my peripheral vision until he shrugs, climbs into the car, turns it on. Hip-hop blasts from the inside, muffled by the closed windows, and he reverses onto the street, spinning tires, and blasts past me. I watch as the car recedes, hitting a big pothole and taking the turn at the end of the street a little hard. I walk to the end of the block and verify the cell didn't fall out.

That's a good start.

I'VE DOWNED TWO cups of coffee in a Dunkin' Donuts when my phone buzzes. A text from Bombay containing a blue link. I click it and Google Maps app opens, with a pulsing blue dot.

Signal dropped out there.

I pull up directions from my location, and it's not too far. I toss the nearly-finished coffee into the trash, think about it for a second, and get a couple of donuts to go. They'll keep in the cold, and anyway, I feel like I've got a little surveillance ahead of me before I report back to Reese.

I shove a vanilla frosted with sprinkles into my mouth as I drive, going slow because the plows haven't been down here yet, a little afraid of what I'm going to find.

It's been a while. A little too long. Spencer and Ginny could both be dead at this point.

It opens a void in my stomach. Makes me think of that day in the locker room with Ginny. Stopping that roid-rage fuck from snapping her neck. So much of my life changed that day. I don't blame her for the things I did or the person I became. I made my own choices. But I wonder how different things would have been without her influence. She gave me my first bump of coke. She gave me cash money to hurt people—people who did bad things so they had it coming, but still. She saw the potential I had to inflict pain, to rage, and she encouraged it.

And now I'm headed to save her.

Because what else could I do?

It was a big moment for Ginny. We never discussed it. Never referred to it again. But I think that was the moment she decided she'd had enough. She would live the life she wanted to live and she wouldn't be made to feel like a victim. She surrounded herself with strong people, but she learned how to fight, too.

She's stronger than she looks.

Which is what I'm hoping.

I'd love to get to the end of this and not find her body. Even if sometimes I wonder whether she invited that kind of thing with the life she chose. Because I'm not stupid. I know she wants Spencer back. But there's more to it than that. There has to be.

Makes me wonder exactly what it is I'm saving.

Well, fuck it. Task at hand. The rest I can sort out later.

The roads get bleaker. Fewer homes. More woods. Civilization dropping off. I know I'm getting close to the dot. I can't see the road underneath me but it feels rougher. My tires are catching better. Gravel?

I reach an empty stretch of road with woods on either side. This is the spot. There is literally nothing in either direction. I sigh, then ball up my fist and jam it against the steering wheel. Once, twice. Maybe the phone fell out, or died. I climb out of the car. Maybe there are some tire tracks I can follow.

There's only one other set besides mine, and they veer off the road, into the woods. Follow them and, a couple of yards up from the road, find a metal fence, rusted a deep brown so it's easy to miss among the trees. There's a small sign affixed to it that says: "Private Property."

There are furrows in the snow. The fence has been pulled out and pushed back. The tire tracks continue beyond it, over narrow, steep terrain.

I look around. The woods look passable, the trees close enough together to keep me somewhat obscured. As much as I think it's a dumb idea, it's better to have a good lay of the land. I back up the car, turn around, find a place to stash it that it's not visible from the road, get out, and begin the trek.

I FIGURE I'VE WALKED at least a mile before I find the house. It's huge. You probably couldn't call it a mansion, but you might not be wrong if you did. Victorian, wood frame, asymmetrical, like it was built by a crazy person. The different sections painted different colors, once brilliant but faded by the sun. Some of the awnings are yellow, others purple, one wall deep forest green, the front is all bare brown shingles.

The dealer's SUV is parked out front. No other activity from the house that I can see.

I find a tree stump and sit, bunch up the jacket around me. Fifteen minutes and I'll go. I want to look. See if I see anything that might end up being helpful.

The house is in a clearing, surrounded by trees. It's completely silent. I pull up Google Maps. There's no cell signal but I can still view the map I pulled up earlier. No houses anywhere around here. I'm not an expert on heroin processing and distribution, but if I was going to do it, I might want to do it here.

Nothing happens in the fifteen minutes that I wait. No movement from the windows. No one comes out. It's getting late. The snow is coming down hard. I'm going to have a hard time driving in this. Should probably get going before I end up stuck.

I stand up and brush off my coat when there's movement on the other side of the house.

Two figures march through the snow, moving carefully. I

recognize them straight off.

Paris and Athena.

Athena is carrying a shotgun.

So it's like that.

Still not showing any signal but I dial 911 anyway, hit send. Put the phone to my ear. Nothing. Paris and Athena are posting up by the front of the house and there is no way I can backtrack out of here and find a signal in enough time before this explodes.

With Brick dead, I don't see how this is anything other than revenge. Paris is probably strapped, too. And I figure the two of them intend to bust in there and fire until there's nothing left moving.

On the off chance Spencer and Ginny are alive and inside, I have to get in.

Oh well.

Party time.

TWENTY-ONE

I CIRCLE AROUND TOWARD the back of the house, sticking deep in the woods, moving slow so I don't attract attention. Paris and Athena have both got their heads down. Planning their assault, I guess. Hopefully, they don't split up. If they both go in the front, I can go in the back. The house is big enough I might be able to avoid them.

I reach the far edge of the house. Any further and I won't see them anymore. I duck down and wait. After a moment, Paris and Athena climb onto the porch. Good. I keep moving, out of their view, then pick up my pace and move toward the back of the house. There's a shed at the far edge of the property along the woods. I ease my way up to it, peek inside. Nobody there. I circle around to the door and find it locked.

It'd be nice to have a weapon. I take out my lockpick kit, not really happy to be so exposed—someone could look out the window of the house and see me—but it's worth the risk. I concentrate on the sounds behind me. Wait for the crunch of a boot or the retort of a shotgun. All I hear is a slight whistle. Wind between the snowflakes.

I manage to work through the lock within a few seconds and duck inside, pulling the door closed behind me. Lots of lawn maintenance equipment, bags of fertilizer, a gas grill. I look around, trying to find something I can use. There's a shovel hanging on the wall. Too big. Next to that, a machete and a pickax. Both a little grisly for my taste.

Garden trowel? Fuck.

I'm about to give up and grab the machete when I see something in the corner that catches my eye.

A cricket bat.

I pick it up. Has a nice heft. It's British, which makes it feel classy. There's a ball of heavy twine and a box cutter on a workbench in the corner. I shove them in my coat.

Back outside and it's still silent, the snow coming down harder. It piles up around the house, building on the roof, making it hard to see. I run toward the back of the house, and just as I'm about to reach the covered deck, the back door opens.

I move low and throw myself forward into the snow. Hit the ground, realize how fucking stupid that was. Whoever it was can look over the bannister, see me sprawled out like I'm making a snow angel, and shoot me in the head.

I wait for a face to peer over.

There's a clicking sound, then a scratch. And another.

A slight crackle.

Zippo.

Smoker.

I get into a crouch, press up against the porch, out of sight.

Look out across the field and see my footsteps leading to the house. I'm wondering how obvious they are when the cigarette flings into my field of vision, landing cherry-down in the snow, sizzling as it extinguishes.

From above me someone mutters, "What the fuck..."

A head pokes over. My dealer friend. He recognizes me. For real this time. Before he can react, I jab him hard in the forehead with the flat end of the bat. Enough to daze him. I jump up, grab his coat, and pull him over the railing.

It seems like a good idea.

Except he falls on me and the two of us tumble into the snow. Both of us scramble, trying to get to our feet, tripping over each other. I catch a stray elbow in the side of the head, nearly go down, but manage to take a knee. He's trying to stand. I throw my fist into his stomach, and then hit him with an uppercut. My leverage isn't great, but it's enough to make him falter.

I get to standing, but before I can do anything else, he tackles me. I push my chin to my chest so I don't hit my head on the ground and he climbs on top of me. I try to buck but he's got all his weight on my hips. I hammer my fist onto his thigh. He grunts but doesn't move. Reaches his fists back. I put my hands up to protect my face as he wails on me.

I'm twisting, turning, trying to get away, my stomach crushed so hard I want to puke, and he's slamming me with his fists, a few of them sneaking through my block.

There's a sound from the house, like someone smacking a ruler on a desk.

Game on.

Lucky for me, he does something very, very stupid. He pauses. Turns. Not sure what he's hearing. I know exactly what it is. Soon as he lets up, I pop my fist into his throat. His hands go up and I swing into his stomach. Then, as he reels back, I drive my fist into his crotch. He rolls off me, lands with a thud, gasping for air. I climb on him, push a knee into his back, try to ignore the pain and the dizziness. Get to work tying up his hands, then work on his feet. He struggles and squirms but can't yell out.

More gunfire from inside the house.

The guy is wearing a knit cap. I pull it off his head and cram it in his mouth. Blood trickles from a small wound on his forehead.

"You keeping people here?" I ask.

He grunts at me through the hat so I hold up my fist.

He nods furiously.

"Where?"

He mumbles at me so I pull the hat out of his mouth. He spits in my face so I jab him in the chin. He turns his head away from me, sucks on his lips.

"You have to know you're not in the position to fuck around," I tell him.

"Upstairs."

"You lying to me?"

"Maybe."

I shake my head. Get up. Rear back with the cricket bat, like his head is a ball and I aim to knock it out of the park. He gets the idea.

"Upstairs. Both of them."

Both of them.

I pick up the hat and shove it back into place.

"You keep your mouth shut, you may live through this," I tell him. He yells something at me through the hat, jerking his limbs, trying to get free. I leave him in the snow.

I climb onto the porch, look through the window on the back door. Darkened, ornate kitchen. No one inside. I open the door and ease in, hear yelling and commotion from the front of the house. Another volley of gunshots. I can't make out what it is but it sounds like a standoff, two sides trying to exert authority.

Silence.

A shotgun blast rattles the windows.

Two sharp gunshots return in kind. They both explode through the wall in a torrent of dust and slam into the fridge. I get closer to the floor.

More yelling.

I look around the kitchen, then the hallway. There's a staircase at the front, facing the front door. There's also an arm. The arm appears attached to a body, which I suspect is sprawled out in the living room. Can't see anyone else.

This is not good. Seems I can't get upstairs without going to the front of the house. Which is where all the people with the guns are. Maybe I could go outside and climb in a window? There was a trellis and a low-hanging section of roof. That's a good way to break my neck.

I look around some more. It's a big old, old house. It makes me think of a house I saw on TV, with a servant's staircase—a smaller staircase leading upstairs from the kitchen. There are a few odd doors in here. I move along the wall, stay low, crack them open. More gunshots cover the sound of my movements. At least they're not moving the fight into the kitchen.

The first door leads to a staircase down to the basement.

Second, boiler room.

Third, pantry.

Fourth—bingo.

A spiral staircase barely wider than my shoulders.

Saved by home renovation shows.

I step into the stairwell and ease the door closed behind me, climb the stairs, find the door at the top locked.

The lock is completely different from the kind I'm used to. It looks like it takes a skeleton key. I have no idea where to even start with this. My lock-picking experience starts and ends with modern tumbler locks. I drop down, peek under the door. Looks like an empty room. Put my ear against it and listen. Nothing on the other side. Not many options left. I put my shoulder into the door, pressing hard.

It takes nearly a minute. My shoulder aches, but finally the door mechanism busts and the door flings open, slamming against the wall louder than I'd like. I fall into the room and find the scrawny guy from the house I visited with Samson. He's got something in his hands, which are extended out and pressed between his knees.

A silver handgun.

He looks at me, terrified and confused. The gun is rattling from his shaking hands. I consider charging at him but it's too much ground to cover.

"Where are they?" I ask.

He trembles in response.

Really not feeling good about that gun in his hand. I move toward him slowly. Hands up. "I'm not going to hurt you, kid. But the people downstairs will. Go down this staircase and head out the back and you'll make it out of here alive. Understood?"

He stares at me like I'm a ghost suddenly manifest in front of him.

"Understood?" I ask, louder.

He nods vigorously. Gets up. Still holding the gun. I take a step forward to close the distance a bit, keep the cricket bat down at my side but ready to swing, so I can disarm him if he brings his arm up.

"Drop the gun and go," I tell him.

He doesn't drop the gun.

I flick out the bat and smack his hand. He rears back and grimaces. I probably broke a finger, but no avoiding it. The gun falls from his grip and he rushes past me. But instead of going to the back staircase, he runs to the front.

I'm about to run after him but there's no use.

He gets to the top and there's a shout from downstairs.

By the time he reaches the bottom, gunshots thunder through the house, followed by a scream and a heavy thud.

Fuck.

Running out of time here.

I check the door the kid was sitting outside. Figure him for the guard. It's locked. I'm suddenly less worried about making noise. Reach back and kick hard. It doesn't move. Do it again, putting my hips into it. On the third kick, the door splinters. On the fifth it cracks.

On the sixth, it flies open.

The room is nearly pitch black, the windows covered in tinfoil. It smells like piss and shit. There's a small lamp in the corner casting off meager wattage. There's a bucket, too—probably the source of the smell—and piles of discarded fast food bags.

There are two mattresses. And two figures. The pair of them disheveled, in cast-off jeans and t-shirts, barefoot. They both sit up.

Spencer's face twists in confusion.

Ginny smiles.

"Darling," she says. "What took you so long?"

I smile back. "These accommodations don't seem up to your regular standards."

"It sounds like World War III down there. Maybe let's get out of here before we start with the comedy routine."

She's right. Ginny scrambles into the hallway, followed by Spencer. They're barefoot, but there are worse things. Ginny picks up the gun that was discarded on the floor, slides the magazine out, nods, and clicks it back into place.

"I'm a little surprised you're still alive," I tell her.

"They've been interrogating us. Figured I would break sooner or later. They know nothing about me." She looks at Spencer and smiles. "About either of us. Now what's the plan?"

"You really think I thought that far?"

I cross to the back staircase. Edge along the wall. Look down. There's a body at the bottom of the stairs, face down, kinked up in the narrow space. Dead. I catch a whiff of smoke.

Both stairways are unsafe. No one in this house is our friend. We could escape out a window, down the roof. Easy to slip and fall. Plus, they're barely dressed. Nearly a full minute has passed since there was a gunshot, but the smell of smoke is getting stronger.

I turn to Ginny and Spencer. "Check the bedrooms. Try to get some clothes and shoes. Last resort is we go down the roof. But I'm going to check the front staircase. See if enough people killed each other we can sneak out of here."

They disappear into the adjacent rooms and I move to the front. Get on my hands and knees and crawl down until I can just barely see the living room.

It is fucking bedlam.

Beautifully ornate. Oriental carpet. Wood trim. Gorgeous stone fireplace. There's a coffee table piled high with glassine bags stamped in red ink. Can't make it out from here but I'm betting it's pizza.

Nearly everything is splattered with dark red sprays blood. I count five bodies. None of them is Paris or Athena.

It's quiet, too, like whatever's currently happening has moved on to another part of the house, or maybe even ended. Smoke is coiling across the floor. Figure that's got to mean the fire is in the basement. Probably where the processing operation is.

I dare to stand, take a step down the stairs, and Athena appears.

Her face contorts in rage. She raises the shotgun at me and fires.

It clicks.

First she looks down at the shotgun and frowns.

Then she looks at me and her eyes go so wide they nearly fall out of her head.

"Thought we killed you," she says.

"Nope!" It sounds jovial. For some reason, I'm not nearly as mad at her as I should be.

"You a zombie? White Walker? What's the deal?"

"You sent Spencer to steal my wallet and he shot me with naloxone."

She nods. "Motherfucker. Well, better than you being a zombie." She reaches into her jacket, pulls out a shell and goes to load it in the shotgun. "Almost feel bad about having to finish the job now."

"Wait."

She pauses, raises her eyebrow.

"I've got no beef with you. Never had beef with Brick. I was here to shut this shit down just like you. We're on the same side. So, I don't know, in the spirit of good will, how about not killing me?"

"You not with this crew?"

"I told you at the start of all this, I'm not with anybody. I'm with Spencer."

"He okay?"

"He is."

"Where's he at?"

"He's okay."

She lowers the gun a little. "Paris is dead. Motherfuckers caught her in the back of the head."

For a moment, Athena's façade crumbles and the sadness shines through. I know that feeling. It's almost enough to make me want to put a hand on her shoulder. Comfort her. Give her something that'll make her feel better.

I don't, because she still has the shotgun.

"You set the fire downstairs?"

"Yeah."

"Where's the man in charge? Where's Kid Vicious?"

She shrugs. "Dunno who the fuck he even is. Just know there were people here need killing."

"So what now?"

"Now I get the fuck gone."

"You going to let me go?" I ask.

She thinks about it for a moment. Says, "Yeah, sure."

She clomps into the living room. I'm about to ask if she'll at least apologize for trying to kill me that first time—not that it's really necessary, and is probably pushing things further than they need to go—when she comes back into view, Paris slung over her shoulder, limp like a doll.

Athena makes for the front door.

I call after her. "Hey."

She barely turns. Regards me in her peripheral vision.

"Did you kill Timmy?"

"He dead?"

I let that linger. Examine the undercurrents of surprise and concern. I guess that answers my question. It hits me like a fist in the gut. It was so easy to think that Timmy's death could be chalked up to this stupid fucking drug war. Turns out he lost the war to himself.

"Yeah," I tell Athena. "He's dead."

She mutters something I think sounds like, "Too bad." I can imagine it's hard to muster up a lot of grief when you're already carrying more than a hundred pounds of it on your shoulder. She makes for the door, leaves the house.

The smoke is getting thick. Hopefully, she sticks to her word. Hopefully, there's no one else alive in this house, because soon, there won't be. I go back up the stairs, find Ginny and Spencer in a back bedroom looking out the window. They're dressed now. Ill-fitting boots and layers of sweatshirts. It'll do.

"I think we can make it down," Spencer says.

"No need," I tell them. "Front is clear."

We make our way for the stairs, Spencer running ahead of me, clearly looking to get out of the house as soon as he can. He makes it down to the bottom of the stairs and there's a hard crack. He jerks forward like someone kicked him in the back.

Ginny and I both duck. There's someone lying in the hallway now, gun drawn. Fucker wasn't there before. Ginny roars and leans over the bannister, firing wildly as blood seeps out of Spencer's left flank. He's not moving.

Ginny's not hitting anything but the floor, splitting the blonde hardwood. Somewhere, a home renovator is weeping.

I look over and catch a glimpse of the person with the gun rolling away, back toward the kitchen. Don't think. Jump over the bannister, land hard, roll into the living room as the sheetrock explodes above me, white dust swirling in the air to mix with the thickening black smoke. I look up at Ginny and nod. She leans over and returns fire, giving me some cover so I can pull Spencer out of the range of the shooter.

He's bleeding but I feel a pulse. I grab a throw pillow off the couch and press it down hard on his back to stop the bleeding. He groans and tries to move away.

Ginny yells at me from the stairs. "Ash? I think I got him."

I peek around the corner. The figure is prone. I'm about to give Ginny the all clear when the guy's hands jerk up. Another bullet slams into the wall, narrowly missing me.

"No, you didn't."

"Sorry, darling," Ginny says.

I look around. Not a ton of options. Best I can think to do is loop around through the dining room, into the kitchen, come up on this guy from behind, and hopefully he doesn't shoot me.

"Ginny, you got any bullets left?"

"I think so."

"You'd fucking better. On three." I lean down to Spencer. "Hang in there, buddy." I get up, ready to run, and call, "One-two-three!"

Ginny and the figure trade bullets. I circle around, nearly tripping over bodies along the way, until I make it to the hallway.

It's the first good look I get at the guy with the gun.

He looks like an accountant. Jeans and a t-shirt. A beard. An unremarkable face. Tennis shoes. He looks like he drinks light beer and is very proud of his propane grill.

He sees me, raises the gun, and fires. I freeze.

It clicks.

Getting real lucky with people not counting their bullets today.

He tosses the gun aside and that's when I see the blood pumping out of his leg.

Must have caught a bullet in the femoral. I say that like I'm a doctor. But there's way too much blood for it to be a flesh wound. Gushing out like a busted pipe. The guy is so pale he's nearly green, and he's exerting a massive amount of strength to move his limbs.

"Come into my...fucking house," he says, choking on the

words.

The smoke is billowing from under the door leading to the basement. It's thick and choking now. He coughs. I lean down next to him.

"You're him? Kid Vicious?"

He laughs, looking down at the widening pool of blood. "Started as a joke. Someone called me that. Hated that…fucking name."

I want to feel bad for him. Really, I do. He'll be dead soon. But then I remember that he was planning to kill a whole bunch of people to make that name stick. I look around for a dishtowel or something, anything to stop the bleeding, because for as much as I think he deserves it, I'm not going to stand by and watch.

I can't.

But by the time I turn back to him, he's gone.

I head for the stairwell. Ginny is standing with Spencer now. Good to see that he's on his feet. "Get him out of here. I'm going to check the bodies. Make sure no one's still alive."

"Ash, we really should go."

"I'm not leaving anyone to get burned alive. I'll be right behind you."

The two of them make for the door. Getting hard to see now.

Makes me think of my dad. How he'd watch movies like *Backdraft* and get so angry. Said you can't look around inside a house or a building that's on fire. There's too much smoke. You crawl around on your hands and knees, searching by touch.

I'm seeing now how right he was. The smoke is crushing. It pushes into your eyes, your lungs. It's like a living thing that wants to hurt you.

I grab a towel off the counter, run it under the tap, hold it to my face. Breathe through that. Stay low and run from one body to another.

Everyone dead.

In the living room, I take one last look at the pile of heroin. It looks like they're packing it into bundles to go out. Hopefully, that means only a few made it into circulation. I grab a handful of the empty bags and head out the back door for the guy with the tan. He's not there. He could be among the dead inside. I could barely make out anyone's face. Could have gotten away.

I circle around to the front of the house. Ginny and Spencer are standing in the snow, watching. I join them. This big beautiful thing, flames licking out the windows, smoke billowing out the doors. I take a deep breath, cough hard. My nose is running. I reach down and grab some snow and use it to clean my hands, my face.

A basement window shatters.

It's going to take some time to trek back to the road. And then we need to get Spencer to a hospital.

But it's so easy to stand here and watch the house burn. Like all of this is finally, finally over.

"You okay?" I ask Spencer.

"I think so," he says. "Thank you."

"Hey, you save my life, I save yours. Now we're even."

I feel something on my shoulder, turn to find Ginny's hand.

Ginny, the queen of the Lower East Side. Stripped of her armor, face covered in grime and soot, limbs thin, face gaunt, days' worth of beard growth. But still wearing diamond earrings. Not willing to surrender.

"We should go," I tell her.

We stand there a few moments longer, watching the flames envelop the house while the snow falls in circles around us, the mix of hot and cold oddly pleasant.

TWENTY-TWO

BY THE TIME we make it to the foot of the road, a fire truck is moving toward us at a brisk but careful pace, the wide tires cutting rivulets in the snow. I open the gate for them. The truck slows down a bit alongside us and the chauffeur peers out the window. I point up the road.

"Place is shot up," I tell him. "Everyone was dead before the fire got going."

The chauffeur nods and they continue on their way. They're being tailed by ambulances and police cruisers. I wonder if someone saw the smoke. Maybe Athena called it in. Doesn't really matter at this point. The only thing that matters is that it's done.

"Fuck," Ginny says under her breath.

I'm sure she'd like to avoid going to the hospital on this. She's going to have a lot of explaining to do. Spencer, too. Gunshots don't get brushed off. Personally, I think the cops and paramedics are for the best, because Spencer is fading, blood spilling down his side, his skin sallow. If it weren't for Ginny holding him up, he'd have hit the floor.

"No sense in drawing things out," I tell Ginny.

She nods, throws Spencer's arm over her shoulder, and moves toward an ambulance. Without looking back, she says, "We'll talk."

"Sure."

A few of the police cruisers follow the fire truck. One of them stays behind, along with an ambulance. I go to the cruiser and the cop who climbs out gives me a curious look.

"Don't need ambulances up there," I tell him. "Everyone is dead."

After that, it's chaos. Cops asking us questions. EMTs checking us over. Ginny and Spencer end up in one ambulance that tears ass down the road, while I end up sitting on the back of another, sucking down canned oxygen. My throat is raw and scratchy, like I smoked twelve packs of cigarettes in an hour. It does not make me miss smoking. Minor smoke inhalation, the EMT tells me.

It's not long before Detective Perry is there, in a long black overcoat, boots crunching in the snow, furious look on his face.

"You," he says.

"Me," I tell him, moving the mask aside.

"Can he take that thing off?" Perry asks the EMT.

The EMT nods. I hand it over, a little sad, because the rush from the oxygen is nice. I hop off the back of the ambulance and Perry gestures for me to follow him. We walk toward the gate.

"What in the hell is going on here?"

Used to be, I would follow that up with a smartass comment in the course of evading the question. Tell him I was out for a hike. If I was in a really pissy mood, I'd say I was on my way to meet his mom. Which is about as juvenile as it is satisfying.

Instead, I tell him a story.

I fudge some of the details. Tell him I was looking for my friends but didn't have any idea what I was walking into. Two crews got in a gunfight and we made it out of there. That it was the tip of a deadly spear. It helps when I hand over the empty stamped dime bags and explain the fentanyl plot. I suspect they were hot on this trail. The way he nods, throws out a little grin here and there, makes me think I'm filling in some missing puzzle pieces.

After it's all done, he takes a deep breath, looks up the road. There's smoke drifting above the tree line. I can smell it from here. Another memory of my dad. The way he could take a whiff of a fire and tell you exactly what was burning.

Polyester couch.

Lacquered furniture.

Garbage disposal.

My sense of smell isn't that developed. All I smell is campfire, maybe a hint of chemical underneath.

"Tomorrow," Perry says. "You come down to the station. I want a full statement. On the record."

Not a request.

"Sure thing," I tell him. "So that's it?"

"That's it."

"Little surprising."

"Why?"

"Figured I'd be leaving here in cuffs."

"Most of what you say tracks," he says. "Anyway, Reese vouched for you."

That brings a smile to my face.

"According to Reese, you're a good kid trying to do the right thing," he says, raising an eyebrow. "I don't trust you. You haven't earned it yet. But I trust Reese, and that can be good enough for now."

I like Perry. He could very easily fuck me on this, and he hasn't. Not really par for the course in my experience with cops. I stick my hand out to him. He regards it for a moment before grasping it in a meaty palm. Gives it a solid pump and nods.

"See you in a few."

"Yeah," I tell him. "You will."

I STEP INTO MY empty apartment. Find the futon Bombay said another tenant was getting rid of and offered to drop off for me. It's nice. Wood, and stable. The mattress is a little lumpy, but hey, free bed. And free couch.

I lay down, breathe deep through ragged lungs.

It's done.

Spencer is safe. So is Ginny. Things are settled with Athena, and Kid Vicious isn't going to hurt anyone.

It didn't get done pretty, but it got done.

I laugh at the popcorn ceiling, then tear up a little. My body releasing the tension that's been building up over the past few days. I feel sick. I feel like I could sleep for a year. I feel so good right now. I pull out my cell phone. Call Reese's office. After a few rings, it goes to voicemail.

"Spencer is safe. Figure they took him down to SIUH. And the thing with Kid Vicious is over. Went up in flames. Big house fire on the south shore. Can't miss it. So…thanks for putting in a good word with Perry. You're the only reason I'm not in lockup right now, probably… Talk to you soon, I guess?"

I hang up. Put my head back. I'm dozing off, my face coated in drool, when there's a knock at the door. I stumble over and open it, find Bombay and Lunette, holding a pizza box and a six-pack, respectively.

"Housewarming?" Lunette asks. Then she scrunches her nose, sniffs. "You smell like a burning laundromat."

"Long story." I look around the empty apartment. "Shouldn't we wait until I get some furniture first?"

"Oh, I'm sorry," Lunette says, putting her free hand to her chest, adopting a look of mock insult. She turns to Bombay. "Apparently, we went to the wrong apartment. The Queen of fucking England here would rather wait until the chaise is delivered."

"Whatever," Bombay says. "More pizza for us."

"You assholes," I tell them, stepping aside. They come in and walk to the center of the living room, where they sit on the floor, flip open the pizza box, lay out some beers. For a moment, I feel like maybe I want to skip the pizza—I'm a little run down on the whole pizza thing.

But then I realize I will never be tired with pizza.

We eat and we talk. Not about heroin, not about missing people, not about whatever melodrama is currently vexing me. We just bullshit.

It's nice to bullshit.

By the time the box is empty, all I want to do is sleep for a hundred years, so for as much as I want to stay here, do this, be with them, I ask if they'll leave. They agree to move the party next door. As they're prepping to go I fall onto the futon. I don't even hear the door close.

THE SNOW HAS stopped and the roads are mostly plowed. Still, it's slow going to SIUH. I was hoping to get there early, for the start of visiting hours, but Perry wasn't messing around. It was a long interview. Dude is thorough. But hey, he did not put me in jail, so there's that.

By the time I make it, the parking lot is full. It takes me forever to find a spot on the street. The few spaces that are dug out and empty have parking cones or garbage cans in them, neighbors staking claim to their work.

After twenty minutes of circling, I give up and drive out of sight of Hylan Boulevard, deeper into the suburban streets until I find a spot, and make the long walk to the hospital. Step inside and head for to the waiting room on the second floor where Reese said she would meet me,

When I step off the elevator, she's sitting in one of the green hospital-issued torture devices that passes for a chair, a cup of coffee in her hand as she skims something on her phone. On the seat next to her is another cup of coffee.

She glances up. "Black, right?"

I sit, pop the lid off, let the steam spill out. Take a sip. Terrible and just right.

"Thank you," I tell her.

"So what happened?"

I run her through it. Tracking them to the house. Not having a cell phone signal. Being forced to act. My statement to Perry. When I'm done, we sit there in silence a bit.

"That was real stupid," she says.

"I know."

"But Spencer's alive," she says.

"That's all that matters," I tell her, sipping my coffee.

She puts her coffee cup on the floor by her feet and sticks her phone in her purse. Turns to look at me. "You really want to do this?"

"I do."

She nods. "You're going to come to my office three days a

week. You're going to do the menial shit I don't like doing. That
means data entry. That means vacuuming. That means scrubbing
the toilet. That means going out to get my coffee when it's raining
and I don't feel like getting wet. I'll keep you in coffee but I'm not
even going to pay you just yet. I need to know you're serious. You
do that for three months, I'll believe you're serious."

"Deal."

"Really?" she asks. "I figured there'd be some pushback on the
salary. Or lack thereof."

"Good thing I'm serious."

She smiles. "Reason I wanted you here was because Spencer's
parents came in. Figure you're the one who found him, you ought
to be around for this. It's the best part of the job. Telling the parents
their kid isn't dead."

She stands up and gathers her stuff. As she does that, I pull out
my list, cross off two more items.

~~Find a place to live?~~
~~Get a job?~~
~~Find Spencer Chavez again~~
~~See my mom~~
Check on Crystal

Before I can spend too much time falling down a sadness hole
concerning the last item, she turns to me and throws an eyebrow.
"You coming?"

"Yeah."

I cram the list in my pocket. We walk down the hall, lit so
white the walls glow blue.

"Thank you," I tell her.

She shrugs. "I think you might be good at this. Long as you

stop doing stupid shit."

"Stupid shit got me this far."

"Don't push your luck," she says.

"Fair enough."

We turn into Spencer's room.

And everything goes sideways.

The room is dim, the curtains drawn. He's lying in bed, his hair slicked back, face clean. IV in his arm and he looks pretty good for someone who got shot. The couple standing over him—mother and father—are all smiles and joy at having their son back, after long enough they probably assumed him dead.

They look nothing like the couple in the lobby of Ginny's building.

TWENTY-THREE

PEOPLE CAN CONVINCE themselves of anything. They can sort through facts and pick and choose the ones that suit them. Sometimes they can do it with things that aren't even facts.

Here's a fact: pretty much from the beginning of this I figured Ginny's intentions on this weren't altruistic. It was the way the pieces didn't always fit together, but also, it's Ginny. I was so desperate to prove working for her wasn't backsliding that I focused on the only thing I could.

The part of the job that was most easy to defend.

Finding a missing kid. Helping out a family.

Because who can argue that those are good things?

Looking at this now, on the other side, clear-eyed, I know what the goal was. I knew the whole time. But I want to hear it from her. She's going to look me in the face and she's going to tell it to me. No more games.

Night is falling as I approach her building. The block is empty. Funny how that happens. New York is supposed to be the city that never sleeps. But there are plenty of pockets where humanity disappears. And then, anything can happen. Anything does.

The SUV is parked at the curb, silent. When I'm within ten feet of the door, Samson steps out. He closes the door and the two of us stand there. His leather duster whipping a little in the wind, the air slicing our exposed skin.

"I need to see her," I tell him.

"She's resting."

"I don't care."

He takes off his glasses, folds them up, puts them in the inside pocket of his coat. Then he takes his coat off, balls it up, and puts it on the hood of the SUV. "You're not going in."

"You really want to do this?" I ask.

Fingers tingling. Heart racing.

"I know you saved her life," he says. "If you think that's going to make me take it easy on you, it's not."

"So it's like that?"

"It's like that."

"I really thought we had a shot of being friends," I tell him.

"You never were as smart as you gave yourself credit for."

The two of us stand there, squared off. I can smell the leather of his coat on the wind. I glance up and down the block. Just the two us.

I smile at him. He smiles back. It's a little funny to smile at each other like that. Not like we're friends, but like we've finally reached a mutual understanding.

And we charge.

AS I STEP off the elevator, I do my best to hide the limp.

The apartment is dark. The museum closed for the evening.

I hear footsteps on the other end, and then Ginny appears. She's put back together—a simple blouse and pencil skirt, subtle makeup, blonde wig. Like she's going out for a drink, not to work. The armor gets a little more ornate when she's going to work.

She stops when she sees me, confused.

"Ash," she says. "I didn't expect you."

"We need to talk."

"I supposed we do," she says, moving toward the couch, falling into it and kicking her stockinged feet onto the coffee table. She nods towards a duffel bag on the table. "The rest of your money. I was going to have Samson bring it to you, but you can take it now."

I sit on the couch across from her. For a moment I can't even bring myself to speak. It hurts too much. And not just the recent body blows.

I mean all of this, and how it's about to change.

That hurts more.

She sees it in my face. Her expression switches from bemusement to concern.

"Ashley?" she asks. Her voice sounds almost like I remember it. The higher register disappearing.

"I met Spencer's parents. At the hospital."

She looks at her hands in her lap. She's taken on the demeanor of a child who got caught pilfering sugar from the pantry. "I see."

"Tell me."

"Ash…"

"Tell me. All of it. You owe me that much."

Ginny nods. Stands. I keep my eye on her. Because she's gone from reprimanded child to caged animal. Like she's afraid of me. And maybe she should be. She probably has a gun stashed around here somewhere. Home protection. Any sudden movements on her part, any opening drawers or lingering too long near a piece of furniture, and I'm going to have to move.

"I want the island," she says. "Of course I want it. It's the biggest market in New York City right now. How could I not want it?"

"So you used me, for what?"

"I didn't use you. I paid you. I employed you. Like before."

"No, not like before. I didn't know all the facts."

"You think you ever knew all the facts?" She circles the couch and stands in front of me. "Here's the truth. You coming home was a stroke of luck. I sent Spencer in there to get intel for me. Only thing is, I was dropping him into a pot that was about to boil over. Brick and Kid Vicious were about to go to war, and neither side was too fond of me. So he got jammed up. When I heard you were coming back, I was thrilled. You were exactly what I needed."

"And what's that?"

"The kind of person who's going to find Spencer for me, but want to destroy the drug trade along the way." She gives me a look, smiles. "I know you, Ash. You like to play this game like you have 'morals.'" She throws air quotes around the word. "I knew you'd go in there and bang shit up enough to clear a path for me."

"That couple in the lobby?"

"They own the bodega down the block," she says, smiling, triumphant. Her voice taking on an edge, filling the space. "I paid them a few hundred bucks to stand there and look sad. It is so easy to play on your sympathies. I figured that's all it would take to get you to move on this. And I was right. Thank you, by the way." She nods toward the bag. "I threw in a little extra, to make up for your troubles." Her voice takes on a condescending tone. "Because you did such a good job."

I clench my fists. Totally involuntary, anger coursing through my veins, making my muscles taut. She makes note of this.

"Should I call Samson in here?" she asks. "Or should we go a few rounds? Last time we threw down, it didn't end too well."

"I wouldn't worry about Samson just yet," I tell her, which causes her to raise an eyebrow. "As for you, last time, I'd been up for three days on a bender. It wasn't exactly a fair fight. Not to say you wouldn't get your licks in, but I'm running closer to full speed right now. You really want that?"

She doesn't have to say it. The way she stands frozen in place explains it well enough.

I stand up and she takes a step back. I consider the duffel bag but leave it. I've taken enough of Ginny's money. Tainted with the blood of innocent people. People like Timmy. She didn't kill him but she's indifferent to his fate. She wants to be the one handing out death in little glassine envelopes.

People can convince themselves of anything.

Like they can't change.

Their lives come to resemble cages, so it gets to be where everything you look at, it's like you're looking through bars.

Thing is, most times all you have to do is open the door and take that first step out.

"When I leave this room, we're enemies," I tell her, my heart twisting in my chest. "Staten Island is my home now. I'm not going anywhere. And I'm not going to stand by while you hurt people."

Her voice drops to nearly a whisper. "Ash, darling. I am a very dangerous enemy to make."

"So am I."

She scoffs. "You think you're a hero now or something?"

I want to give her a clever answer to that, but I can't think of anything.

She averts her eyes from me, takes out her phone. Clicks at the face of it and puts it back in her pocket. "I'm sorry that you feel this way."

"I'm sorry, too. Truly."

And that's not a lie.

I didn't stay in touch with a lot of people from high school. Ginny and Bombay are it. It's special when something lasts that long. When it's something you want to carry with you. But then it runs out. Doesn't matter the circumstances. It's sad when that happens.

I turn toward the elevator, leave the duffel on the table.

"Ash."

I stop.

"Do you regret it?"

She's asking about the locker room. I turn and it looks like Ginny might be approaching something akin to tears.

"Are you stalling?" I ask. "Giving Samson time to get up here? He's not on his way."

Her eyes go dark. "What did you do to him?"

"Put him through the windshield of your car."

Ginny goes ramrod straight. For the first time in my entire time knowing her, she is rendered speechless.

"Use the money I'm not taking to fix it," I tell her. "We're more than square."

We stand there for a moment, the air heavy with history whistling out of the room, like air out of a balloon, into a vacuum.

"See you around, Ginny."

I step into the elevator and press the button for the lobby. My shoulders stay clenched until the doors close and I'm sure I'm not going to catch a bullet in the back.

TWENTY-FOUR

MORNING BREAKS. I slept well, even though I probably shouldn't have. I made an enemy of someone no one wants to make enemies with. I like to think Ginny won't come after me, that years of friendship might mean something.

But I like to think a lot of things.

I cross the hallway to Bombay's, let myself in, find him sitting on the couch in his boxers and a t-shirt sipping a cup of coffee. Lunette is on the chair in the corner, wearing a bathrobe. I pour myself some coffee, sit down on the couch next to Bombay. We watch as a pretty couple trades witty banter as they tear down drywall in their soon-to-be dream home.

Neither of us talk.

We don't have to.

Sitting in that silence is the most settled I've felt since I got home.

I want to say this to Bombay and Lunette, to tell him how much it means to be sitting here with them. I don't say anything. I don't know what to say. I want to enjoy it.

The show ends. I swallow the last swig of my coffee. Bombay asks, "Plans for today?"

"Nap," Lunette says, stretching.

"Could use some furniture," I tell him.

"Could use a job, too, bro," he says. "Get your own coffee."

"I'm going to be temping for that PI three days a week."

He smiles at me. Raises his hand to give me a high five. We slap our hands together.

"Good job," he says. "You still going to need me on the computer stuff though?"

"Actually, I'd like you to start teaching me."

"You gonna pay me?"

"No longer having to do it for me should be payment enough."

He puts the coffee down. "I know a place. Not too far from here. They sell furniture. I think they deliver, too. Want to roll up there?"

"Sure. We can visit my mom after. See how's she's doing. I'm sure she'll be happy to see you, too." I turn to Lunette. "You want to come for a ride?"

"Nah, I have some stuff to do. You boys have fun."

My phone buzzes. Phone call from a number that's not programmed in. I consider sending it to voicemail but then figure, hey, live dangerously.

"Ash?"

"That's me."

"This is Emily Chan. We met the other day. At your friend's house?"

"Right, right. Sorry. I should have called but things have been a little…hectic."

"Well, I have your friend. I'm actually down at the One-Two-Oh precinct today. Want to meet me there and you can pick him up?"

"Yeah, I'm right up the block. See you in a few minutes."

I click off the call. Bombay and Lunette look at me funny. I ask Bombay, "You down to run a few errands before we hit the furniture store?"

He shrugs. "Got nothing to do today."

Best to get moving. As I'm crossing the apartment to put my empty mug in the sink, Bombay calls, "Hey."

I turn.

"This is good," he says.

Lunette smiles. "Yeah. This is good."

I smile back at them and for the first time in a long time, feel like I've earned that.

THE WIND WHIPS my clothes against me, skin tight from the cold. Bombay huffs into his hands. Our old high school sits before us, already empty on account of Christmas break. I tighten my grip on the ceramic urn. It's painted to look like blue marble, but it feels cheap, like if I drop it, it's going to break.

Used to be there was a break in the fence behind the football field, back where the track kids threw shot-put. Now it's gone. This is the closest we're going to get without trespassing.

"Why here?" Bombay asks.

"Remember that day in art class?"

"Mr. Reitz?"

"Yeah, with Mr. Reitz. He had scavenged a bunch of shit from the bio lab. And there was a static sphere?"

"I don't think I was there for that."

"He got this static sphere thing. It was like a big metal ball. And it was broken, and you remember Mr. Reitz, he really didn't care if we fucked around. So me and Timmy got to playing with it, trying to fix it. And we did." I laugh a little at the memory. "So we decided it would be funny to rig it up to the doorknob. To shock the next person to come in. The art lab was all the way down in the corner of the building, so we figured it was going to be another student."

Breathe in. Breathe out. "So we found this flexible metal tubing, but we couldn't fasten it to the sphere, so Timmy is standing there with his fucking shoes on his hands, so he won't get shocked. And we turned it on and stood there waiting for someone to touch the knob. It was like ten minutes before someone showed up. Of course, it turned out to be the a vice-principal."

Bombay laughs, slaps me on the shoulder. "I remember that. You got in so much trouble."

"Yeah. It was kind of worth it. It was Mr. Kazepis who got shocked. He was a dick."

"He was. But you still haven't answered my questions. Why here?"

I look out over the field behind the school, covered in pristine snow.

"We were happy here," I tell him.

I kneel down, pull up the corner of the fence, wave Bombay down with me. He grabs it with both hands and pulls up, giving me enough room to stick the urn through and upend it, dumping the gray ash into the snow. I pat the urn a few times to make sure it's empty and we put the fence back.

The ash collects in piles. Gray at the peaks, black down by the base where it gets wet. It sits there, soaking into the snow.

"We good?" Bombay asks.

"Yeah," I tell him. "We're good."

WE'RE TURNING ONTO Victory Boulevard, traffic snarled on roadways cut narrow by massive piles of snow gleaming white in the sunlight, when my phone rings. My mom. Speaking of. There's a cop car parked by the side of the road so I pass the phone to Bombay, let him answer.

"Hello, Mrs. McKenna. No, we've been through this, I'm not calling you by your first name. My parents raised me better than that. Yeah. Okay. I'll tell him."

Bombay puts the phone against his chest.

"She says there's someone at the house. Wants to see you. Says it's important."

My stomach wrenches.

Fuck.

No.

Ginny wouldn't do that. I know we basically declared war on each other last night but she wouldn't stoop so low as to go after family.

Samson though. He might.

And he was pretty pissed when I left him.

Or at least, he was going to be when he woke up.

I slam the pedal to the floor, find a narrow space between cars, and duck down a side street. The car fishtails a little in a patch of snow and then we rocket up the block.

"Whoa, what the fuck?" Bombay says.

"Me and Ginny got into it last night," I tell him. "Could be trouble. I'll drop you at the bottom of the block."

"Fuck that, bro. It's your mom. We go in together and we go

in hard."

I reach across and smack him on the chest.

"I love you, brother," I tell him.

"Love you, too."

Playing the side streets, we make short time to the house. Under four minutes, and miraculously don't end up wrapped around a telephone pole. I pull the car in front of the house, onto a bank of snow, scraping the chassis so hard I feel it in my spine, but I don't care. We dive out of the car and run toward the house.

The front door is unlocked.

I crash into the living room, Bombay right behind me.

And I stop.

Sitting in the center of the living room floor is Rose.

I breathe out hard. My knees weaken, buckle.

Last time I saw Rose was somewhere in Oregon, in the back of a car on a dark country road. I read her a story and she fell asleep. I kissed her mother goodbye and watched their car disappear, my heart shattered, pieces of it clinking onto the roadway. They were off someplace to be safe. Someplace away from me. Because at that point, I figured it was the only way to protect them.

Rose looks up at me and smiles. She looks different. Her hair is longer. Her face is a little more grown up.

"Hi, Ash," she says.

I try to say something but I can't. It's all I can do to breathe.

It gets even harder when Crystal comes into the living room, like this is the most normal thing in the world.

Her hair is different. The last time I saw her, one side of her head was shaved to stubble, the other side draped like a curtain, going down to the small of her back. Now it's a pixie cut, black highlighted with purple.

But those blue-green tempered glass eyes are exactly the same.

And they light up when they see me.

"Howdy, stranger," she says.

My mom follows behind Crystal, beaming. "Well, that was fast."

"Yeah, Ma, sometimes it's helpful to clarify, you know, who exactly is here."

Through, truthfully, if I knew it was Crystal, I might have made it faster.

We all stand there in cautious silence. Finally, my mom throws her hands up in the air. "Bombay, this is Crystal. Why don't you help me in the kitchen. And, Rose, I think I might have some cookies in the cupboard. If that's all right with you, Mom?"

Crystal glances back and nods.

My mom smiles. "Let's give these two a second to talk."

Rose runs after the promise of cookies and Bombay follows, probably also interested in the cookies, making a quick introduction to Crystal along the way, and then it's the two of us in the living room.

"What the fuck is going on?" I ask.

She laughs. "It's nice to see you, too." Takes a few steps toward me. "Been meaning to visit New York for years. Thought it would be nice to see it at Christmas. And as long as I was here...I looked you up. Wasn't sure where you were. But I found your mom. Friended her on Facebook. And when she started posting how happy she was that her son was home..."

"I looked for you on Facebook."

"I'm using a different last name."

I take a step toward her. The distance between us closing. My vision goes blurry.

Tears sneak up on Crystal's eyes, too. "I had to see you. I'm sorry if this is a little presumptuous, to show up like this..."

Everything this past year has been such a fucking nightmare. I've been running so long and so hard. I was so tired. And finally, finally, it feels like I reached my destination.

This is it.

We close the distance. I take her hand.

"I'm glad you're here. I missed you." I glance toward the kitchen, hear Rose laughing. "I missed you both."

"Good," she says.

She leans in for a kiss, presses her lips to mine, and it tastes like all I could have ever wanted in this entire world.

TWENTY-FIVE

THE SUN PEEKS through the blinds, gold bands falling across the bed. It's getting warm, even with the air conditioner humming softly on the far end of the room. I roll over, tangled in blankets. Crystal is on her stomach, breathing softly. I unwrap from the blanket slowly, careful not to wake her. She doesn't stir. I stand up, pull my charging cord out of my phone. Check the time. Four minutes until my alarm is set to go off. Been doing that a lot lately. Waking up like an actual adult.

I tiptoe through the apartment because Rose will wake at the sound of an eyelash hitting the floor, but then I remember she's having a slumber party at my mom's house. It gave me and Crystal the opportunity for a little adult time: Thai takeout from down the block, some wine, Netflix, then passing out on the couch, her nudging me awake somewhere around three in the morning so we could trudge inside to bed.

The best kind of night there ever was.

I shower, sneak back into the bedroom and get dressed. Even though Turk hates me wearing shorts in the office, it's too hot for pants. I used to loathe days like this in Manhattan. The way the city holds the heat, radiating off the brick buildings. The way it amplifies the smell of the trash. The way it makes everyone want to kill each other.

But on Staten Island, it's not so bad. Maybe it's being surrounded by water, with fewer tall buildings to block the breeze. Maybe it's that lack of heated brick and stone looming over you at all times. The heat here feels so much more bearable.

It's early still so the roads are light. It takes me less than ten minutes to make it up Victory and then down Forest. I park in the shade under a tree so the interior of the car won't get too hot, stop off at the Dunkin' across the street, get some coffees and Munchkins, make it to the office and open things up. The air is stiff so I turn on the central air, get things moving. Go to my little desk in the back and look at the pile of stuff Turk left me to do.

I sip on my iced coffee, tap the space bar on my keyboard to wake up my computer. The background is a selfie of me and Rose and Crystal on the Wonder Wheel in Coney Island. The phone in my outstretched hand reflected in my sunglasses. Crystal's hair plastered to her forehead with sweat. Rose's cheeks flushed red, the color of freshly-picked apples. I see the picture every day and every day it makes me smile.

The workload today looks light. Mostly filing. Things have been quiet. Even though I'm past the donkeywork stage, even though Turk has been letting me do stuff a little more in-depth— door knocking, stakeouts—I like doing the grunt work. There's something calming about filing. About making sure everything is in its place.

Anyway, it's not like there's anyone else to do it. Turk's daughter used to help with that stuff, but soon as I showed up, she went back to doing kid stuff. Which is exactly what she should be doing. Though sometimes if she sees me cleaning the office, she'll give me a hand.

She's a good kid. So is Rose. I like being surrounded by good kids. Gives me hope.

My phone buzzes.

Have to run an errand. Going to be a few minutes late. Hold down the fort.

I write back: *10-4, captain.*

As I'm sorting the stack to make it easier to file, there's a sound from the front of the office. The front door. I pick up my coffee and make my way down the carpeted hallway to the waiting room.

Standing in the middle of it is a woman. She's young, maybe early-thirties. Blonde hair. Pretty. White tank, jean shorts, sandals. Eyes rimmed in red. She's been crying. She looks at me with that look people usually have on their face when they come in here. Like it's their last option. That mix of fear and hope that jabs me right in the fucking heart every time I see it.

She starts to speak, but chokes on her words. Fighting back more tears.

Takes a deep breath.

"I'm sorry," she says. "It's my brother. He's missing…"

I cross the room to her, take her hand, sit her down on a chair. Pull another chair over so I'm sitting across from her, our knees almost touching. I give her a small smile, press her hands together between mine. Her shoulders unknot a bit.

"It's okay," I tell her. "I'm here to help."

ACKNOWLEDGMENTS

Five books in three years. I nearly lost my mind, but I didn't. And that's thanks to a couple of people: My publisher, Jason, for believing in me, and this series, and letting me see it through to the end. My wife, Amanda, my best and most important reader. My mom, for all the work she's done to promote these books, and my dad, and his buddies in the FDNY, for setting the standard for real heroism. My daughter, for making me a better man—Ash starts in a dark place and grows toward the light, and that evolution was thanks to her influence. I could sit here for hours and name countless readers and writers who gave me words of kindness and encouragement, especially when I needed them, but that'd be a whole other book, and I almost hate to do this for fear of who'll get left out, but a couple of folks deserve special thanks, including Todd, Nik, Alex, Renee, JDO, and the Malmons. Also, thanks to Danny for the hand, and Joey and Joe for the intel. I am endlessly thankful to the bookstores and reviewers who took a chance on me and promoted my work. Finally, most importantly, I am thankful for the readers who went on this journey, or just picked up this one book, but either way, forgave me the growing pains of a writer finding his way. Ash has grown a lot over the course of this story, and so have I.

ABOUT THE AUTHOR

Rob Hart is the author of four previous Ash McKenna novels: *New Yorked*, *City of Rose*, *South Village*, and *The Woman From Prague*. He is the publisher at MysteriousPress.com and the class director at LitReactor. Previously, he has worked as a political reporter, the communications director for a politician, and a commissioner for the city of New York. His short stories have appeared in publications like Thuglit, Needle, Shotgun Honey, All Due Respect, Joyland, and Helix Literary Magazine. His non-fiction has appeared at LitReactor, Salon, The Daily Beast, Mulholland Books, Criminal Element, The Literary Hub, Electric Literature, the Powell's bookstore blog, and Nailed. He has received both a Derringer Award nomination and made multiple appearances in Best American Mystery Stories. He lives in New York City.

Find more on the web at
www.robwhart.com and on
Twitter at @robwhart.